Unforgettable

GRANGER'S CLAIM: Colt Granger ~~~~~~~~~~ and his Montana claim against the murderous outlaws that are terrorizing settlers in the West—and have their own personal vendetta for Colt . . .

BANDIDO CABALLERO: Once a Confederate spy, Tom Fallon has found a new career stealing gold from the French and giving it to Mexican rebels. He's becoming a legend on both sides of the border as the mysterious gunslinger Bandido Caballero . . .

THE HARD LAND: Though Jess Sanford left Simon Bauman for dead, the man is still alive. And there's one thing more relentless than the law: a shamed son with all the wealth of the Bauman family behind him . . .

IRON HORSE WARRIOR: Hunting for his brother's killer, Chance Tenery takes a job on the Union Pacific Railroad and begins a long fight for his honor, his life, and the woman he comes to love . . .

(continued . . .)

ANGEL FIRE: When Kurt Buckner agrees to escort a woman to the Colorado Territory, he finds that hostile Indians are no danger—compared to the three men who want her dead . . .

POWDER RIVER: Case Gentry is no longer a Texas Ranger. But the night a two-bit gunhand rides up to his cabin, he has to bring back every instinct to survive . . .

GUN BOSS: Raised by an Apache tribe, Trace Gundy must call upon the fighting spirit he learned as a boy to avenge the loss of his beloved wife . . .

THE RUGGED TRAIL: Ex–Confederate soldier Hawken McClure watched as the carpetbaggers took away everything he fought for—and now the ex-soldier for the South is ready to give them a whole new war . . .

TRAIL BROTHERS

JACK BALLAS

BERKLEY BOOKS, NEW YORK

This is a work of fiction. Names, characters, places, and incidents are either the product of the author's imagination or are used fictitiously, and any resemblance to actual persons, living or dead, business establishments, events or locales is entirely coincidental.

TRAIL BROTHERS

A Berkley Book / published by arrangement with
the author

PRINTING HISTORY
Berkley edition / January 2000

The Penguin Putnam Inc. World Wide Web site address is
http://www.penguinputnam.com

ISBN: 0-425-17304-6

BERKLEY®
Berkley Books are published by The Berkley Publishing Group,
a division of Penguin Putnam Inc.,
375 Hudson Street, New York, New York 10014.
BERKLEY and the "B" logo are trademarks belonging to
Penguin Putnam Inc.

PRINTED IN THE UNITED STATES OF AMERICA

10 9 8 7 6 5 4 3 2 1

1

QUINT CANTRELL STRAIGHTENED, arched his back to get the kinks out, looked with satisfaction at the last post to which he'd secured the strand of barbed wire, then pushed his hat back and wiped sweat from his forehead. He looked at Art King, his partner.

King tipped his head toward the northeast. "Rider comin'." With the warning, he thumbed the thong from the hammer of his handgun. Cantrell followed suit.

The rider, a lean, leather-faced man, rode closer, hands crossed on the saddle horn. "Howdy. Lookin' fer directions to Lion McCord's place—the Bar I.M. Hear tell folks hereabouts call it the BIM."

Cantrell glanced at the rider's hands, slipped the thong back over the hammer of his Colt, then eyed the rider. "You been ridin' on BIM range the last thirty miles. Why you lookin' for it?"

The slim man tilted his head against the bright sunlight. "Lookin' fer the man what married the owner's daughter. Cantrell's his name."

Quint let a slight smile crack the corners of his mouth. "You lookin' for 'im peaceable?"

The rider nodded. "Got a message fer 'im. Brung it all the way from Fort Sumner—'nother rider passed it on to me there. Reckon he wuz 'bout the third man headin' this way."

Quint nodded. "You found your man. I'm Cantrell."

The stranger studied him a moment. "Yep, you're big 'nuff, but I figgered you'd be 'bout ten foot tall, an' mean enough lookin' to whip a grizzly."

King stuck in his two cents' worth. "Don't let his six-foot-somethin' fool you, mister. When he's mad, an' lookin' at you, he looks jest the way you figgered."

The rider glanced at King, then back to Cantrell. "I'm called Branch Winters by my friends."

Quint told the man his partner's name, then waited.

Winters nodded toward King, then said, "Like I told you, I brung a message. Man by the name o' Brad Mason down in the Big Bend o' Texas's in a heap o' trouble. Bandit by name of Manuel Soto's 'bout take over his ranch. Steals his cows, shoots his riders, burns his grass. Don't know the reason, but from what I hear Mason needs help an' is too damn proud to ask fer it." Winters swabbed sweat from his neck using his bandana, then frowned. "Hear tell Mason's ranch is one o' the biggest in the country, but Soto's got a reg'lar army. An' Mason's men, the more peaceable ones, are leavin' him. His crew's 'bout down to thirty now. Ain't 'nuff to stand up to them bandits what're made up o' Mexican an' white border trash."

Cantrell looked at King. "Gotta see Lion." While gathering his horse's reins, he glanced at Winters. "You ridin' the grub line?"

Waters nodded. "Yep, till I find a job. Figgered to see if Mr. McCord wuz hirin'. Left Texas to git outta the heat. Heard tell this Colorado country wuz better, but from the feel of it don't know as I made a good decision."

He made a sweep with his right hand to take in the San Juan Mountains, behind and to his right. "Man, to look at this here country, looks like the man up yonder picked up a piece o' heaven an' jest flat dropped it in the middle o' everything, despite this here summer heat."

Cantrell grinned. "Okay, you found both—grub an' a job." His grin widened. "Gonna tell you right now, though, when this high-country cold seeps into yore bones, you gonna wish mighty hard fer some o' that Texas heat, or for some o' this here weather for that matter." He toed the stirrup, kneed his horse toward the southwest, and said, "Let's go let Lion meet his new hired hand."

Cantrell felt free to hire and fire men for McCord, not because he'd married his daughter, but because Lion held a good-sized chunk of Quint's money, money he'd earned the hard way: on cattle drives, and rounding up his own herd of longhorn Mavericks.

Quint knew Lion trusted him. Someday McCord and his wife Venicia would pass the BIM on to Elena and him, so Lion figured any decision Quint made would be for the good of his daughter and the ranch. Cantrell looked up from his musings. The headquarters buildings were just over the next rise.

They had covered the ten miles in about two hours, with Winters admiring the grass, spruce, creeks, and the snowcapped mountains all the while. Then he gave an exaggerated sniff and shook his head. "Damn, if I'da done that in west Texas, I'da been sneezin' till tomorrow with all the dust. Up here all I got wuz the smell of them evergreen trees. Yep, think I done found heaven despite this here midsummer heat."

After Cantrell took Winters to meet the foreman, Wyatt Mann, he and King rode to the ranch house. Elena met him at the door. She came into his arms, kissed him, then swept them both with a glance. "Didn't think y'all would be finished till this weekend."

"Gotta see Lion. He busy?"

"Quint, you know Papa is never too busy to see you. Take Art on back with you."

"You better come too, Elena. Get Venicia. You've all gotta hear what I got to say."

He would have bet that when she turned away, she said, "My man's gonna tell me about some trouble, an' he'll be right in the middle of it."

Only a few moments later they all sat in Ian McCord's office. His nickname, Lion, fit right down to the mane of white hair framing his face. "All right, Cantrell, what's so damned important you an' Art left the fence you took outta here yesterday to mend?"

"First off, Lion, I hired you a new rider, second I'm gonna need 'bout ten o' yore best fightin' men—I pick 'em. Then gonna need to take off for 'bout a month—with them men I pick."

Lion scooted his chair back a few inches, reached in his bottom drawer, pulled out a jug of his best liquor, set three glasses on his desk next to the bottle, and poured each man a glass full. "You got trouble, son, you can take the whole damned BIM crew—you know that."

Before he could finish, Quint jumped in. "I ain't fig-urin' to be close-by. Gonna take them men 'bout a thou-sand miles from here, down to the Big Bend.

"Pa Mason's got a whole mess o' trouble comin' down on 'im—gun trouble, Mexican bandit trouble. I figure to get 'im loose from it."

Elena hadn't said a word until now, but she stood abruptly and, hands on hips, stared down at him. "You thinkin' to make that ride down there without me, Quinton Cantrell?"

The way she stood, and the way she looked, Quint knew from hard experience that whatever her argument was, she would win. Still he had to try. "Elena, this's gun trouble I'm goin' about. Ain't no place for a beautiful lady." He nodded. "Yep, I'm gonna make that ride without you."

She pinned him with a look that said this wasn't the end of the argument, and to hide the fact he expected more out of her, he took a swallow of his drink, and looked at McCord. "Figure to send a couple o' riders to tell Cole an' Clay their pa's in trouble. Think they'll want to know."

Lion nodded. "Pick your men. When you leavin'?"

"Come daylight, Lion. We'll spend the night gettin' supplies, loadin' the chuck wagon, then ride out."

Again Elena muttered. "Good, I've been wantin' to meet Cole's and Clay's wives. And ever since I met you, I've wanted to meet their father, the man who raised you as his own. Know from what I've heard 'bout those ladies Cole and Clay married, they won't let their men go off alone either."

Quint knew then he'd lost any argument about whether she'd go.

When they rode into Fort Sumner, people along the street, ankle deep in dust, stopped to stare, not only at the hard-bitten, salty crew, but at Elena. Cantrell smiled. His wife would win the prize for beauty anywhere.

They stopped the wagon in front of the general store. Quint helped Elena down. "Bein' you're the one cookin' fer us, you better see what they got in there we can use. We'll stay here tonight an' head out again in the mornin'. I'm gonna get a drink."

She eyed him a moment. "Bring a bottle to the room. You an' I'll have a drink before we go to bed." He grinned, then nodded and headed for the saloon.

Even though it had been over a year since he rode the Outlaw Trail, there would be men who remembered him. He pushed the thong off the hammer of his Colt, stepped through the batwing doors, and moved to the side. He'd never stolen anything in his life, but he'd had to shoot a few of those who had. If there were some in here who'd ridden the owl-hoot, they wouldn't take kindly to it if one of those he'd shot had been their partner.

He scanned the darkened room, saw no one he knew, and went to the bar. "Whiskey, best you got, an' one for my partner here."

King pushed to the polished surface beside him, his mouth slit only a little wider than usual, which was about as close as he ever came to smiling. He eyed the glass the barkeep poured liquor into. "Gonna take more'n one o' them to cut the dust outta my throat, Cantrell."

Abruptly, those within earshot stopped talking. The bartender quit pouring. Still holding the neck of the bottle over the glass, he looked at King. "Did you say 'Cantrell'?" He turned his look on Quint. "You Quint Cantrell?" His voice came from deep in his chest, and carried to every corner of the room. Total silence reigned.

Quint went quiet inside. He nodded. "Yeah, I'm Quint Cantrell. Why?"

The big redheaded barkeep finished pouring their drinks, then shook his head. "Don't know whether you got trouble or not. Heard even while you rode the owl-hoot you wasn't really wanted by the law—it wuz them Hardester brothers put the price on your head, but, Cantrell, they's been at least six men come through here the last month or two askin' fer you. You might want to ride like they wuz trouble around every curve in the trail."

While he talked, Quint gave King a slight grin, then looked back at the big redhead. "One o' those men caught up with me. Don't worry. There ain't gonna be any trouble." Cantrell and King picked up their glasses and knocked back their drinks.

The voices started again, along with the clink of poker chips and rattle of glasses. The barkeep grinned, and poured them another drink. "On the house." His grin widened. "Figured for a while I might get my saloon shot up again."

Cantrell sipped this drink, rolled it around in his mouth, and said, "Not bad whiskey, better give me a bottle to take to the room." He paid for all except the house drink, and he and King headed for the door.

Outside, Cantrell looked at Art. "Whoever started carryin' word 'bout Brad needin' help sure made sure there'd be somebody git up to our neck o' the woods with it. Wish I knew who he was so I could thank 'im."

"Don't reckon he wants thanks. He figgered to do Mason a favor an' he done it."

Cantrell, Elena, and the crew spent the night, and with

supplies replenished, they again headed into the heat before daylight.

Twenty-seven days after leaving the BIM, Quint and his crew pushed along a narrow trail edged by chaparral—the brush held the heat on the road like an oven. Dust swirled into the riders' faces, clothes, and hair. Cantrell motioned his riders around him. "Stay close to the wagon. Keep your eyes busy—try to see through this tangle of cactus, scrub oak, an' mesquite. We gettin' close to Pa Mason's ranch headquarters now, an' if there's bandits around we gonna find 'em." He pushed a smile through his dust-caked face. " 'Course they more'n likely gonna be the ones who find us."

The words were no more than out of his mouth when shots punched through the soft sounds of horses' hooves, trace chain clanks, and saddle leather creaks. The shots came from the thick brush bordering the rutted, dusty road.

Art King, driving the wagon, whipped the team into a dead-out run. Rifles spewed their deadly messengers, accompanied by the whir of bullets sounding like bees when they passed close enough to a man's head. A look at Elena in the wagon bed, cooly firing at those attackers she could see in the brush, swelled King with pride—he'd helped raise the brave young woman. Pure guts made up the crew of the BIM.

Cantrell, every muscle tight with fear for his wife, rode his black gelding into the face of the attackers, firing and jacking shells into the chamber of his Winchester, his knees clamped tight to the barrel of his horse. Two men spilled from their saddles in front of him. He urged his horse faster, at the same time motioning King toward the open gates of Brad Mason's ranch yard dead ahead. He fired, and then levered off another shot at the bandits. One fell.

A glance showed him his crew riding their horses belly to the ground, some firing handguns, others using Winchesters held like pistols. Then he saw the wagon's tailgate disappearing inside the walled ranch yard.

He now gave all his attention to the bandits climbing aboard horses and heading deeper into the cactus-infested brush, all firing over their shoulders at him and his men.

Cantrell penetrated the chaparral only a few yards, pulled rein, and yelled at his men to quit the chase. The deeper they got into the brush, the more they'd play into the hands of the bandits.

The crew gathered around. Sitting his horse, waiting for them to draw closer, Cantrell snorted the acrid smell of burnt gunpowder and dust from his nostrils.

Once the men were sitting silently in a circle around him, he tipped his head toward the attackers disappearing into the heavy chaparral. "Reckon we know now what that rider meant when he said Brad Mason wuz having a *little* trouble with bandits down this way." He flicked a glance to cover each of his riders. "Any o' you catch lead?"

A grizzled old-timer sitting his horse next to him shook his head. "Hell no, Cantrell, if you didn't catch none, ain't no way we'd've caught any. You wuz almost in the middle of 'em when they took out fer the Rio Grande. Figger they gonna cross soon's they kin reach it."

His gut beginning to relax, Quint nodded. "All right, first let's see how many o' those dog droppings we sent to hell—know I got three. Then we'll find if Ma Mason's got supper fixed." He reined the big black into the brush and yelled over his shoulder, "Don't none o' you get more'n fifty yards into this. They might be a couple o' them hangin' back to get a shot at us."

A search among the clusters of prickly pear and stunted trees surrendered another five bodies—two of them gringos.

"All right, men, let's head for the barn." He kneed the black toward the gate, now feeling tiredness permeate his body, pushing out the energy that had flooded him with the first shot.

He'd no more than stepped from his horse when a big, burly, weatherbeaten man grabbed him around the shoulders and hugged him, only to be pushed aside by a matronly gray-haired woman.

She kissed his cheek, squeezed his shoulders, and stepped back. "What brought y'all all the way from Colorado down here to the Big Bend? Lordy, that's a long hard trip, and to think you brought your almost new wife with you."

Cantrell grinned. "Ma, I'll tell you all about it soon's you feed us. I been looking forward to one o' yore meals slam across two states."

"Well, don't just stand there, come on in. Brad'll pour you and your men a drink while I get Inez to set table."

Quint nodded. "Sounds good, but set places only for Elena, Art, an' me. My men'll eat with your crew; they wouldn't have it any other way." He grinned. " 'Course they'll be mighty obliged for that drink Pa's gonna pour us. After supper I'll tell y'all why we come such a long way."

After they'd eaten, and sat in the Mason's large front room, Brad poured the three men a drink and had Inez bring the two ladies a lemonade. "Not that I ain't glad to see you an' your young wife, Cantrell, but why you here?" Abruptly he frowned and sat forward. "Bet the word's done reached that Durango country we got a shootin' war goin' on 'tween us an' them outlaws."

Cantrell raised an eyebrow and smiled. "I reckon you nailed that shoe on tight. I gathered up ten o' Lion McCord's best fightin' men to come down here an' help get rid of them Mexican bandits you got a problem with. Wuz gonna leave Elena with her ma an' pa till I got the job done, but she wouldn't stand still for that. Fact is she raised enough hell to raise the roof a mile."

"Mr. Mason, when Quint and I married, we said it was for good or bad. If he thought for one minute he could leave me behind, he doesn't know me as well as I think he does."

Quint smirked. "Reckon I knowed all the time you wouldn't stay home. You couldn'ta stood it that long without me."

Elena glared at him. "Wait'll I get you alone."

His smirk changed to a grin. "Now that's somethin' I'm lookin' forward to." Her face turned a bright red.

Mason's shoulders sagged. "Quint, you know even though we ain't got our blood mixed, I figger you as much my son as I do Cole an' Clay. That's the reason I didn't ask for help—I don't want none o' you gettin' hurt." He nodded. "Yeah, yore ten men'll help, but we're facin' one hulluva lot more men than you an' me's got." He shook his head. " 'Fraid it's a losin' battle, boy.

"Manuel Soto, along with Benito Santana, leads them bandits, an' he's got a bunch o' the meanest hard cases either side o' the border. They run across the border each time they make a raid. Our law, our Army, the Rangers—

nobody can cross the river with any legal reason to back 'em up without gittin' the Mexican gov'ment crossways with our'n. That'd turn a hornet's nest loose, might even cause a war."

Quint took a hefty swallow of his drink, gasped, and put his glass back on the table. He looked at Pa Mason through slitted lids. "You write either Cole or Clay lettin' 'em know you got trouble?"

Brad shook his head. "Hell no, I ain't askin' none o' my boys to come down here an get shot at." Then he bristled like a mad porcupine. "An' I'm tellin' you right now, boy, I ain't askin' nobody for help. I always took care o' my own troubles, ain't gonna stop now."

Quint grinned. "Bet you they'll both be here in less'n a week—with as many, or more, men than I brought."

Ma, her face crinkling like old leather, her eyes misty, shook her head. "Oh, Mr. Mason." Quint had never heard her call her husband by his first name. "Mr. Mason, I hope those boys don't hear about the troubles we have. We spent a lifetime trying to keep them outta trouble, now seems we're gonna put them into the worst shootin' kind of situation ever."

Elena placed her hand over Ma's. "Mrs. Mason, I know your feelings well, only yours are three times as bad as mine. I've seen Quint shot, dressed his wounds when I thought he'd up an' die on me, seen 'im leave in the middle of the night to go fight four men thinkin' I wouldn't know what he was about." She nodded. "Yes'm, I know, but our men bein' the way they are is part of the reason we married them."

Ma looked at her a moment, brushed her sleeve across her eyes, and shook her head. "Call me 'Ma,' Elena.

You're part of the family." She smiled through her tears. "And it surely looks like Quint picked well for himself."

Elena grinned. "I figure Quint might tell you I picked *him*." She sighed. "An' now I reckon it's gonna be part of our burden to see them ride off, while we wait here hoping they'll come back sitting their saddles rather than slung across them."

"Hey! 'Nuff of that kind o' talk. Let's git to know y'all." Brad put his gaze on Art King. "Figure you an' Quint's pretty good partners. How'd it happen?"

King, not used to talking, looked at Elena for help. She shook her head and grinned. He grimaced. "Well, I'll tell you. He patched me up from gunshots—I patched him up from the same kind o' hurts, an' since then we jest sort o' drifted into it. Looks like he brung me down here so's he can take 'nother try at makin' me suffer. He's the damndest, 'scuse me ladies, he's the gosh-dangdest meanest man anywhere when he's got you at his mercy an' diggin' into you for a chunk o' lead." He sat back, then obviously thought of one more thing. "My ma's full-blooded Apache, so I'm a pretty good Injun, but Quint Cantrell is good, maybe better'n me at bein' a Injun any day o' the year. Maybe that's the reason we partnered up."

Quint cut in. "Naw. I jest felt sorry fer the pore old Injun. Figgered he needed somebody to take care o' him."

King's face turned red as a dust-laden sunset. "Why gol-dang . . ."

They all sat back and laughed—now no longer strangers.

Cantrell looked at Mason. "What you want me an' my men to do first, Pa? You know what we're facin' more'n I do, so tell me what you want us to do."

Mason twisted his mouth to one side. "Like hell. Quint, you never paid any attention to what I told you in the past, don't reckon you gonna start now. What you figger to do?"

Feeling the devil come up in him, Cantrell grinned. "Why, Pa, glad you asked. Figure we'll go skunk huntin'. Try to thin Soto's army down some 'fore Clay and Cole get here. Don't want 'em to have all the fun."

Ma placed her hand over Elena's and squeezed. Her knuckles turned white. Cantrell remembered the times she'd pulled him, Clay, and Cole down beside her and tried to teach them to use proper grammar. Cole was the only one who took her lessons to heart. He'd gone on to the United States Military Academy at West Point, while Quint and Clay had concentrated on guns and knives.

They talked long into the night, talked until Ma said there would be another day and that she'd see them at breakfast.

The next morning, after they'd eaten, Cantrell went to the bunkhouse, rounded up his men, and walked down to the corral. He didn't waste time. His glance swept the tightly gathered group. "Check yore handguns, rifles, knives, an' bring plenty of shells. We gonna pick up sign on that gang what took us on yesterday, track them down, an' leave as many as we can fer the coyotes to eat. We ride in an hour."

The ones he figured to find didn't outnumber him and his men by more than twice. With surprise on his side, Cantrell thought to be able to more than hold his own.

White around the lips, Ma gave him a hug; Elena held him close to her a moment, kissed him, and told him to be careful.

When he'd cleared the door, she looked at Ma. "Before

he knew I loved him, we were on the way to Santa Fe to shop for Christmas. My mother, Venicia, and a crew about like the one we brought here with us were headed down there. Papa had put Quint in charge.

"When we left Chama, New Mexico, we had warning of a bunch of outlaws waiting for us on the trail. Quint slipped out of camp one rainy night, and took them on by himself. He didn't know it, but he took my heart with him that night. Mama told me then to not let anything stand in the way of letting him know how I felt, and not to worry—he'd be back safe. Her words were 'That man still has the bark on. He wears his shirts out from the inside. It'll take one helluva bunch to take him down.' I reckon I've grown to believe nothing he sets his mind to will ever defeat him." Her words were much braver than the chills running up and down her spine indicated.

She turned her back to the door. "Let's have a cup of coffee while you tell me what kind of boy Quint was."

Cantrell wasted no time at the corral. His men had a big dun gelding saddled for him. Giving their own horses time to rest, they'd borrowed some of Mason's.

Quint led out, heading toward the last place they'd seen the bandits disappear into the brush. Art King rode beside him.

Art reined his horse in and stepped from the saddle. "I'll track 'em fer now. You rest me after a while."

Quint took the reins of the bay King had ridden only a short distance, nodded, and said, "Don't get too far ahead, partner. Don't want you where I can't take care o' you if you get in a little trouble."

King stared at Cantrell a moment, disgust written all over his rawboned, leathery face. "Figgered you'd let me take a slug or two just so's you could dig 'em outta me."

He shot Quint a look that passed for a grin—only a crinkle at the corners of his eyes. "Gonna wait fer the shootin' to start when you're leadin' out ahead o' us. I brought some o' the rottenest whiskey you ever tasted to doctor you with."

Cantrell didn't try to hide how he felt. "You be careful out there—you heah?"

King's pace ate up distance as though he were riding horseback. The men he tracked made no effort to cover their tracks. "Too danged scared with tryin' to git outta that there firefight we had 'em in," he muttered.

When he began to pick up fresh sign, he slowed his pace, then brought his Apache training into play. When he stepped on a horse dropping, still fresh and moist, he crouched low to the ground and eased forward; after about a half hour the hum of conversation came to his ears.

Dropping to his stomach, he slithered toward the sound. Soon, he heard words in Spanish, broken, but enough to tell they talked about the shoot-out they'd had on the trail. He put some of the sentences together, enough to know they were worried that Mason had recruited more fighting men. Then one of them said, "We go find Santana. He want to know all Mason does."

Then another of them, arguing loudly against the man's suggestion, said, "No. We stay here an' do like the boss tell us. We stay right here while some go shoot at lone riders. Santana get mad like hell he find out we run from such a bunch."

King waited until he was sure they would stay put long enough for him to gather his men for an ambush. A quick glance at the ground he'd crawled over sent a shiver up his spine. "Damn, I bet they's more rattlesnakes in here than cactus. Shore don't wantta run into one." His muttered words were more prayer than talk.

2

KING REACHED BEHIND his back to his belt, and pulled his Bowie. If he ran into a rattler, he wanted at least a small chance, short of using his Colt, which would draw Santana's men like flies to a cow paddy.

He slithered much like the snakes he feared. Sweat streamed down his face into his eyes, trickled between his shoulder blades; dust, the ever-present dust, attached itself to the droplets and streams of sweat, to cake solidly on his face and clothes. He covered about twenty-five yards before getting up to his knees. He shook his head and dropped back to his belly. "Don't get to gol-danged anxious, King," he muttered. "Git yoreself full o' holes thata way."

He blinked sweat from his vision, then stared straight ahead. A rattler, about four feet long, lay stretched across his path. He stared at the scaly thing, sweating even harder. His back muscles kinked.

He shifted direction enough to miss the snake by ten feet, not wanting to argue about a little old thing like who had the most right to be there. All the while he sucked in short, choppy breaths. Chills ran over his body. His eyes stayed glued to where the snake sunned itself. When he figured he could safely get to his feet, careful to not make a sudden move, he brought his knees under him and stood. He saw two more snakes before making it back to Cantrell's side.

"You go next time, partner. Ain't nothin' in there to be scared of 'cept rattlers an' border hard cases."

Cantrell looked at him a moment. "Found 'em, huh?"

King nodded. " 'Bout fourteen of 'em way I figger it. We can take 'em easy." He pulled his bandana from his neck and swabbed sweat. "One of 'em wanted to head for the border, but the rest wuz too damned scared o' what Soto or Santana would do if they come back with their tails 'tween their legs. They all stayed."

Cantrell frowned. If he led his men straight for the bandits, chances were they'd get shot all to hell. "Seems they're a mite shy o' gettin' their boss mad at 'em. Let's help 'em stay on that bandit bastard's good side."

He hooked a leg around his saddle horn. "Tell you what we're gonna do. We gonna ride a wide circle 'round 'em—get 'tween them an' the river." He wiped the sweat from his forehead. "You ain't none o' you gonna like this, but we gonna leave our horses and go in afoot." He swept them with another glance. "Reckon we better wait'll we see how they're set up 'fore I tell you how I figure to take 'em on."

He pulled his leg free of the horn and looked at King. "You better lead outta here. Take us to where we'll be barely outta hearin' of 'em, then I'll tell you what I got planned."

They strung out behind King while he wended his way around and through the chaparral. After about forty-five minutes he drew rein. "Best I can do, Cantrell. What you got figgered now?"

Quint pushed his hat to the back of his head. "First, don't want none o' you close together. Leave 'bout ten, maybe fifteen, foot 'tween you an' the next man. King, you lead us in. I'm gonna stay with you till we see their horses. Want all o' you to stay clear till I can stampede them nags across their camp. Soon's I get them ponies runnin' toward 'em, y'all come in shootin'." He glanced at each of them. "Figure I got a good chance o' makin' this work, 'cause I done it once before down 'tween Chama an' Santa Fe." He again pinned them each with a look. "Got it?"

He pulled his hat down over his eyes. "Gonna tell you right now, they might be some o' you what won't be set-tin' down to eat supper with us. That bothers you, toe the stirrups and slake outta here—no hard feelin's."

A kid, no more than twenty years old, Sam Rawlins by name, shuffled his feet a couple of times, got Cantrell's attention, and said, "Reckon you 'splained that to us 'fore we left the BIM. Didn't see nobody pull leather then, don't reckon to now."

Quint slanted a look at the kid. "Didn't figure you to be one I wuz talkin' to anyway, Rawlins. Reckon I always thought you'd stick."

The boy's face glowed from the praise.

Cantrell looped the reins through a mesquite limb, assigned one of his riders to stay with the horses, and said, "Let's get after it." He noticed that most of the men pulled rifles from saddle scabbards, jacked shells into the chamber, and followed. With the job he'd chosen for himself, his Winchester would be next to useless. His every target would be in range of his Colt .44.

He stopped, walked back to the old-timer, Burkett, and held out his hand. " 'Preciate usin' your handgun for a while since you seem to favor that Henry."

Burkett thumbed the thong off the hammer of his Colt, lifted it from its holster, and handed it to Cantrell. " 'Spect you to bring it back to me when this is over, lad."

He pushed a grin through his fear. "Burkett, ain't a man in this outfit gonna be more careful than me." He glanced at the sun. "Let's go. We oughtta get there soon after sundown. Don't none o' you start poppin' caps till I open the ball."

They hadn't been started more than a few minutes when Cantrell cocked his head to listen. A smile creased his lips. For all the sound his men made, they might as well have been in the next county. Another few feet, he came on a game trail, or maybe one used by cows headed for water. The path wound its way in the general direction he wanted to go, so he followed it.

Before deciding to come in from this side, he'd checked the wind to be sure they were downwind of the bandits' camp—and the horses. He sure as hell didn't want the ponies getting spooked, or letting the camp know anyone sneaked up on them.

By his best guess, about ten minutes passed before he smelled smoke, then the flicker of a fire danced through the foliage of a tree about fifty yards ahead. He dropped to his stomach and slithered closer—close enough to hear the soft murmur of Spanish words.

He held still, hardly daring to breathe, and searched the area for horses. His eyes made two sweeps of the area before he picked out their dark shapes a little to his right, about fifteen yards closer than the campfire.

His back and chest muscles tightened. His guts felt as if an eggbeater whipped through them. Dust threatened to make him sneeze. He choked it off and eased closer to the ponies, hoping they were tethered to the same rope.

Again he stopped and scanned the area for anyone with the horses. No one. He moved closer. Stopped. A bandit left the fire and walked toward the remuda. Cantrell reached to his back and pulled his Bowie. He lay only a few feet from the hooves of the nearest horse. If the bandit had thoughts of checking each horse, he would come mighty close to stepping on him.

Cantrell flattened himself to the ground, wishing there was a hole he could crawl into. He waited. The outlaw did exactly what Cantrell hoped he'd not do. He walked to each horse, patted its neck, crooned soft words to it, then moved to the next one. When he came to the horse in front of Cantrell, he patted the strong neck, his back turned slightly to Quint.

Cantrell sucked in a deep breath, pushed himself up, and pushed the Bowie out ahead of him with the leverage of his knees behind the blow. The blade went to the hilt, stopped only when Cantrell felt his hand against the bandit's back. As soon as the knife entered the outlaw's back, Quint wrapped an arm around and covered the bandit's mouth with his hand. Only a low moan came from the man. Cantrell lowered his prey to the ground, careful to not excite the horses, and wiped the knife blade on the man's shirt.

He felt for the borrowed six-shooter shoved behind his belt, pushed the thong from his own Colt, stepped close to the horse nearest him, cut the tether, then went to each horse, freeing it. He grabbed the last horse by the mane, swung to its back, sheathed his knife, and drew both handguns. The yell that erupted from his throat would've made a Comanche swell with pride.

Every horse in the remuda bolted toward the fire. Bandits scrambled to get out of the way, and at the same time tried to reach rifles, or handguns laying by their saddles. Some fell under the hooves of the frightened animals. Others were knocked down by the shoulders of the charging beasts. Gunfire winked from the brush surrounding the camp.

Cantrell, legs gripping the barrel of his horse, fired at a man spinning away from a horse. He missed. Another of the outlaws came under his gun. He didn't miss. Quint fired weapons with both hands, rode to the far side of the fire, slipped from the back of the frightened animal, and stood spread-legged at the rim of firelight, firing into any man that moved.

The terrified bandits, those still able, turned their guns on Cantrell. His left leg went numb. A streak of fire burned his ribs. Then it felt like he'd taken a punch from a big man, right in his gut.

Abruptly, all movement and sound ceased. Cantrell wondered if he'd gone deaf. He felt that he stood alone in the world. Then his men, one by one, drifted from the heavy brush, all looking at him with awe.

"What the hell you need us for, Cantrell? You tried to do it all yourself." The man throwing words at him was Burkett.

Cantrell shook his head. "Just wanted to make sure we got 'em, down to the last man." He looked at the gun in his left hand, still smoking. "I'll clean yore Colt 'fore I give it back." He looked at the crew. "Check these bandidos. Any still breathin', tie 'em on a horse an' head it for Mexico."

King moved to his side, his voice low, and tender. "You took a couple, partner. Lie down. Let me see how bad."

Cantrell cast him what he hoped was a sour look. "Ain't got time to mess aroun', King. We'll check 'em later." Pain washed through him, only now making itself known. He grimaced. " 'Sides, only reason you want me to lie down is so you can whittle on me with that damned knife o' yours, an' pour some o' that rotten whiskey on me, an' in me."

The acrid odor of gunsmoke mixed with irritating dust hung heavy over them. The men walked to each body, made certain there was no danger from it, and moved to another, until all bandits were checked.

Only two lived, and they were headed for the Rio Grande as soon as they could be tied to a horse. Art King hadn't left Cantrell's side. "What you wastin' them horses fer? Them two rannies gonna be dead 'fore they get a mile from here."

"I want 'em to get back to Santana—let 'im know there's others drawin' cards in this game. Besides, they're two we ain't gonna have to bury."

"We gonna bury the others?"

Cantrell nodded. "Yeah. Figure their stink'll blow back to the ranch if we don't. Don't want Ma or Elena havin' to smell 'em."

King looked a question at him. "You checked to see if anybody other'n you took lead?"

Cantrell nodded. "Already checked. Didn't have to ask. I seen 'em standin' in the firelight with no blood showin'. They're all right." He made a quick count of bodies lying in grotesque shapes around the fire. Fourteen. "You men find a dry wash, dump these piles o' cow dung in it an' cave dirt over 'em, then we'll head for our horses. We oughtta get back to headquarters 'fore mornin'. Y'all take the day off when we get there."

" 'Fore we do anythin', partner, you gonna let me take a look at them holes in you."

Quint didn't argue this time. He felt like he would pass out if he didn't sit somewhere right sudden. He eased himself down to lean against one of the bandits' saddles.

Rawlins looked from the dead bandits to Quint. "What's our next move, Boss?"

Cantrell pushed his hat back and scratched his head. "Don't know, son, gotta think on that tomorrow. Right now I'm gonna let this damned Apache look at them holes causin' me to leak blood faster'n I can make it."

The first place King looked was Cantrell's stomach. He looked up and grinned. "Ain't no hole here. Bullet hit a cartridge in yore belt. 'Sploded it, an' glanced off somewhere."

Quint nodded. "I figure the one on the side is only a crease. How 'bout my leg?"

King slit Cantrell's trouser leg to his crotch, peeled the cloth back, and frowned. He worked his hands along the bone as best he could, nodded, and looked up. "Leakin' blood pretty good, but didn't hit the bone. Slug went all the way through. Soon's we get back to our horses, I'll waste some o' my good whiskey on it to keep it from putrefyin'."

Cantrell shut his eyes. "I knowed damned good an' well you wuz gonna get around to that."

Later, Cantrell's leg bandaged, the bandits' weapons gathered, and horses put on lead ropes, the Big Dipper told Quint it was about four o'clock when the sentry hailed them from the top of the wall surrounding the ranch yard.

"Cantrell here."

"Ride on in. Everything go all right?"

Cantrell, now through the gate, and knowing his voice showed tiredness, and pain, said, "The boys'll tell you 'bout it in the bunkhouse."

They had unsaddled, rubbed their horses down, turned them into the corral, and gathered around the pump to wash up when Cookie rang the triangle for breakfast. King took care of Quint's horse.

Cantrell was limping toward the sound of the call with the rest of the crew when Elena ran across the yard to throw herself into his arms.

Then, in the dim light she stood back and looked him up and down. "Besides those holes in your clothes, an' blood all over you—you all right?"

Quint groaned. " 'Course I'm all right, 'cept for that savage damned Apache tryin' to kill me. He's the one cut my jeans up, an' tore my shirt. Gonna have Lion dock 'is pay fer 'em."

She clamped hands to hips. "Oooh, Quint Cantrell, you're the most exasperating man in the world . . ." She couldn't say more. His lips covered hers. After a long while she stepped back, caught her breath, and said, "Cole and Laura, along with twenty riders, came in a little after sunset last night. He was upset that you'd, in his words, 'started the ball without him.' "

She took his hand in hers. "Breakfast's ready up at the house. I'm gonna take a look at the work Art did on you, then we'll eat. Laura's up. Cole's already eaten, an' Ma an' Pa are waitin' for us. They heard you ride in."

After Elena made sure Quint was all right, the cook danced from one foot to the other while all the hugging and handshaking went on, obviously fretting that her meal was getting cold. Finally, reaching the limit of her frustration, she pushed her way into the middle of them. "Eef the *señores y señoras* don't sit an' eat, I'm going to throw it out."

A few minutes later, all seated, and all trying to talk at once, Elena gave Quint a hard look. "Know what, cowboy, last night Cole told me all the crazy, dumb things the three of you did before leaving home. Most of it included guns and knives." She raked a couple of eggs from the platter to her plate, heaped some country fried potatoes alongside the eggs, and speared a steak from another platter. "An' you can bet soon's I finish breakfast I'm gonna corner Art King an' see if you didn't do the same thing last night with those Mexican outlaws."

"Aw now, Elena, ain't no sense in you botherin' King 'bout that li'l ole fight. I wuz jest in the wrong place when them Mesicans wuz throwin' all that lead. So I took a couple li'l ole chunks o' lead anybody else coulda caught."

She eyed him a moment. "Yeah, but nobody else did." She nodded. "Yep, I'm gonna talk to King."

Quint shaped his face into his most sober look. "As for what Cole's done told you, *mi amor,* don't listen to him. He's the one what taught me all I know 'bout fightin'. Fact is he led me into most o' them fights."

Cole rolled his eyes skyward. "Ma tried all these years to teach you proper grammar, an' you still talk like you never saw the inside of a schoolhouse."

"Well, they's a good reason for that. While you wuz goin' to that fancy Army school at West Point, me an'

Clay wuz learnin' somethin' useful, like how to use a Colt, an' Winchester, an' Bowie knife. Fact is, neither one o' us ever got good as you with any o' them."

Cole took a swallow of coffee and looked at Elena. "Honey, you have to understand, we never get together but what this argument comes up.

"The truth be known, Quint Cantrell may be the fastest and most accurate man alive with those weapons he mentioned." He nodded. "Yeah, I taught him everything I knew, but he took it up from there and made an art of it."

Elena looked Cole straight in the eye. "I'm gonna tell you something. If you taught him, I owe you a deal of gratitude, because I've had occasion to be glad he knew what he did. Besides, Papa tells me he'd hate to see the two of you ever have to face off. He figures both of you would die."

Cole shook his head. "That's how reputations get built." He looked at Quint. "You send Clay word 'bout Pa's troubles at the same time you sent me the message?"

Quint nodded. "Yeah, figure he'll be here in three or four days." He grinned. "Bet money Molly'll be with 'im. From what he told us in Leadville, I'd say she's a whole lot like our women."

Ma cut in. "Well now, I'd say you've all done yourselves proud with the women you picked, and when the grandbabies come along, I expect to see y'all back down here so I can spoil 'em."

Elena and Laura blushed.

They finished breakfast, drank the big coffeepot dry, and Quint pushed back. "Cole, you an' me better get our heads together for a little war talk. They musta taught you somethin' at that soldier-boy school you went to while me an' Clay done all the work 'round here."

Elena stood. "Laura and I'll help Inez red-up and do the dishes." She studied her hands a moment, then looked at Laura. "Cole tells me you make the best apple pie this side of heaven. If we can find dried apples, I'd like you to teach me."

Laura looked at Cole and grimaced. "Gonna tell you somethin', Elena, that man most ate the whole county outta dried apples *before* we married. I reckon by now, only a year later, there isn't a dried apple in the valley." She nodded. "Yeah, if Ma'll show us where the fixin's are we'll whip up several of them. Think maybe the crew'll like some too. Cole's got our crew to wantin' them much as he does."

While they headed to the kitchen, a separate room with a dog run between it and the main house, Cole and Quint went to Pa Mason's study to talk and learn how large a problem they had. Pa went along to fill them in on the way they were being fought, and what he'd found the best way to fight back.

As soon as they were alone, Quint packed his pipe, lit it, and looked through the smoke at Cole. "What you got in mind?"

Cole pinned him with a look. "Way I see it those people across the river will remember me. You and I spent a lot o' hell-raising time over there. I don't think they'll remember you. Back then you were a lanky hundred-and-seventy-pounder." He swept Quint's two hundred thirty pounds with an appreciative look. "No way any will remember you." He stood, went to the cabinet, and poured them each a glass of his father's whiskey. "I think you should go down there and see what the situation is. Then we can plan how to get the most for our money."

Quint nodded. "Sounds good to me." He frowned. "But jest so you make yourself useful while I'm gone, figure you oughtta have the men, including those I brought, scour the brush for bunches like we took on the other night."

"When you leavin'?" Cole asked.

Then, before Quint could answer, Cole shook his head and pinned him with a look. "You forget any of the *correct* Spanish grammar the Fernandez family taught us while we were down there?"

A faint smile crinkled Quint's lips. He answered in pure Castilian Spanish. "You must not forget, *señor. Mi esposa y a ella familia es* one of the oldest Spanish land grant families in the New Mexico Territory. We speak *español* back home as often as we do English."

Cole shook his head. "Damned if I can figure out how you can speak fluent Spanish, an' still speak your native English like an outhouse dog."

"Don't talk English—talk Texan."

Cole shrugged. "Yeah, and both you and Clay have put a bunch of gray hairs in Ma's head because of it."

Quint stood. "Reckon I better go tell Elena her favorite boy ain't gonna be around for a while." He gave Cole a hard look. "Don't want you tellin' her where I've gone, or what I figure on doin', you got it? If she knew, she'd sit back on her haunches an' sulk like one o' them old East Texas loggin' mules—then she'd start raisin' more hell than you ever seen."

Cole grinned. "Sounds like Laura." He frowned, then he looked at Quint. "You reckon the *señor,* or perhaps the *señora Fernandez* would know anything that might help us?"

"Figured to give 'em a visit while I'm down there."

• • •

Cole called his and Quint's men around him and told them the plan—as much as the plan concerned them. He singled out Martinez as being a good woodsman, then looked at Art King. "According to Quint you're a better Injun than most. You got any others in your crew with that kind of talent?"

"Reckon we got another couple o' us. What you got in mind?"

"In a minute." He frowned, wishing Clay was here. He was certain his little brother would have a couple of men who could fit the job. The fact was Clay himself could, as well as that sidekick of his, Snake McClure.

He looked at the men gathered close to him. "Okay, men, hunker down, I'm gonna tell you most of what's gonna be going on, and most of all, I want to caution each of you—there's not a job here that's not deadly dangerous. I don't want any of you getting careless and getting hurt. Now check your saddle leather, weapons, take a saddle bag packed with shells, and get ready like you're goin' on a trail drive. All right, let's go."

Quint came out the door as Cole was entering. Quint eyed him and said out of the corner of his mouth, "Get yore gear an' get the hell outta there. Them women o' ours have purely got their backs bowed agin' us doin' whatever they figure we gonna do." He shifted his bedroll to the other shoulder. "I jest told Elena to look fer me when she seen me. *That made 'er even madder.* She wanted to know where I wuz goin' an' what I wuz gonna do. I left before she could really build a head o' steam."

Cole chuckled. "Damn, you reckon she and Laura are kin somewhere in the past?" He gripped Quint's shoulder. "All joking aside, boy, you be more careful than you've ever been. I'll take care of things on this side of the border."

Quint made a playful swipe at Cole's shoulder, and left.

Cole went to his room, the same one he'd had while growing up, packed his gear, sucked in a deep breath, and went to the family room, where the women were sitiing, to let Laura raise her particular bit of hell with him.

It took her about ten minutes of uninterrupted caustic mountain-cat comments before Cole could get his chance to say anything. "Laura, we came down here to give Pa a hand at fighting this border trash. I figure to do what we came for. When Clay gets here, he's gonna be with me. Quint has a special job to get done . . ."

"And if I know him, it's the most dangerous," Elena cut in.

Cole looked her in the eye. "I won't lie to you, sis. He's sticking his head in a noose," he shrugged, "but then aren't we all."

She stood back and looked at him. "Cole Mason, reckon I knew when we left home it was gonna be this way, but—but, well hell, it's not easy. In the year we been married, I guess every time Quint leaves the house I don't know whether I'll see 'im ridin' or being carried slung across his horse come sundown."

Her eyes teared up. She turned her head, wiped her eyes, then pinned him with a look. "Y'all be careful, you heah?"

He pulled both her and Laura to his chest, held them a moment, then spun and went through the big heavy door.

When he passed the corral, a rider rode past him wearing a huge, floppy sombrero, trousers belled at the bottom, and a black bolero jacket. The rider raised his hand in farewell. "*Vaya con Dios, Señor Cole.*"

Cole stopped, stared at the rider's back, and murmured, "So that's how he figures to play it." Then louder.
"*Vaya con Dios, Señor Quint*. I hope He holds your hand
all the way."

As Cole and his men rode from the ranch yard, Quint,
with his black gelding eating up the trail, was already
three miles toward the border. He felt safe posing as a
high-class Mexican. His sun-darkened skin would pass,
and his Spanish would put many from the old country to
shame.

He decided to head directly to the Fernandez *rancho*. If
they didn't know anything, he'd return to Ojinaga. From
what he'd been told by Pa's hands, Santana's *rancho*
spread for miles on each side of the town.

He crossed the river, thought to skirt Ojinaga, then
decided to ride into town, have a drink—and listen. He
rode to the tie rail in front of the first *cantina* he saw, La
Paloma, "the dove." Now *that* was a good name for the
gates of hell. Before stepping from his saddle, he pushed
the thong off the hammer of his Colt. There might be
some in town who would remember the hell-raising
youth who had treed the town more than once.

At the bar, he tossed the bartender a five-centavo piece
and said, "*Cervesa, por favor.*"

"*Sí, señor,* but it is not very cold."

"*De nada.* I'll have it anyway."

He had lifted his drink to his lips and taken a swallow,
when a whip-lean *vaquero* pushed to his side. "See
you're ridin' a Texas rig, you a Texian?" The question
was neither friendly nor unfriendly, but Quint dropped
his right hand to his side.

"*Amigo,* when I'm in Texas, I'm a Texian, when in

Mejico, I'm a *Mejicano,*" he hardened his voice, "and I'm gonna tell you right now, whichever I call myself is none of your damned business. *Comprende*?"

The *vaquero* turned his side to the bar, putting his right hand in the clear. "*Señor,* I do not like your words,"

"And, *señor,* I don't give a damn what you like, or dislike. I came in here for a *cervesa.* I figure to drink it and leave peacefully—'less you have other ideas."

The slim Mexican made a sweep for his handgun. Quint stepped in close and brought his right up into the hard stomach in front of him. The *vaquero* stumbled backward, tripped, and fell to his back. He gripped his six-shooter in his right hand, tried to clear leather. He didn't make it. Quint pinned his hand to the floor with his boot.

They had been speaking in Spanish; now Quint switched to Texan. "Gonna tell you somethin', cowboy. You ain't very good with that handgun o' yores. I coulda, maybe shoulda, killed you." He kept the hand pinned to the floor. "Now turn loose that gun easy-like, an' I'll let yore hand go."

The fingers slowly uncurled from the walnut grips. The *vaquero* stared into Quint's eyes—then he grinned. Quint frowned. "What the hell you grinnin' at?"

"You, *señor.* You're a bad man, but not so bad, eh? *Sí,* you could have keeled me, but I am happy enough to grin when you don't." Quint removed his boot from the cowboy's hand. The young Mexican stood. "Shake hands, *señor*? We be friends?"

Cantrell extended his left hand, leaving his drawing hand free. Still grinning, the *vaquero* shrugged. "Ah, you are very careful. *De nada,* I still weesh to be your *amigo.*"

Quint liked the kid's spunk, and realized he may have overreacted to the kid's question. Cantrell gripped the extended hand. "Okay. Sorry I was so unfriendly, had a long hot ride, an' this heat don't do nothin' to make a man able to take a lot from nobody. Name's Juan Cantello. Buy you a *cervesa, amigo?*" Quint had decided to use the alias during his ride in. Too many in the area would remember the name Cantrell.

Still grinning, the kid nodded. "*Sí.* I have never turned down a drink. You buy, then I buy." He tapped his chest with his thumb. "*Mi nombre es Pablo Molero.*"

They had four beers while Quint learned the kid worked at the Fernandez rancho, was a top hand, and thought the sun rose and set in his employer—also his uncle.

When Cantrell made a motion toward the bartender, the kid shook his head. "I must be riding, *señor. Mi patron* weel be looking for me, ready to work *mañana.*"

"You care if I trail along? Your uncle is also my friend. I am headed to visit with him a day or so."

"I would like that, *señor.* Ees maybe feefteen kilometers to hees *rancho.*"

3

WHEN CANTRELL AND Molero gathered their horses, hostile eyes glared at Quint. The muscles between his shoulders tightened. Now speaking Spanish exclusively, he glanced at Pablo. "There are many in this town who dislike *Americanos, sí*?"

Molero nodded. "*Sí, señor,* ever since Manuel Soto take all theez land, he has some very bad hombres riding for heem, some of them *Americanos*. And many of heez *ganadero,* cattle as they are called in *Tejas,* wear American brands."

Cantrell's mind flicked to the numbers of cattle Brad Mason had lost. No wonder Soto's cows wore American brands.

He toed the stirrup and swung his gelding alongside Molero. "What's this Soto look like?"

Pablo shook his head. "Don't know. Nobody I know ever sees heem. A very hard man rides *segundo* for him, hombre named Benito Santana. He is good with the *pistola,* and rifle. He even keel heez own men when he gets angry." He shrugged. "But where thees Soto ees, nobody knows."

Cantrell pondered that problem while they rode. How could a man with the land and cattle Soto had remain invisible? The hostile looks pierced his back until they were well clear of town.

Before they got to the Fernandez *hacienda,* Cantrell told Molero that if he heard him called by a name other than Cantello, to keep it under his hat. Pablo agreed.

At the heavy, carved door to the *hacienda,* a servant announced Quint, still using the name Cantello, then escorted him into the living room, a room Quint remembered well.

Vasco Fernandez came into the room, a slight crease puckering his forehead. "*Señor* Cantello, have we met?"

Cantrell smiled. "Of course, *señor.* Many years ago, my best friend, Cole Mason, and I visited your *hacienda* on more than one occasion." He tapped his chest. "It is me, Vasco, Quint Cantrell. Have I changed so much that an old friend has forgotten me?"

Fernandez stepped back and studied Quint a moment. "Yes, yes you are Cantrell," he gripped Quint's hand, "but why the Cantello name?"

"I will explain to you, *señor,* but I must ask you to call me only by the name I now use."

Fernandez called for a *serviente* to bring tequila, and pulled Quint to one of the massive chairs. "Are you in trouble with the *federales,* old friend?"

Cantrell shook his head. "Nothing like that." The servant brought a tray with sliced limes, salt, a bottle of tequila, and glasses. He placed the tray between the two chairs. When he left the room, Cantrell told Vasco why he was there.

He put salt on the back of his hand, bit into the lime, knocked back the jigger of tequila, and leaned closer. "You have met this Manuel Soto?" At Fernandez's head shake Quint frowned and lowered his voice further. "I must find this man. I intend to destroy him. He has hurt the man who raised me, *amigo*. I can do no less."

Vasco placed his hand on Quint's forearm. "Old friend, you have chosen a very dangerous enemy. No one I have talked with has seen Soto, but all know the brutality, and rapacity, of his *segundo*, Benito Santana."

He leaned back in his chair, and shook his head. "Quint, the man has all the gunmen and outlaws in this part of *Mejico* working for him. We are all afraid. Afraid for our families, our land, our cattle—but we don't know what to do. If we call a meeting, try to organize against him, he counters by killing our men, or burning our *haciendas*." He knocked back his drink and poured another.

Cantrell frowned, stared into his glass, then looked his friend in the eye. "Cole and I brought thirty-seven men with us from New Mexico Territory and Colorado. I realize this is not many to fight the likes and numbers of Soto's men, but we're going to try. I figure we can whittle them down slowly then launch an all-out attack on what he has left."

Fernandez stood, took a turn about the room, then came back and stood in front of Quint. "Cantrell, when you get ready for that, give me a week's notice, and I'll give you enough men to help balance the scales." He nodded. "Yes! I'll have them if I have to drag them along at gunpoint."

Quint, his face sober, let the shadow of a smile crinkle his eyes at the corners. "That's more than I hoped for. I'll let you know, and remember, I'm Juan Cantello, son of one of the oldest ranchers down Saltillo way. Now, enough of trouble, let's talk of the good times we had in the past."

Cantrell spent three days with Fernandez. When he rode from the *hacienda,* he felt he and the Masons had a much better chance of ridding *Mejico* and the Big Bend of Manuel Soto—but he still had no idea who the man they must rid themselves of might be.

He rode into Ojinaga in mid-afternoon. Sweat soaked his shirt and ran from under his hat. He needed a good cold beer. He rode to the best *cantina* in town—and into trouble.

He went to the end of the bar, stood with his back to the wall, and signaled the bartender for a *cervesa.* A glance swept the room. Five dirty, unshaven Americans sat at a table in the back of the room talking, their heads close together. Quint picked up the name "Santana" in their discussion. Then one of them stood and walked to stand in front of Cantrell. "You a Texian?" Then, not waiting for an answer, he said, "We don't like Texians down here, an' we don't like them Spaniards who think they better than us."

Cantrell eyed the would-be badman a moment, and assuming the man spoke Spanish, he tried it on him. "Ah but, *señor,* I'm not a Texian, and in either case I don't *think* I'm better than you and that scum you sit with—I know damned well I'm better."

He softened his voice. "And I'm telling you right now, this is the second time I've come into this town for a drink, and have had someone interfere. I think you must need a lesson." As the troublemaker reached for his gun,

Quint dropped his glass and swung the flat blade of his straightened hand in a backhand motion against the man's throat.

The scum's eyes bulged. He grabbed for his crushed Adam's apple and tried to suck air past the constriction in his throat. Failed. His face purpled. He sank to his knees, then fell forward onto his face, clutching at his chest, his throat. Horrible gurgling noises came from him. His face blackened. He kicked twice, straightened his legs, and lay still.

Cantrell took one step backward, placed his back to the wall, and waited for the dead man's friends to come at him. They did.

The four stood, flipped the thong off their six-shooters, and took careful, measured steps across the room toward him. Cantrell held his breath. His guts churned. His scalp tightened against his skull. They drew closer.

Cantrell figured that when they got within ten feet they'd stop and make their play. At the moment he thought they would stop, he drew his Colt in perhaps the quickest draw he'd ever managed. They stopped. Three of them crouched, as though ready to buck the odds. One of them had better sense.

"*Amigos,* if that hombre can shoot good's he can draw, we gonna all be buzzard bait if y'all try fer them guns."

The curved clawlike tenseness left the hands of the three gunnies. At the same time, Cantrell let a little of his pent-up breath escape past slitted lips. "Your friend uses his head for something other than a hat rack. You're smart to follow his advice. Now, if you want to show me how smart you really are, leave those six-shooters in the middle of the floor where you stand, and walk back to the table you just left."

The eyes of one of the gunnies lit up like this was what he'd been waiting for. Cantrell shook his head. "Tsch, tsch, *mi amigo*, you've never seen the day you were good enough. You—any of you—twitch wrong, and I'll blow all of you to hell."

The gunny who'd had the notion wilted. They unbuckled their gunbelts and stepped back, then turned and walked to the table they'd left only moments before. From the corner of his eye, Cantrell watched the bartender blow out a breath through puffed cheeks, pick up a couple of glasses, and pour two drinks. At the same time, a slim Mexican scuttled for the door, looking over his shoulder at Cantrell. Quint would've bet money that man was going to tell Santana what had happened. The tall Texan shrugged. He might as well meet the feared Santana now.

"Bartender, have someone collect those *pistolas,* and bring them to you, *por favor.*"

"*Sí, señor.*" He glanced toward the door. "And, *señor,* you are about to meet the man for whom those five work. Do not shoot up my *cantina, por favor.*"

Cantrell chuckled. "Only if he insists on it." He turned his gaze toward the batwing doors still swinging back and forth from the heavy-handed entry of the man coming toward him. He'd only a moment ago slipped his Colt into its holster. It rode easy in the leather only an inch from his right hand.

Santana, as tall as Cantrell, was heavier through the shoulders, barrel-chested, with lank black hair hanging from under a greasy black sombrero that framed his high-cheekboned, square face. He stared at Cantrell through flat, black eyes.

"You 'ave keeled one of my men, *sí?*"

"If that pig lying there belongs to you, Santana, the answer to your question is yes." Cantrell still spoke the fluent Spanish he had learned while staying with the Fernandez family.

Santana frowned. "You have heard of me, yet you do not appear afraid."

"The man never pulled on a pair of boots who could claim I showed fear of him. You're only one man. You have some reason I should be afraid of you, let's hear it."

Santana studied him a moment, then shook his head. "A man like you, I want to work for me, but from what I see I don't think you work for any man."

Cantrell relaxed only a mite. "Guess that depends on the job."

The big outlaw *segundo* looked Cantrell up and down. "You speak English good's you do Mexican?"

Quint shifted from Spanish to Texan. "Naw, don't speak English a'tall. I talk Texan pretty good though. Spent some time up yonder punchin' cows fer a man named Rance Senegal. Learned to talk listenin' to his men."

Santana's head bobbed slowly. "*Sí*, I think you are the man I need."

"*Señor*, I might work for you, but I'm tellin' you right now—I don't come cheap."

"Ah, *Señor* Cantello, none of the good ones come cheap." He turned to the bartender. "Bring a bottle and two glasses to that table." He glanced at Cantrell and nodded toward a table. It stood in the middle of the room.

Quint let a crinkle show at the corners of his lips. "No. I will sit back there, and my chair will be the one against the wall."

Santana laughed, a low rumbling sound which came from his stomach. "Yes. It will be as you say. If you'd sat where I suggested, I'd have known you were not the man I wanted."

"What kind of man you looking for?"

Santana studied Cantrell a moment. "They call you Cantello, no?" Quint nodded. "Cantello, in *Tejas* there is a saying, 'I ride for the brand.' " Now that they were seated at the back table with a bottle in front of them, Santana poured them a drink. "What I want for the man I hire is one who rides for the brand. Me, as far as you're mindful of, I *am* the brand. You weel not ride for Manuel Soto or anybody else. You ride for me alone." The outlaw knocked back his drink, smiled, and said, "Too, *señor,* the man must be very quick with his guns."

Cantrell, sensing something more here than had been said, pushed his luck. "Ah, but I thought you worked for Soto."

A sly smile crossed Santana's face. "Perhaps, *señor,* I am not one who believes in riding for the brand—but again perhaps, I am one who would demand it of the man I hire. That man will work for me and me alone."

Cantrell pinned the big outlaw with a look that would have gone slam through most men. "Santana, you the man who pays me, you the man I work for. First, I want to know what I gotta do for yore money, then I'll tell you what it'll cost you and if it's something I will do."

Santana took a swallow of his drink, studied his glass a moment, then looked into Cantrell's eyes. "Do you know this man who calls himself Manuel Soto?"

Cantrell shook his head. "Don't know 'im, don't know anybody who does. Fact is, I ain't never met a man who ever saw 'im." He sat back, rolled a twirly, and lit it. He'd have liked to smoke his pipe, but these Mexicans seemed to favor *cigarillos* over a pipe. "You know him, *señor?*"

Santana shook his head. "I 'ave talked with him on several occasions, but have never seen him. He always meets me on his grounds, always has his face hidden, always has me leave where we meet before him, and it's always where he can see me until I'm out of his sight."

He again shook his head. "He pays me well, and gives me enough to pay the crew, but no, I do not know heem. Eet ees for that I wish to hire you. I want to know where he goes when he leaves here, and who he eez. *Comprende?*"

"You think perhaps he is an *Americano?*"

"I do not know, *Señor* Cantello. He speaks fluent Spanish, but he can also talk in the English."

Cantrell shrugged. "Tell you the truth, *señor,* I don't see how I can help you. I gotta have some way to know I'm on the right trail."

Santana leaned forward. "Perhaps I can help. Stay close to me, be my shadow, and after I meet with him, follow him."

Santana poured another drink, knocked it back, and leaned forward, his eyes slitted. "What I really want to know, in addition to who he is, is what kind of game he is playing. What are the stakes? Or is he playing the game for someone else?"

Cantrell twirled another cigarette, lit it, and looked through the veil of smoke between them. "Gonna lay it on the line, Santana. I'll take the job, but it's gonna cost you enough that I'll be happy with what you pay me. Ain't gonna try to get more outta you, an' ain't gonna take a chance on you figuring I'm gonna try for some o' the big pot at the end of the job. I do what you hire me for, give you what I find out, an' we ride off to follow our own trails." He swallowed some of his drink. "My price is ten thousand American dollars."

Santana, about to take a swallow of his drink, choked. "Ten thousand American dollars? Hell, I can hire twenty men for that."

Cantrell forced a shadow of a smile to his lips. He pushed back from the table and stood. "All right. Hire 'em." He let the smile crinkle his eyes and widen his mouth. "If all twenty of them put together are good as me, have at it." Not turning his back to the outlaw, he edged toward the door. Santana stood.

"*Una momento, señor.*" He pulled out the chair Cantrell had vacated. "Sit down. We must talk further."

Cantrell shook his head. "Ain't changin' what I give you by one damned *centavo*. If you're willin' to talk on those terms, I'll sit."

Santana twisted the chair toward Cantrell and waved his hand for the big Texan to be seated.

They talked another thirty minutes, and this time when Cantrell stood, he had the agreement he wanted—five thousand when he started, and five thousand when he deliverd the information to the outlaw. Santana told him where and what time he was to meet Soto the following night. Then after that meeting he and Quint would again meet in the cantina—only in a back room. He'd pay him his first five thousand then.

The place Soto was to meet Santana was an old, falling-down *jacal* outside of town about a mile. Cantrell wondered how he could get to the place undetected. He'd bet every cent the big outlaw agreed to pay him that his employer would have him watched.

When he left Santana, he went to the hotel, rented a room for a week, then went to the general store, bought a bait of jerky, and took it to his room. After about eight o'clock, he turned the lamp down, blew it out, and waited.

Long into the quiet of early morning, with the *cantinas* closed and all the people gone to bed, Cantrell slipped on his boots, cracked the door leading into the hall, and studied its silent length for almost fifteen minutes. Nothing stirred. He slipped from the room and headed for the back stairs. He checked the desert along the back of the hotel, then eased down the steps.

Once outside, he again studied his surroundings. Each yucca, clump of prickly pear, and ocotillo came under his gaze before he moved out into the desert.

The old tumbledown shack Santana had directed him to soon materialized through the dark. Cantrell circled the *jacal,* made certain no one had been sent there other than himself, and slipped into the dark, one-room hovel.

Before sliding down the wall to spend the rest of the night sitting, he walked around to make sure there were no rattlers wanting to occupy grounds he claimed. Finally, he sat to await the coming of daylight, and the passing of the hot day, before the two bandits were to meet. He wouldn't follow Soto this time. He wanted to check Santana out, see if he was playing straight with him. So far he figured his employer as either cagey or foolish. Santana had certainly brought Quint into the fold rather hastily.

Cantrell smiled into the dark room. Here he was, wondering if Benito Santana would play it straight with him, and all the while he wondered how he could outsmart both the outlaw and Soto.

4

CANTRELL DOZED THROUGHOUT the day, wakened occasionally to chew a few bites of jerky, stand, work the kinks from his muscles, and again sit—and sweat. The adobe walls trapped the heat such as to make an oven of the *jacal*. But he'd stood worse.

The sun's huge, fiery orb finally slipped below the ridge of low mountains, but it would be hours before the desert cooled. The stillness of twilight settled over the desert, then faded to a velvety darkness. The moon would not rise until about eleven, to paint the acres from hell with its silvery, magical sheen.

Darkness had not gripped the land more than a half hour when the soft clopping of a horse broke the silence, stopping just outside the walls, and followed by a soft curse. The first man had arrived.

Only minutes later a horse approached from the south. Cloth again scraped the adobe wall. Cantrell guessed the first to arrive had stood. Little above a whisper came the question "Santana?"

"*Sí, señor,* ees me. You have *pesos,* for me and the men?"

"*Sí,* but also information. My people across the river tell me Mason is bringing in fighting men by the dozens. Three bunches have already arrived, a total of about forty men, and more may come."

Santana chuckled. "Ah, *Señor* Soto, where they have increased their number by forty, we still have three to one. We don't let numbers worry us. They will lose the fight we make with them."

Soto made some remark Cantrell couldn't catch, then said in English, "Gonna tell you, my outlaw friend, they better lose, after all the *dinero* I'm payin' you."

Then, to Cantrell's surprise, Santana asked, "Why you payin' me all theez money, *señor*? I can take my men up there an' fight them, wipe them out. That what you want?"

Soto's voice hardened. "Why I'm payin' you all this money is none of your damned business. We'll play this game accordin' to my direction, or the money will stop. *Comprende?*"

Santana's voice lowered to a soft purr. "*Sí, señor,* I understand."

They talked only a moment longer, then Soto told Santana to head out, that he'd leave in a few moments.

Wanting now to smoke his pipe, which he'd not done for several hours, Cantrell waited—and so did Soto. Not until the sound of the big bandit's horse died in the distance did Soto leave. Cantrell waited another half hour before he headed back to town. He'd be able to pick up the tracks of the unknown man come daylight; only a wind would erase them—and it seemed the wind would never blow again. He smoked his pipe while waiting.

On his walk back, Quint thought of the words he'd heard. The words themselves meant little, it was the animosity he read into the tones of each of their voices. If he could identify Soto, maybe he could work them against each other.

Back in town, he went directly to Santana's room. Only a light tap with his fingernails brought the bandit chieftain to the door, gun in hand. "What you wake me this time of night for? I've not closed my eyes yet."

Cantrell looked at the gun. "Put your six-shooter away. Thought you'd like for us to talk out of the way of unfriendly eyes."

"Where the hell were you while I met with Soto? My rider never saw you leave town."

Santana pulled the curtain and lit a lamp. Cantrell grinned at him. "So you thought to have me followed? Tell you what, Santana, I figured you would do just that, so I left last night. I was at your meeting, sitting inside the *jacal* not three feet from you." He twirled a cigarette, lit it, and stared at the big outlaw. "Wanted to prove you got a man who can think. Too, I wanted to see if you trusted me. Figure you know I can think. And there isn't any doubt now that you don't trust me."

He took a drag on his smoke, knocked the ash from it, studied the red coal a moment. "You wantta back outta the deal now, we'll forget it; if you don't, then give me my five thousand dollars, and I'll get on with the job you give me."

Santana poured them a drink from the bottle sitting at his bedside. "*Señor,* when I give a man this much money, I like to have the feeling in my stomach he isn't going to ride away an' leave me holding the bag, as the *Americanos* say." He knocked back his drink, and poured another. "*Sí*, I will have you followed." He grinned. "You outsmarted me once, but don't figure to do it twice." He swallowed his drink and poured them each another. He reached into the saddlebags laying on the bed and pulled out a leather sack that clinked with the sound of gold. "You're still hired to do the job we talked about. Here is your first pay. Don't try to get away without finishing the job, or there will be nowhere you ride but what I'll find you."

Cantrell stared at him a moment, then in a soft voice said, "Don't ever threaten me, *amigo*. I don't like it." He put the bag of coins in his pocket and stood. "I'll see you when I got something to report." He left the room, not turning his back to the outlaw.

Cantrell had no more than cleared the door of Santana's room, when across the river, only a few miles to the north, the rattle of wagon wheels drew the attention of Cole. He looked at his father. "Pa, you have anyone out with the buckboard tonight?"

At his father's head shake, Cole smiled. "That'll be my little brother then." He stood, went to the door, looked out, pulled the door wide, and shouted. "Sure took you long enough, little brother. What'd you do, hang back thinkin' Quint and I would get all the fightin' done 'fore you got here?"

"Nah, figgered you an' Cantrell'd get things so messed up you'd need me a little later to straighten everything out."

Cole sprinted to the side of Clay's horse, pulled him from the saddle, and bear hugged him until Clay worked his hands between them and pushed him away. "Damn, big brother, glad to see you too." He twisted to halfway face the wagon. "You ain't met my wife yet. This here's Molly Claibourn Mason. Molly, this here's my big brother. I done kept him safe from gitten hurt more times than I can count." Before Cole could think of a proper retort, Clay turned to one of his riders. "Cole, you remember Snake McClure from up Leadville way. He's one o' us who kept you from gettin' yore damned head shot off."

Then, the whole family cut into the greetings, Ma Mason in the middle of it. After making certain everybody knew everyone else, Clay swept the ranch yard with a glance. "Where's Quint?"

Cole looked at Elena, then to Clay. "We sent 'im down to Ojinaga to see if he could find out what's behind this concerted attack on Pa's ranch. He's been gone about a week. We lookin' for 'im back any day now."

Clay studied his brother a moment, then turned his eyes on Elena. "Ma'am, know you're some worried 'bout yore man, but don't be. I guarantee you he's gonna stay till he finds what he went down there for. Might even be next week 'fore he gits back." He grinned. " 'Sides that, they ain't 'nuff Mexicans down yonder to brace Cantrell an' git away with it."

Elena, recognizing that Clay was trying to assuage any worries she might have, looked him in the eye. "Thanks, Clay. You Mason men and my Quint are what we women dream of." She nodded. "I know how my man is, and I know there are few his equal with weapons—but I still worry. I've dressed gunshots in his hide too many times not to worry."

Clay scraped dirt in a circle with his boot toe, then looked at Elena straight on. "Ma'am, I wasn't tryin' to hide what I know Quint'll do. I know how he is when they's a job to git done. He jest lowers his head an' bulls his way in. Don't know as how I ever seen 'im scared o' nothin'. 'Sides that, they's only one thing Cole an' me agrees on, an' that's that Quint Cantrell is the best man with six-gun or knife we ever seen."

A grin broke his solemn expression. "Hey, 'nuff o' this here long-faced stuff. Let's go in an' see if we cain't drink enough o' Pa's whiskey to make necessary a ride into Presidio for more."

The next morning at breakfast, Elena noticed that both Clay and Cole came to the table wearing sidearms, and stood rifles against the backs of their chairs. She looked at Cole. "You expectin' trouble here, or the two of you goin' lookin' for it?"

"Goin' lookin' for it. We figure those men we ride with won't consider the odds before charging in on the rustlers. We want to make sure they do."

The three wives and Ma stood and watched Clay, Cole, and Snake ride through the gateway. Ma swept the wives with a glance. "Poo now, y'all quit your worryin'. I've seen those two and Quint ride out more times than you could believe, ridin' out to find the troubles which have often ridden our shoulders." She nodded. "They'll be back safe."

Though she and Clay had been married less than six months, Molly had seen the kind of man she married before and after their wedding. Now she'd met one other just like him. She squeezed her eyes tight shut to hide any moisture that might give her away to her sisters-in-law or Ma. "You know, the General—that's my grandpa, an ex-Confederate general—well, he once told me Clay was the hardest man he'd ever seen. I believe him, for I saw Clay hang a man all by his lonesome for tryin' to do me harm." She sighed. "Now I've met one more like him. I can't believe it's possible."

Laura, still looking at where she'd lost sight of them, nodded. "Believe it, Molly. I married the eldest. He can be as hard as he has to be."

Then Laura's face took on a glow, a softness, then she nodded. "Yes, he can be hard, but he can also be the most tender, lovin' man alive. I think I would lie down and die if anything should happen to him."

"Hey," Elena cut in, "nothin's gonna happen to our men, or the crew." She placed hands on hips and looked at the others. "We all brought rifles with us. Let's get them cleaned, loaded, an' ready to shoot if any of that bandit bunch decides to attack the ranch. Our guns'll kill them as easily as the men's will."

While the wives cleaned their rifles that morning back at the ranch, Cantrell had a leisurely breakfast, saddled, and left Ojinaga. He smiled, knowing that one of Santana's men followed. If he wanted to lose the bandit, he had no doubt he could do it easily, but for now, let Santana's man suffer the heat.

He rode directly to the *jacal,* dismounted, studied the tracks, and again climbed to the saddle. The soft dust gave up no identifying hoofprints, but he didn't need any to track the horse Soto rode, unless it got into an area where several horses had walked. Soto had left in the same direction from which he'd approached the night before. South.

Cantrell figured he could head north and cut Soto's

sign, but he didn't take the chance. He followed the tracks and, as he had thought, they circled back to the north after only an hour.

At the Rio Grande, Cantrell found Soto's horse's tracks in soft, wet ground. He crossed the river and stopped at an adobe building with a sign made of weathered, cracked wood that named it as a café. He looped his horse's reins around the hitch rack and went in.

He sat at a table with his back to the adobe-thick sidewall, a wall thick enough to stop a bullet. In this rough border town, most who could find a place to shield their backs took it.

After ordering a steak, beans, rice, tortillas, and coffee, he studied those who busily shoved food into their mouths. He knew none of them, and after a casual glance his way, they went back to eating.

While sitting over a second cup of coffee, Cantrell wondered how he could find the man with such a well-hidden identity. That he was smart went undisputed. He could be the town banker, a lawyer, run the mercantile store—hell, he could even be the blacksmith, or a rancher. Whoever he was, he had his hands on a lot of money, and was willing to spend it, as evidenced by the payroll he maintained across the border with the bandits.

His cup empty, Cantrell stood, paid for his meal, and went to the saloon. The big beefy man brought him his glass of suds, studied him a moment, obviously trying to think where he'd seen him before, shrugged, and went back to pouring drinks. He was the same man who'd served him gallons of beer in years past.

Quint held his breath, then let it out slowly when the man failed to recognize him. He carried his drink to the back of the large room and sat where he could see those who entered. The term "hard case" would have fit any man in the room. Cantrell dropped his hand below table-top level and flicked the thong off the hammer of his Colt. Might as well be safe.

He sat there for over an hour, had two beers, and had thought to leave when a tall, thin, ferret-faced man pushed through the batwings into the dark room. Cantrell settled back in his chair. He knew the man—but not from around here. He'd seen him several times along the out-law trail, in places like Brown's Hole, Jackson Hole, and the Hole in the Wall. The man, Clem Barnett, was poison-mean, and would know Quint with a glance. Cantrell had killed his partner.

Quint tipped his hat forward to almost cover his eye-brows, and watched. Barnett bought a bottle, picked it and a glass up, brought it to the back of the room, and sat at the table next to Cantrell.

Barnett filled his glass, knocked it back, filled it again, swallowed it in one gulp, and then did this again several times. Cantrell figured the outlaw's eyes should by now be accustomed to the dark, and he would be getting more than a little drunk—and mean. He was right on both counts.

Barnett glanced his way, looked away, then swung his head back to stare hard at him. "By damn!" He stood, knocked his chair over, and reached for his handgun. "Cant—"

Before he got the full name out, Cantrell drew, slipped his thumb off the hammer, and thumbed it back again. He didn't fire again. Barnett stood staring at him, eyes bulging, a black hole only now oozing blood from his shirtfront. Trying to squeeze off a shot, Barnett's hand loosened on the grips and his pistol dropped to the floor.

He followed it, his face buried in the dust, spit, and grime of the rough puncheon decking.

The man at the next table looked at Cantrell, grinned a thin-lipped smile, and said, "Friend o' yores, I reckon."

Quint picked Barnett's half-empty bottle from the table, handed it to the thin-lipped man, and said, "Have a drink on Clem Barnett—he never wuz p'ticular who he drank with,"

The thin-lipped hard case acted like he wanted to make something of Cantrell's words, then glanced at the tied-down holster and took the bottle from Quint's hand without saying a word.

By then a swamper came, pulled the body to the back door, swabbed the blood from the floor, and went about his usual cleaning. The batwings again swung inward.

A short, thin *vaquero* stood to the side a few moments, then went to the bar, got a drink, and scanned the room. His eyes rested on Cantrell only a moment, but long enough for Quint to be sure the man was the one Santana had sent to track him.

Quint stood, went to the man, motioned to the table at which he'd been seated, and looked him in the eye. "Might as well make your job easy as possible. Come to my table, then you can tell Santana you followed me closely." He spoke Spanish so there would be no doubt the man understood.

The *vaquero* looked confused, opened his mouth as though to say something, picked up his drink, and followed Quint to his table. "I'll be in this town for some time, so to save you and your boss trouble why don't you go on back, tell him I'm staying in the hotel, and will do the job he gave me—but I don't want interference."

He took a swallow of his beer, gave the *vaquero* a

straight-on look, and continued. "Also, tell him get me word of his next meeting time and place. He'll know what I mean."

The Mexican, apparently thinking he'd done exactly as Santana had directed, finished his beer and left. Cantrell sat there long enough to drink another beer, went to the hotel, signed for a room, put his gear on the chair, and stretched out on the bed.

Where should he start? Soto was a name known throughout the area, but where was the face to go with the name? Should he start with trying to find an obviously wealthy person, or a person with vast land holdings? He thought on his problem for a couple of hours and was no further ahead than when he'd lain down.

He swung his feet to the floor, buckled on his six-shooter, and went down to the lobby. A newspaper lay on the seat of a chair. He picked it up and read every word in it, but came across nothing that gave him an idea how to go about finding the man he sought.

Making his way out onto the street, he came face-to-face with Cole. Careful to show no recognition, he brushed by his old friend and said from the corner of his mouth, "Room three. Half an hour."

He walked on down the street to the general store, bought pipe tobacco, and returned to the hotel. He had only a few minutes to wait until there was a light tap on his door. He cracked the door an inch or so, then opened it to let Mason enter.

"What you come down here for, Cole? Ain't nothin' but stray dawgs, hard cases, an' dust in this here town."

Mason glanced about the room, settled on the bedside table, and apparently didn't see whatever it was he was searching for. "Hoped you brought a bottle to your room." He looked back to Cantrell. "Rode down here hoping to see you, partner." He grinned. "Had a helluva time convincing Elena to stay put."

"What you need to see me 'bout?"

Cole shrugged. "Mostly to see if you were all right, see if you needed help."

Quint shook his head. "Damn, you'd think I wuz a helpless baby." He then told Cole all that had happened since he left the ranch. He nodded. "Figure 'tween us we might have a idea what to do next."

Cole leaned forward. "First, I'll tell you Clay, Molly, his sidekick, an' a few riders showed up." He grinned. "Quint, that Molly o' Clay's is a thoroughbred. All them women fell into friendly ways like they'd known each other forever.

"Clay's ramroddin' half the riders we brought with us. I've got the other half, and we're keeping all of Pa's riders at the ranch to see nothin' bad happens there. Clay and I are using surprise tactics taught me at West Point by General Lee. We're whittling down Soto's troops slowly, but considerably." He shook his head. "But they still outnumber us 'bout four, maybe five, to one."

Cantrell packed his pipe and offered Cole his tobacco. Pipes lit, Quint smiled. "Hell, Cole, four, five to one makes it 'bout even with the kind of men we got. I'd say let's ride down yonder to Ojinaga an' wipe 'em out, but that wouldn't settle nothin'—we don't know who Soto is, or what his game is." He stood.

"Tell you what, you stay here, I'll go to the saloon, get a bottle, an' you an' me'll see what we can come up with." He'd hung his gunbelt over the back of the chair when he came in; now he buckled it about him again and left.

Less than ten minutes later he was back. While pouring

them a drink, he looked across his shoulder at Mason. "I'm callin' myself Juan Cantello around here. Nobody knows me from when you an' me raised so much hell while growin' up. Figure it's best we're not seen together or they'll soon know that I'm Cantrell. I'm s'posed to be a fast gun from down Saltillo way."

Mason nodded. "Fair enough. I've gotta get back to my men anyway. Hell, they might decide to invade Mexico if I'm not there to hold 'em down." He knocked back his drink and held his glass for another. "Now let's see if we can come up with how to identify this Manuel Soto."

They talked for an hour, and finally decided on a plan. They had another drink, then Cole stood, gripped Quint's shoulder, looked him in the eye, and said, "*Mi amigo,* I wish it made sense for me to side you in this down here," he shrugged, "but don't reckon so. I'll tell Elena not to worry."

He stepped toward the door. "I'd say be careful, but knowing you that would be a waste of words. You're always careful, but still stick your nose into more trouble accidently than most men find on purpose."

Cole opened the door a crack, checked the hallway, and left.

About the time Cole left Quint, Clay lay flat on his belly peering into an arroyo. In the bottom, at least twenty men, half of which were *Americanos,* the rest Mexicans, sat around a fire. Farther down the gulch, a couple of riders held about forty head of cattle, all of them, from what Clay could determine, wearing Brad Mason's B-bar-M brand. He rubbed his fingertips up the grip of his Winchester, tempted to open fire on the bunch, then mentally shook his head. Taking on those odds was something only Quint Cantrell was fool enough to do. He inched back from the lip of the ravine until certain he could not be seen, and in a long stride headed for his men, dodging yucca and prickly pear clumps along the way.

The sun, now only an hour above the horizon, seemed bent on drying and cooking all under its rays. Clay stopped, pushed his hat back, and mopped sweat from his forehead. He pondered the best way to attack. Finally, he smiled, pulled his hat back down to shade his eyes, and headed back to camp.

Once there, he gathered his men around. One by one, his gaze locked on them. His face feeling stiff as weathered leather, his gut beginning to tighten, he again swept them with a look. "Y'all ready for some fun? They's 'bout twenty o' Soto's men in a ravine a mile from here. They got 'bout forty o' Pa's cows down the arroyo from 'em. The walls up from 'em are pretty steep. We stampede them cows into 'em an' we gonna have us some fun shootin', watchin,' an' laughin'."

Martinez said in a low voice, "Clay, what you say eez nothin' to laugh 'bout. Me an Cole done that once up yonder in Tomahawk Canyon. It's a bloody, unhuman thing to do."

Clay stared at his boots. "Know it, Martinez, but we in a war. In war you win any way you can."

A half hour later, hunkered behind a clump of prickly pear, Clay looked along the lip of the ravine. He could see all of his men except those he'd sent to stampede the small herd. He turned his glance toward the sun. It looked as though it would bury itself in the rocky, arid hills, the edge barely touching the tops of them. Then the blood-curdling Texas yells sounded from down the dry ravine.

Those at the fire grabbed for weapons. Clay's men along the rim opened fire. The first volley, four bandits fell, and one of them crawled toward his saddle. Clay put a bullet into his legs.

The cows, bellowing in fear, horns clanging together, ran in a crazed line straight toward the rustlers' camp. Now, all thought of rifles forgotten, the bandits tried to climb the sides of the ravine. Clay's men, almost like at a turkey shoot, cut them down. The sound of rifle fire was ear-splitting, then rapid six-gun fire, only a little less sharp, increased the volume.

Two of the rustlers ran ahead of the stampede for the high wall ahead. Sharp hooves churned them into the dust. Clay turned his head. There would be only blood-sodden clothing where the two had run. This was harder to stomach than he'd thought.

Abruptly, all sound ceased except for the cattle beginning to turn and mill about at the end of the arroyo. Dust churned up from the bottom. Clay stood and yelled for his men to gather around. Slim, Brown, and Martinez were the last to join him. Martinez looked to the bottom of the draw. "You still theenk theez is fun, *amigo*?"

Clay shook his head. "It had to be done, Martinez." He studied his boot toe. "No, it wasn't no fun. Don't wantta have to do nothin' like it again." He straightened his shoulders. "C'mon, we gotta see if any o' them still live."

An hour later they sat in their own camp. They drank coffee in silence. Clay pulled a bottle from his saddle-bags, went to each of them, and spiked their coffee with a strong jolt. "We'll head back to the ranch house in the mornin', see how Pa an' his bunch're doin'."

5

BRAD, THIRTY MEN, and the ladies, manned the adobe walls around the ranch headquarters. They'd been at their stations since the night before. All were tired, their faces haggard from lack of sleep. Sporadic fire from the chaparral searched for human flesh along the high, thick fence.

Elena climbed down the pole ladder, clutching her rifle in one hand while grabbing for ladder rungs. On the ground, she walked to stand below Laura and Molly. "Let's see if Ma's got supper ready. We'll bring it out here. Three or four of the men can sit at the base of the wall and eat while the rest keep those animals at bay." She stepped toward the house, then turned. "Bring your rifles. We'll take time to clean them while Ma dishes up."

Her shoulders sagged with tiredness; she wished Quint was here. She straightened her shoulders, and with an effort pasted a smile on her face. No point in letting Ma see how the strain was getting to her.

They got the men fed. Each of them cleaned his rifle

after eating, and took a fresh supply of ammunition back to the top of the wall.

After helping Ma clean up the dishes, Pa told them to get some sleep. He and the men could hold off any attempt the bandits made to breach the walls.

Molly shook her head. "Nope. We'll spread our blankets out here. Wake us after 'bout three hours an' we'll let some of the men rest awhile."

Elena and Laura agreed, and by sunrise all of them had gotten a few hours' sleep.

They suffered through the second day of the siege. Thus far only two of Brad's men had gotten hit; minor creases along the shoulder of one and a burn across the neck of another. Brad wondered how long luck would stay with them. He glanced at the sun. Soon another night would set in, with the constant tension of when, and if, the bandits would charge the walls.

Clay had led his men to within a mile of the ranch when he held up a hand. They stopped, silent. He cocked his head. Rifle fire! His first impulse was to ride hell for leather to where he knew his wife was in danger, but he knew that would be a damned fool thing to do.

"Men, the ranch is under attack, an' we don't wantta go bustin' in there." He searched the face of every man there. "Most o' us has fought Injuns; fact is, most o' us has spent our whole life fightin' somethin'. I figger we leave our horses here, go around such that we got the wall circled, then slip toward it until we can ease up on 'em one at a time an' put our knives to work." He again searched their faces. "Any o' you got a better idea, let's hear it."

One of the men said, "Sounds good to me. They ain't

gonna figger to look fer one man behind 'em—they gonna look fer a whole bunch."

Each of them nodded. He squatted and drew a circle in the alkali dust. With barely enough daylight left for them to see by, he sketched in more detail. "Okay, supposin' this here's the ranch wall, here's where I want each of you to start yore move toward it." He proceeded to assign each man a specific place to start toward the wall. "When you don't hear nobody firin' close to you, come back here. We'll ride to the *hacienda* together." He stood. "All right, let's get at it."

About to head for his station, he stopped, took his rifle to an old gnarled post oak, and stood it against a scraggly limb. "Reckon it'd be a good idea to leave our rifles here. We'll make less noise that way." He gave them a crooked grin. " 'Sides, this here's gonna be close-in work—knife, or six-gun." He spun on the toe of his boot and headed out.

In his sector he could hear that there were five rifles firing, each of them about twenty-five or thirty yards apart. Clay pondered the best way to attack. Should he take out the middle one first, or start at the end of those in his area? He decided to start at the end.

He moved at a right angle to where he could start his approach, then he went into a crouch.

One foot in front of the other, he slipped his booted feet along the hard ground, with only a fraction of an inch of dust overlaying the weather-packed surface. His feet found the spines of a dead ocotillo bush, toed it aside, and moved closer toward the sharp sound of the long gun.

The velvety black softness of night now surrounded him. He wished his mission could ultimately claim the same velvety comfort of victory. Then, along with the nerve-clattering noise of the rifle ahead, he could see a tongue of fire erupting from its muzzle.

Clay froze, stared at the spot where he'd seen the flash, and turned his head only a fraction of an inch to try and see the shooter. After a moment the bulk of the man separated itself from the softer dark of the night.

Clay's hand moved to the razor-sharp Bowie knife at his back and eased it from the sheath. He stepped toward the back of the rifleman. All of his concentration on the target, he moved silent as smoke.

Only an arm's length separated them, when his foot found a dry twig. It snapped. To his ears the sound exploded into the dark, sounding as loud as the rifle in front of him. The bandit whirled to face him.

No need for stealth now. Clay stepped toward the man, the knife grasped in his right hand, and clubbed it to the side of the outlaw's head. The bandit dropped.

In the same fluid motion with which he'd clubbed the man, he stooped, swept the blade across the man's throat, and felt it go through until it touched neck bone. The bandit lay like a saddle blanket carelessly tossed to the ground. Clay headed toward the rifle fire to his left, circled, and came in on that bandit's back. In less than an hour he had that man taken care of, and the third. He moved toward the fourth outlaw. The smell of cordite grew stronger the closer he got to the man.

Less than ten feet in back of the bandit, Clay put his foot down, and before lifting the other, he cocked his head to listen. The only rifles still firing were those remaining for him. His men had done their job—thus making his job harder. He'd taken on more targets than the others, knowing it would be harder, but not anticipating that he'd be doing it with the other rifles silent.

He looked at the dark form in front of him, thought to use his throwing knife, then discarded the idea. He couldn't chance missing his target. He stepped silently to the bandit's back. His knife again did its work.

The last of the five still fired, but sporadically. Clay wondered how long it would take the outlaw to determine that his was the only rifle firing. Standing almost fifty yards from where he'd seen the last flash from the bandit's gun, Clay didn't have to wonder much longer. A thrashing through brush, and the soft steps of careless feet in the dust, told him that the man had quit his post. Hunkered beside a prickly pear clump, Clay waited.

Not a yard in front of him the dark bulk of Soto's man materialized. Clay's hand swept to his handgun. He drew and thumbed two shots into the chest of the squat man in front of him. This time the smell of cordite came as a welcome thing, because he knew this man was the last of the threat to the womenfolk.

Molly leaned her head against the parapet of the wall, wondering where Clay might be on this treacherous night. At least she had a thick adobe wall to shield her. What might he have to keep bullets and knives from his body? A chill ran up her spine.

Tired enough to doubt her own senses, she raised her head from the wall. Her ears strained for the sound of gunfire. Only silence rewarded her. She walked along the catwalk to find Brad Mason. After looking closely at seven men, she found him slumped over his rifle stock—asleep. She touched his shoulder.

"Brad, the firing's stopped. What can it mean?"

Mason stirred, pawed at his eyes to wipe sleep from them. "Wh-what you say, Molly?"

She repeated her question.

He pushed his head up enough to see over the wall, shook his head, and again tilted his head to listen. "Don't know, child. They may be rebunching, or pullin' back for ammunition. Not likely they'll quit. They had us by the tail with a downhill drag. Nah, they wouldn't a quit."

Molly nodded, her shoulders slumped a bit more, and then walked back toward her place along the wall.

Clay spotted the shadowy forms of his men and their horses while still more than twenty feet from them. "It's me, Clay. Somebody light a fire. Reckon we can fix breakfast, drink a little coffee, have a drink outta one o' them bottles you men got in yore saddlebags. When Mr. Sun gives us enough light so's them at the ranch can see who we are, we gonna go see how they got along." While talking, he'd made a quick count of his men. They were all here.

"Any o' you take lead, or a knife cut?" Not a man spoke. He nodded. "Figgered y'all wuz good Injuns. You ride for Quint, Cole, or me, you gotta be."

They sat around the fire, ate, drank coffee laced with the strong whiskey, and told lies until Clay stood. "Time we get to the ranch, we'll have 'nuff light for them inside to see who we are. Saddle up."

When still a quarter of a mile from the wall, the sun only now showing a bright rim above the eastern hills, Clay held up his hand, palm outward in the universal peace sign. Those inside could see that long before they could put a face to the riders. He held his hand in that fashion until the gates swung open.

Before he could swing his leg over the rump of his horse, Molly toed the stirrup, swung up behind him, and clasped him in her strong young arms. "Oh, Clay, I knew it had to be you out there when they stopped shootin' at us."

He swung his leg over the pommel, jumped to the ground, and held his arms up to help Molly down. They shared a long, hungry kiss. Though tired to the bone, Clay wanted her with every bit of his body.

He looked at her smudged face, let a smile crinkle the corners of his lips, and pulled her to him again. "Reckon y'all had a right rough time of it. Want all o' you to get some sleep now." He twisted to look at his men. "You men get to the bunkhouse and turn in. Me an' Snake'll keep watch." He looked at Brad, who only then walked to the men bunched around. "Pa, get yore men to the bunkhouse. They need to sleep till that old sun goes to bed. I'll give a yell if anything looks like we're in for it agin'."

Snake edged his horse closer to Clay. "Somehow, I knowed you an' me wuz gonna be the ones shortchanged on sleep."

"Ah hell, Snake, we gone without 'fore." Still holding Molly close to his side, he said, "Course if you're too tired to side me, reckon I can handle it alone."

Snake bristled. "Why, damn you, Clay, you know good an' well if you gonna be up there on that there wall awatchin', I'm gonna be right there with you."

Clay chuckled. Snake backed his horse and peered at him. "Now see there, you done it to me agin. Roped me in tight 'fore I knowed you had a rope on me." He reined his horse toward the corral. "Let's take care o' our horses, men, then y'all crawl in yore blankets."

Still holding Molly close to his side, Clay turned his horse over to one of the hands and headed for the *hacienda*.

• • •

Dark had settled in when Cantrell went out into the street. He stood a moment, and in the dim light read the signs hanging over the boardwalk. One read, "ANSEL RONDELL, Attorney at Law." He walked toward it.

Cantrell peered through the dust-coated glass. A faint lantern glow painted the dirty window. He went in. A slim man, two or three years younger than Quint, about Clay's age, light hair, and a deeply tanned face, stood. "May I help you, sir?"

Cantrell smiled. "No, sir. I'm new in town, an' figgered to meet all the 'portant folks here. You're first." He stuck out his hand. "I'm Juan Cantello."

"Ansel Rondell here, and I'm tellin' you right now, you missed the last train if you figured to meet one of the town's important citizens in this office." He looked toward the coffeepot. "Want a cup of coffee?"

Cantrell nodded. Rondell took two cups off a wall peg and poured. "You need a lawyer, Mr. Cantello?" His voice exuded hope.

Quint grinned. "Business as bad as all that?"

Rondell shrugged. "Worse. These people around here shoot their troubles. I've not had a client in two months. 'Bout ready to go back to punchin' cows."

"Aw hell, man. You got it a lot softer here than pushin' a bunch o' cows around." Quint liked this young man, especially after finding he'd done some cowboying.

Rondell shook his head. "Not softer, Cantello. Hungrier is the proper word. I've eaten more regular ridin' the grub line than here." He sipped his coffee. "What can I tell you about the town?"

Cantrell shook his head. "Don't know. Reckon I just want to get a feel for it. Who swings the biggest stick?

Who's the meanest?" He grinned. "Don't know yet whether I want to try for a job in town, or go back to cowboyin'."

Rondell leaned forward. "Tell you right now, stay with cowboyin'. Course 'bout all you have to put up with bein' a cow nurse is summer heat, thirst, winter cold, rope burns, sleepin' on hard ground, rattlesnakes, stampedes, roundup." He grinned. "Well, maybe a town job wouldn't be all that bad after all."

Quint frowned. "Anybody 'round here know who this man Soto is? I hear a lot 'bout 'im. Seems he's got a lot o' money. The ranchers don't like 'im. The bad men're scared o' him—an' ain't nobody ever seen 'im. Sounds like they're all jumpin' at shadows, scared of ghosts."

Rondell frowned and stared into his coffee cup a moment. He looked up, his eyes troubled. "I can only tell you this, cowboy. Soto's no ghost. I don't know anyone who can point 'im out to you. I know I don't know who he is, but I'll tell you right now, there're some mighty dangerous men afraid of him.

"The name—not the man—started up around here 'bout two years ago. The ranchers started losing cattle. Those who asked questions disappeared—some shot, some just plain gone. The riffraff abruptly had money to spend. Oh hell, Cantello, what I'm tryin' to tell you is, don't ask about him outside of this office. It will only mean trouble for you."

"Rondell, trouble's my middle name, 'bout all I ever had wuz trouble, an' it always come in bunches."

The young lawyer poured them another cup of Arbuckle. "Why don't you stop in to see the sheriff, the banker, Art Kinkaid over at the general mercantile store; get acquainted if you figure to spend some time here."

Cantrell stood. "Good advice." He glanced at the coffeepot. "I'll stop in here for a cup o' yore coffee ever'so often too."

Rondell nodded. "Do that. We'll talk cowboyin'."

Cantrell walked away from the lawyer's office more puzzled than before, but he'd gotten one piece of information that might help him: The name Soto had only appeared on the scene about two years ago.

He walked by the bank. Closed. A glance across the street showed the sheriff's office only a few doors down. He angled across the street, stopped for a late-driving wagon to pass, then went to the door he'd sighted from across the street.

The man he took to be the lawman sat, feet crossed on top of the desk. Cantrell couldn't tell whether he would stand tall from the way he sat, but he knew he faced a powerful man, a man with hamlike fists, heavy shoulders, and a stubborn, pug-nosed face under a shock of red hair.

The lawman uncrossed his legs, dropped his feet to the floor, and peered at Cantrell through steel gray eyes that swept his tall frame from head to toe, and stopped but briefly on his tied-down holster. "You got trouble, cowboy?"

Cantrell shook his head. "No trouble, Sheriff. Just stopped in to say howdy. I'm new in town an' thought to get acquainted. Name's Cantello."

The lawman stood and held his hand out across the desk. "Bart Engstrom, sheriff. Glad to know you—I hope."

Cantrell grinned and shook his head. "Don't figger to bring you no trouble, Engstrom."

The sheriff flicked a thumb toward Quint's holstered

Colt. "You will sooner or later if you can use that six-shooter—an' I figure you can."

Cantrell's face hardened. "I use it only when somebody won't have it no other way. If they bring it to me—then they got trouble."

Engstrom nodded. "Keep it that way." He looked toward the coffeepot. "Coffee?"

The tall cowboy shook his head. "Nope. Done had 'nuff to fill the Rio Grande, buy you a drink, though."

The sheriff pulled his hat from a wall peg, smiled, and said, "Let's go."

Engstrom led them to the closest saloon. Standing at the bar, Cantrell felt the eyes of almost everyone in the room, and they didn't all seem friendly. He picked up his drink, held it in a toast, and said, "*Salud*." He glanced about the room. "Don't seem like I made any friends comin' in here with the law."

Engstrom knocked his drink back and grinned. "Figured you wouldn't. I run a tight town. There's them hard cases, an' there's me. Thought to put you on my side when we come in here."

Cantrell looked into the lawman's eyes. "Sheriff, if I gotta take sides, you ain't done me no wrong by puttin' me sided up with the law. Let 'em cut their wolf loose."

The lawman laughed, a deep rumble from his barrel chest. "Kinda had you figured that way, Cantello. If they bring you trouble, I'll play it square with you. Just stay legal."

Cantrell held his glass out to the bartender, then said, "Engstrom, I ain't never took nothin' that didn't b'long to me—cow, horse, or money. An' I never shot nobody what wasn't lookin' at me, an' already tryin' for his gun."

The lawman studied Cantrell a moment. "Cowboy, I mighta put you 'hind the eight ball by comin' in here with you. Right now, I'd say the feelin's 'bout you in this here room are of suspicion, distrust, or downright anger. This time I'll buy."

They knocked back their drinks, shook hands, and the sheriff left.

The lawman had no more than cleared the batwing doors when a lanky, hatchet-faced man, wearing tied-down holsters, sidled to Cantrell's side. "Ain't healthy in this town to be too friendly with the law."

Cantrell, right hand hanging at his side, flipped the thong from his Colt. "Figger it's a free country, *amigo*. I drink with anybody I damn well please. You, or anybody in this room, don't like who I drink with, cut loose yore wolf."

To Cantrell's surprise, the man laughed, and the laugh took some of the edge off his temper. The stranger said, " 'Bout the way I had you measured. I don't give a damn who you drink with. Just thought to give you a warnin'. Ain't many in this room friends with nobody, me included. Be careful."

Cantrell looked in the mirror behind the bar. The faces he could see stared with hostile eyes at his back. The hatchet-faced puncher looked into the mirror, his eyes locking with Quint's. "See what I mean?"

Cantrell nodded, ordered another drink, tossed it back, and flipped a coin to the bar. He twisted, looked at the puncher, said "Thanks," and walked toward the door.

About ten feet from the batwings, a short, hard-faced man stepped between him and the door. "Don't like your friends, cowboy."

Anger again bubbled to the surface, making Cantrell's scalp tighten, his face hot.

"Seems they's a bunch o' you in here makin' my business yores. I don't like it. You lookin' for trouble, you done found it."

The squat gunman stared at Cantrell, and his eyes held an oily sheen, black, with no emotion. He looked as though he hadn't expected an outright challenge, looked as though he thought there would be some talk first. He hesitated.

Cantrell, his fingers brushing the walnut grips of his Colt, held his look on the puncher, but saw all around him. "You come at me lookin' for a fight, you got one. Draw, or run."

The gunman twisted as though to head for the door—then swept his gun from its holster. Cantrell drew without thinking, and thumbed off two shots, each punching a dark black hole in the man's shirt pocket.

The slugs knocked the gunman back a step. He caught his balance, took a jerky step toward Cantrell, and thumbed off a shot, knocking splinters from the rough puncheon floor. As he eared back the hammer for another shot, his thumb slipped the hammer—and he caught Cantrell's third bullet. A hole in his forehead cut his left eyebrow in two.

He fell backward, his trigger finger tangled in the trigger guard. Cantrell swallowed his anger. He kept his eyes on the rest of the room. "Anybody else?" His voice sounded hard as granite to his ears. "C'mon, I still got three more where those come from. Hate to clean my handgun less'n I done emptied it."

The room stood silent. Every hand in the room lay flat

on the table in front of it, palm down. Then a thin, high voice from back against the wall said, "Gawd, I ain't never seen a gun come outta a holster so fast."

Another voice said, "You still ain't seen one come out that fast. Ain't nobody in this room seen him draw." Then, speaking to Cantrell, he said, "You got no fight outta any o' us. Reckon somebody oughtta git the sheriff, or marshal. Me, I'm gonna sit right here an' have 'nother drink."

There was no need to send for the law; Engstrom pushed through the batwings. His glance swept the room and came back to Cantrell, and he nodded. "Didn't take you long to find trouble, Cantello. How'd it happen?"

"Ask them. I'll tell my side of it over at your office. I'm goin' there now." He pushed through the doors and walked to the sheriff's door.

In the saloon, Engstrom asked for details. A man who had been sitting at a table with the dead man stood. "Reckon I'll tell you, mister lawman. That gunslinger what jest left here bumped into Yancy there lying on the floor. Yancy started to say he wuz sorry, an' that there *pistolero* shot 'im. Didn't give 'im a chance even if he'd been wearin' a gun, an' he wuzn't."

Engstrom pinned the talker with a hard look. "You sayin' the dead man had no gun?"

"That there's 'zactly what I'm sayin'."

From the rest of the people there came a resounding "Yeah, yeah, that's the way it happened." The sheriff looked at each of them, then turned to the doors, only to see the hatchet-faced puncher go out the doors ahead of him.

Engstrom stepped through the doors to see the man

waiting for him in the middle of the street. When he reached him, the puncher turned and walked by his side.

"Sheriff, them in that there saloon must've seen a different gunfight than I seen. That ranny what said he'd tell you his story in yore office give that dead man in yonder every chance to back down. Then when he wouldn't, he give him the chance to draw first—even let 'im get 'is six-shooter out an' almost leveled 'fore he drew." He grinned. "Ain't gonna tell you I seen 'im pull iron, don't b'lieve nobody in there seen 'is gun come outta the holster, but suddenly that there dead man had two holes in his shirt pocket not more'n a inch apart."

Engstrom stopped and looked at the puncher straight-on. "You a friend of the man in my office?"

The man looked him straight in the eye. "Sheriff, I ain't never laid eyes on 'im 'fore 'bout fifteen minutes ago. When you left, after y'all had a drink, I went to where he stood, an' told 'im quiet-like he'd better be careful. He told me to mind my own damned business."

They stepped to the boardwalk. Engstrom nodded to the door. "Come on in an' listen to the way Cantello tells what happened." While pushing the door open, he said, "Don't be buttin' in an' givin' him a chance to tell it your way."

"Ain't gonna say a word, Sheriff. Let's see how he tells it."

They listened to Cantrell's version. Engstrom asked, "You know this man here, Cantello?"

Cantrell shook his head. "Never seen 'im 'fore, 'cept at the bar. He warned me I hadn't made no friends in there."

Engstrom's smile caused no more than his eyes to crinkle at the corners. "You had one, Cantello. This stranger told it almost word for word the way you laid it out." He looked at the cowpoke. "What's your name, son?"

The hatchet-faced puncher scratched his head, then looked the sheriff in the eyes—grinning. "In this town, sir, I'm callin' myself Bob Penders."

Engstrom gave a jerky-headed nod. "Good 'nuff for me, Penders, long's you don't cross me in my town."

Cantrell stuck his hand out. "Glad to know you, Penders. Figure you're four-square. C'mon, I'll buy you a drink." He looked at the sheriff. "That is if the law ain't gonna hold me for some reason."

"Ain't got a reason to charge you with nothin' but self-defense. I allow that sort o' thing in my town. Go have your drink—but I'd advise stayin' away from that same saloon."

Cantrell nodded. "You can bet yore prize saddle on that, Sheriff Engstrom." He and Penders left.

6

WHILE THEY WERE having their drink, Cantrell asked Penders if he knew a man hereabouts who went by the name Manuel Soto. Penders shook his head. "Hell, man, I got in town only a few minutes 'fore I seen you an' the sheriff walk into that saloon. I'd been in there long 'nuff to see what kind they were, an' to see how they looked at you. Naw, I don't know nobody 'round here." He knocked back his drink, reached in his pocket, pulled out a cartwheel, studied it a moment, shrugged, and said he'd buy.

Cantrell saw the way Penders looked at the dollar—as though losing his last friend. "You 'bout broke, cowboy?"

Penders looked at the cartwheel laying on the bar. "Last one." Then he hurried to say he'd find a job hereabouts right soon. "Like I said, I'll buy. I rode down from Marfa. Rode for a man up yonder by the name of Gundy, Trace Gundy. Helluva man to work for. He works harder'n anybody on his spread. That makes a man work even harder."

"That why you quit?"

Penders's face hardened. "Cantello, when the sun goes down at night, ain't a man can say I didn't do more'n my share. I drew top-hand pay, an' I earned every penny of it. Nope. I done left that job 'cause I could see Gundy didn't need nothin' but good herdsmen for right now. Anybody can do that sort o' thing. But Gundy woulda kept payin' me even though he didn't need a top hand right then."

His face hardened even more. "Got in a poker game an' lost all my pay 'cept'n ten dollars 'fore I left Marfa. Now I gotta find 'nother man what needs me."

Cantrell studied on whether to offer Penders a job. Could he trust him? Was he tied in with the Soto gang? It wasn't likely. The cowboy had taken the trouble to warn him, had told the sheriff the straight thing of the gunfight, and had been willing to spend his last dollar for a drink in order to pay his way. Cantrell decided the hatchet-faced man could be trusted.

"Gonna tell you somethin', Penders," Cantrell said quietly. "I know a man up north o' here a few miles, owns the B-bar-M, man by the name of Brad Mason." He stared at his drink a moment, then looked at the cowboy. "For now I'm usin' the name Cantello." He sighed. "I got another name. You head up there and tell Mason that Cantrell sent you an' to give you a job. He'll do it."

Penders's face took on an awed look, his eyes wide and mouth hanging slightly open. "Cantrell? You ain't Quint Cantrell, are you?" His voice came out soft and quiet. Before Quint could answer, Penders nodded. "Hell yes you're Quint Cantrell. After I seen you use that handgun in that other saloon, I ain't got a doubt 'bout you bein' him."

He shook his head, knocked back his drink, and said, "Man, I can tell my grandkids, if I ever have any grandkids, that I had a drink with Quinton Cantrell—fastest man whatever pulled iron."

Cantrell shook his head slowly. "Cowboy, I told you my name because Mason knows me, raised me from a button, an' he'll give you a job on my say-so." He packed his pipe and lit it. "Too, gonna tell you for damn sure, ain't no man can claim to be 'the fastest man what ever pulled iron.' They's always somebody quicker waitin' over the next hill to prove hisself. An' remember, far's you know, my name's Cantello.

"Now 'fore you make a decision, you gotta know Mason's havin' trouble up yonder—gun trouble. There's them what are takin' his cows, shootin' at his womenfolk, shootin' his men, an' tryin' to burn 'im out. You better think on it awhile 'fore you go lopin' off to ride for 'im."

Penders looked him in the eye. "Gonna tell you, Cantello, I ain't never walked around a fight in my life. I ride for the brand. If Mr. Mason's got troubles, an' I'm drawin' my pay from 'im, I got troubles." He fingered his lone cartwheel again, signaled the bartender for two drinks, shrugged, and looked at Cantrell. "I'm headed up that way come daylight. 'Sides that, if they's a man up yonder shootin' at womenfolk, I'd sortta figger to fight without pay."

Quint pushed his hand down into his pocket and pulled out a double eagle. "Figured you that way. Here's a little to get you stocked up on tobacco an' such. Reckon I'll be seein' you when I get up yonder."

Cantrell twisted to head for the door and turned back. "My wife's up yonder stayin' with Mason awhile. Tell 'er I'm doin' fine. Tell 'er not to worry, an' she better damn well not come down here." He flung up his hand in a wave and left.

• • •

Making a quick stop in Ojinaga before heading back to
the ranch, Cole reined in at the first saloon he came upon.
A flick of his thumb removed the thong holding his Colt
in the holster. As he pushed through the batwing doors, a
flicking glance at all in the room told him he knew no
one. But there were many in this part of Mexico who had
seen him, and would know him for the gunfighter Cole
Mason.

He steered clear of the well-lit bar area, walked to a
back table, and sat, his back to the wall. When a girl came
to take his order, he bought himself and her a *cerveza,* but
told her he didn't want company. Men sat at tables on
each side of him. He attuned his ears to listen to their
conversations. The four men at the table to his right were
Americanos; to his left sat five Mexicans—all talked of
the gunmen brought in by the Mason ranch.

Cole's hand brushed the handle of his holstered Colt,
and moved to his belt where he'd stuck another six-gun.
He hoped he wouldn't need either of them.

To his left a man talked. "Ah but, *señores,* we have
many men. *Señor Santana* tells me we now, at this
minute, have many men attacking the Mason ranch. The
pistoleros they have brought in are no equal to our men
with the rifles."

Another spoke. "No. I think you are wrong, Raul. I
hear Mason's *dos hijos* are there with their friend
Cantrell. Those three are worth many men."

"*Sí,* you are right, but only in a battle with the *pistolas.*
We use the rifle against them, they are not much—*nada.*"

"They have brought many men with rifles. They are
killing our men. Santana will not say so, but our numbers

are shrinking. If this continues, they will soon outnumber us."

A man across the table spoke for the first time. "We will take all for Manuel Soto if the *rancheros* and their men don't get into the fight."

Then another spoke. "Who is this Manuel Soto? I have never seen him."

Then in a hissing whisper, Cole could barely make out, someone said, "Do not ask that question. Don't nobody know him—and it is very unhealthy to ask."

After that no one spoke. But Cole had found what he wanted. The Mason bunch was throwing the fear of God into Santana, and perhaps Soto. They were hurting the *bandidos*.

He stood, and only two steps from the doors, one of the *Americanos* at the table that had been to his right yelled. "There's one o' the bastards. Git 'im. That's Cole Mason."

Before the man could finish, Cole drew his belt gun and thumbed off three shots toward the table. A man fell with each shot. Cole slammed through the doors, twisted, emptied his belt gun into the doors, and toed the stirrup. His horse didn't wait for him to get his leg across the saddle, before hitting an all-out run.

Cole hung to the saddle horn, dropped both feet to the ground, bounced, and swung aboard.

The batwings exploded outward. Men poured through them—all firing at anything that moved. Slugs whined past Cole's head. A burn along his left side told him he'd been hit, then another smashed into his shoulder. Same side. He bent low over the cantle, and did something he never did—he put spurs to his horse. The big black horse took flight.

He crossed the Rio Grande. A look over his shoulder revealed no sign of pursuit. It would take time for the *bandidos* to get horses. He skirted Presidio, and when barely to the other side of the town, he saw a large group of horsemen crossing the river and splitting, one group going into the town, the other taking the same route as he did.

Cole thought to pull into the chaparral and try to lose them. He shook his head. He was bleeding. Loss of too much blood and he'd pass out while in hiding. He reined onto the trail that ran close to the ranch and slowed his horse, wanting to save him for an all-out race for the *hacienda*. He headed for home.

After about an hour, the pain in his shoulder worsened, and the hot flow of blood from his side wound gathered around his stomach, above his belt. Only then did he try to staunch the flow. He pulled his bandana from around his neck and stuffed it inside his shirt. His fingers found where the bullet had sliced across his ribs. Not serious if he got it taken care of soon.

Still about two miles from the wall surrounding the *hacienda,* he glanced over his shoulder. A large group of horsemen, perhaps ten men, came into view and began firing. Lead whined past, but not close enough to worry about. He again brought his horse to a full run.

Another ten or fifteen minutes and the gate came into view. He hoped none of the sentries atop the wall would take a shot at him.

Atop the wall, Laura saw the lone horseman round the bend in the trail, riding like all the demons of hell were on his tail. She put her rifle to her shoulder, drew a bead on the center of the rider's chest like Cole had showed her, and tightened her finger on the trigger only a hair. Her eyes widened. She relaxed trigger pressure and yelled to the men along the parapet. "That's Cole. Hold your fire." Then a yell to a man on the ground: "Open the gate."

She took another look along the trail. A group of horsemen rounded the bend behind her husband. "Soon's Cole gets inside, close the gate." She didn't have to call for the men to start firing at those chasing Cole Mason. They busily jacked shells into rifle chambers and squeezed triggers. Two of the pursuers fell from saddles, then another, and another.

The bandits had drawn rein, and turned their horses to ride back the way from which they'd come, when rifle fire from the chaparral emptied the rest of the saddles. Clay stepped from the brush, motioned the men he'd stationed there to come with him to the *hacienda,* and headed for the gate at a dead run. The gate, half closed, began to open again.

As soon as Laura saw Clay and his men take over the firing, she scrambled to the ground and caught her husband's big body when he toppled from the saddle. Four men assisted her, taking him toward the ranch house. Laura stared at the blood soaking the front of Cole's shirt. Her eyes shifted to his white face. His lips showed a tinge of gray.

The men placed him with gentle hands on the large sofa in the middle of the room. Laura started issuing orders: bandages, whiskey, aloe vera leaves, hot water, fresh linens to place under him, and a blanket to cover him. Ma Mason wiped his face with a damp cloth.

Laura cleaned his wounds with whiskey, and when Cole opened his eyes a moment, she gave him half of a glass of the fiery liquid, and insisted he drink all of it. Although the bullet to the ribs had caused a lot of bleeding, it had only creased his side. The one to his shoulder had gone all the way through. Laura cleaned it out, ran a swab through to the other side, put a liberal amount of the aloe vera sap on every surface she could reach, and bandaged it. Cole opened his eyes halfway through the dressing ordeal and grinned at her.

"I'll take another jolt of that whiskey if you didn't waste it all on these little old scratches."

Laura stood back, clamped hands to hips, and pinned him with a hard look. "Damn you, Cole Mason, why do you do this to me? Always gettin' shot, stepped on by a horse, tangled up in your lasso. Oh hell, honey," she threw herself down by his side and slid an arm under his head, "I love you so much, an' you don't do a thing to stay outta trouble."

Cole looked over her shoulder at his mother. "Ma, she only cusses like this when she's of a mind to tell me how much she loves me." He chuckled, winced, and looked into Laura's eyes. "Gonna tell you, little girl, I love you too, an' there wasn't a thing I could do to avoid this."

Ma stood to the side and watched her big, dangerous son babied as though he was in fact a helpless little toddler. Tears crept down her cheeks.

Cole looked from his wife to his mother, grinned, and said, "Now you pour me another belt o' Pa's whiskey, then get yourself in the kitchen an' fix me one o' those apple pies half the punchers in New Mexico would fight for a slice of. Don't know of anything that'll get me well faster."

Laura nodded. "You get your whiskey, an' you get your apple pie, but if you try to get up and around before I say so, you're gonna need a whole lot more doctorin' than I'll be able to give you." She didn't need to look for another bottle; Brad stood there with a full one.

He inched to his son's side. "Know didn't nobody shoot you from in front. Both them slugs came at you from the back."

"Tell you for a fact, Pa, I caught those bullets while I was flat-out runnin' like a scared rabbit. I had half the town of Ojinaga chasin' me."

Brad reared back and looked at Cole. "What the hell you go down yonder for? You know ain't nobody down there'll put up with yore nonsense since you an' Quint raised so much hell in that town."

"Tell you, Pa, I thought maybe I could find out if we're hurtin' Soto's bunch much with our hit-and-run tactics." He smiled. "I found out all right. We're hurtin' 'em good. Also found out a *bandido* by name of Benito Santana's runnin' the show for him. Never did hear of anyone who knew who Soto was, or had ever seen him."

Clay had been standing quietly on the fringe of those smothering Cole with care and concern. He eased to the side of the sofa, stared at his brother a moment, and said, "Damn if married life ain't makin' you soft. Remember times you coulda took on a whole town like Ojinaga." He shook his head. "Next time, reckon y'all better send me. I'll get the job done right."

Molly jumped into the conversation. "Not if I can help it, big man. You're gonna stay right here close to me. 'Sides, if they know Cole, and hate him an' Quint so much, an' shoot soon's they see Cole, you won't be any better off. 'Side from that scar on your cheek, you an' Cole could pass for identical twins anywhere."

"Aw now, Molly, you've hurt my feelin's," Cole chuckled, "I always figured I was better lookin' than my little brother."

While Cole was getting patched up at the *hacienda*, Cantrell pondered his next move. He thought to go and make the acquaintance of the banker the first thing the next morning. Or if he couldn't get in to see him, he could study him from a distance.

The next morning, while he ate breakfast, much of the talk around him centered on a tall, good-looking man who'd shot up a saloon in Ojinaga, killing five. Cantrell's first thought was of Cole, then his thought was verified. A man at a corner table, talking so all could hear him, said, "Just like it use to be. The gunfighter wuz Cole Mason. Only one missin' wuz Quint Cantrell. He'd've been there, they could've cleaned out the town."

Another said, "Mason's back? Well, reckon we can look for some lively times around here for a while."

While paying for his breakfast, Quint felt eyes focused on him, and his tied-down holster. Many wore sideguns, but few wore them like he did, almost as though they were a part of him. He'd thought of leaving his Colt in his room when he went to breakfast but quickly discarded the idea. There were too many here, and throughout the West, who would shoot him whether or not he carried a weapon.

He'd eaten late, and when he stepped from the café he scanned the street. Already the town was busy: buckboards, freight wagons, men sitting horseback, pedestrians on the street and along the boardwalk, stray dogs with tails tucked trying to stay out from under hooves and wheels. He nodded. The town had grown since his last visit.

His eyes strayed to the two-story building across the

dusty road. A man stood at the door taking the lock from it. The banker had arrived.

Cantrell angled across the street, dodging wagons and horses. The banker had pushed open the door and then swung it as though to close it, when Cantrell stepped to his side. "I'd like to talk with you a little, if you got the time, sir."

The man's eyes raked Cantrell from top to bottom, then returned to his tied-down holster. His eyes widened, his lips tightened, and since he was not wearing a hat, beads of sweat coated his forehead.

"I mean you no harm, mister. I'm new in town, and I got a little business to take care of."

The banker jerked his head in what would pass for a nervous nod. "Come on in." Then, as though hoping to make Cantrell leery of making gun trouble, he added, "My staff'll be here in only a few moments."

Cantrell let a smile show at the corners of his eyes and lips. "Like I said, mister, I'm peaceable."

The man motioned him through the open door.

Only a few feet inside the door, the banker faced him. "All right, sir, what is it you want?"

Cantrell's face hardened. "What I want is to talk business. First, I'd like to sit across from you at yore desk. Then I'd like to be treated like you treat most o' yore customers. I want land, an' I got fifty thousand dollars to put into it. Ain't got it with me, but when I find what I want it'll get here a few days afterward—*comprende?*"

The banker's attitude changed like the sun breaking through heavy clouds. His demeanor changed from coward to simpering, butt-kissing fop. His smile, now sickening, surrounded his words. "Why, mister, er I didn't get your name . . ."

"Juan Cantello . . ."

"Ah, Mr. Cantello, I'll be happy to assist you. Right now I know of no land for sale in the area, but . . ." He now rushed to a chair at his desk and pulled it out for Cantrell. "As I was saying, I know of no land, but it would be to your advantage to have your money close-by; that way, when something does come available, we can close a deal quickly."

Cantrell swallowed his disgust. He'd have liked to have this jackass on roundup for about a week—if he could last that long. It took him only seconds to decide that this silly man could not possibly be Soto. He shook his head. "No. I've changed my mind. I won't transfer my money. This town is too wild. I'll keep it in St. Louis till I find what I want." He stood. "I'll ask elsewhere."

The banker's face took on the look of a spoiled child; his bottom lip drooped, his cheeks quivered. "Perhaps you'll reconsider."

"Don't b'lieve so." Cantrell spun and headed for the door.

Outside, he sucked in a breath of fresh air. Damn. How did a thing like that one survive here where real men, the good and the bad, made their living? He turned to go down the boardwalk, and bumped into a man dressed in black suit, white shirt, black bandana, and highly polished boots. "Sorry, mister, reckon my mind wasn't on lookin' where I went."

The man, whose eyes were a steel gray, looked at Cantrell straight-on. "No problem, sir." He stuck out his hand. "Jarred Phillips, the town's only preacher."

Cantrell introduced himself while shaking hands. He studied the preacher, and let a chagrined smile crinkle his lips. "Dressed like you are, I woulda took you for a gambler, but bein' a parson ain' too much different; just bettin' with higher stakes."

Phillips returned his smile. "No offense, Mr. Cantello." He frowned, then looked at Quint's gun. "You're the man who shot a man in the saloon last night, are you not? And the same man who took on one of Santana's men down in Ojinaga the other night."

Cantrell went quiet inside. Why would a preacher interest himself in who had gunfights here and across the border? Too, his look into the man's eyes revealed a cold, calculating brain behind those steely eyes. He nodded. "Yeah, I'm the same man. I don't look for trouble, preacher man—but I don't walk around it either."

Phillips reached for Quint's arm. "No offense, Mr. Cantello. We along the border make it our business to know what goes on on both sides." The arm he'd reached for was Quint's right. He stepped back out of reach before the parson took hold of him. He never wanted the disadvantage of having his right hand hindered, even by a friendly gesture.

While Phillips talked, Cantrell studied him. The hand that gripped his when introduced was strong, although not work-hardened; his eyes had no softness, nor did his walk show the short, soft tread of a town man. There was more to this man than showed on the surface. "You got time for a cup o' Arbuckle's, Mr. Phillips?"

The man of God shook his head. "There are those of my congregation who need my help. I'd best be seeing what their needs are." They shook hands in parting—this time Cantrell felt for and found the hard callous on Philips's thumb. The man practiced with a single-action six-gun—a lot.

7

AFTER LEAVING THE preacher, Cantrell headed toward the livery to see if Penders had left for the B-bar-M, but his thoughts clung to the callous he'd felt on the parson's thumb. Why would a preacher need to practice the use of a revolver? What threat would a man of God feel to make him want to know how to use a handgun? Or maybe the hardened skin had not been made from thumbing a six-gun hammer back at all. Yeah, maybe, but Cantrell, in his infinitely cautious way, decided to believe the obvious.

Then his thoughts went to the minister's eyes. They were not the eyes of a gentle man. The fact was, the eyes he'd looked into were as hard and unyielding as a chunk of granite. He shrugged mentally. He'd always been good at reading a man, and Jarred Phillips was a man it'd pay to watch. He might be no more than what he professed, but Quint decided to be on guard when around him.

His thoughts turned to Elena. He decided to ride back to the ranch, see Elena, and check on the Mason brothers' progress. This was a good time, while the Santana man who trailed him was back in Ojinaga.

The old man at the livery told him that Penders had ridden out before daylight. Cantrell saddled his gelding and left. He checked his backtrail closely to make certain he was not followed, and his thoughts turned back to Elena. Lordy day, how he missed her. He wanted to hold her close, feel her tremble when she tightened her body to his, feel its warmth, feel the softness of her lips—hell, he only wanted to know she was there.

His gelding picked his own pace while Quint studied the surrounding chaparral. Even so, he missed seeing the man hidden in the brush. A voice from the side came at him. "Cantrell. Over here. Ride like you might o' changed yore mind."

The man knew his name, and if he'd wanted to shoot him, he'd had that chance. Quint kneed his horse toward the voice, reined in, took his canteen from the saddle horn, and took a drink. The voice again. "Theez eez Martinez of Cole's outfit. 'Tween us an' the *rancho* eez 'bout eight o' Soto's men. They been down to the *rancho* to take a few shots at our people, an' are only now headed back theez way."

Talking softly, his eyes locked on the trail ahead of him, Cantrell said, "Thanks, *amigo*. Think I'll sit here in the trail an' greet 'em. When I open the dance, y'all start throwin' lead." He stopped, frowned, and peered into the brush. "I said 'y'all' figgerin' you got more'n just you. Got any men with you?"

"*Sí,* I 'ave three men, two across the trail, an' one with me."

Cantrell grinned. "Hell, Martinez, our five 'gainst their eight ain't fair. We got 'em outnumbered more'n two to one. Let's you an' me take 'em on."

Martinez chuckled. "Damn if I don't think you mean it, *amigo,* but eez too late. The men weeth me already 'ave the Weenchesters cocked. Cole, he never show us how to uncock 'em without pullin' the treeger."

Cantrell nodded. "Well, if you an' me's gotta share the fun, I'll ride to the middle of the trail an' wait for 'em."

As though taking another drink from his canteen, he walked the gelding to the middle of the road and waited. In only a few moments the soft sound of hooves falling on heavy dust sounded, then riders rounded the bend in the road. Cantrell knocked the cork back in his canteen, hung it from his saddle horn, flicked the thong from his Colt—and waited.

He held up his left hand in the universal peace sign, and pulled his horse around so his right hand showed on the side toward the approaching riders. He didn't want to fire across his body.

When about fifty feet from him, the lead rider pulled his horse in and stared at Cantrell. "What you do out here alone, *hombre*?"

Cantrell eyed the man a moment. "Why, I reckon I figgered to do a little skunk huntin' bein's it wuz such a nice day for it. Reckon I done found a whole passel of 'em all in one bunch. Hello, skunk." With the words his hand swept his Colt from its holster.

Surprise on his side, Quint had already emptied two saddles before they unlimbered their weapons. By then, Martinez's men were firing. The encounter was over almost before it began. Martinez came from the brush first. He smiled. "You open the dance veree sudden, *amigo.* You veree selfish man, you almost leave no fun for my men."

His face sober, Cantrell shook his head. "You got it all wrong, Martinez. While I wuz growin' up, Ma Mason taught me to never be cruel." He opened the loading gate on his Colt, dumped spent cartridges into his palm, pushed in new ones, and shrugged. "I figgered to drag this encounter out would o' been pure-dee cruel. That's the only reason I opened the dance real quick."

The slim, handsome Mexican slapped him on the back. "We go to the *rancho,* see how Cole is doin'. He took a couple slugs last night getting away from some o' Santana's men in Ojinaga."

Quint squinted between his gelding's ears. "Bad?"

"No. He eez too tough to let a couple o' bullets keep heem down. Even though Laura raised hell, he got up for breakfast theez mornin'."

While riding toward the ranch, Martinez brought Cantrell up to date on all that had happened: Clay's stampede while fighting one of Soto's gangs, the defense of the *hacienda,* Cole's fight. Martinez smiled. "We been beezy."

Cantrell said little of his doings along each side of the border. His thoughts were on Elena.

When the adobe wall came into view, Quint unconsciously urged his horse into a lope. The gates opened and he went through the wide opening ahead of the rest. Before he could climb from the saddle, Elena ran to his gelding's side and reached her arms for him. "Damn, woman, looks like you right happy to see me." He smiled as tenderly as the welling in his heart.

Elena dragged him into her arms. "Quint, I didn't know how much I could miss a person till now."

Quint wrapped his arm around her shoulders. They walked across the wide veranda and met the rest of the family at the door—including Cole, pale, but standing with them. Cantrell turned his look on Cole. "See them *bandidos* didn't put you down for long."

Cole shook his head. "They only knicked me a couple o' times. C'mon in. We'll drink some o' Papa's whiskey an' catch up on what's been goin' on."

They spent the day talking, as families will, and all the while Quint's thoughts were on getting Elena to their room. He wanted her so bad he hurt. Elena must have had the same hungers, because in the middle of the afternoon, she whispered, "Big man, you reckon this day'll ever end? I need to get you alone so we can talk to *each other* the rest of the night."

Quint slanted her a grin. "*Mi amor,* don't reckon I figured to do much talkin'." He shrugged. "But reckon if that's what you want, that's what we'll do."

Her face turned a lovely pink. She gouged him in the ribs with her elbow. The smile she gave him said she agreed with his intent.

That night after supper, as quick as Quint deemed proper, he took Elena's elbow and escorted her from the room.

"Quint, you made what we wanted so obvious. Why, my goodness, Ma, Pa—oh damn, all of them know what you have in mind."

Quint chuckled. "Reckon so, *querida*. If they don't, I figger ain't none o' them loves their mate much as I do you." They had not cleared the room before Quint swung her around and kissed her, at first gently, then all the hunger stored into his body took over. His kiss—rough, demanding—only matched Elena's. He swung her into his arms and headed for their room.

The next morning, Brad, with a total lack of diplomacy, or modesty, greeted them at the breakfast table. He stared at Elena a moment. "Ummm, yore face looks like the sun's tryin' to shine in it, an' that there sparkle in yore eyes tells me you been workin' pretty hard to give us a gran'baby."

Elena's face blossomed to a bright red. Ma looked at her husband, hands on hips, and said, "Mr. Mason, you have absolutely no couth at all. Why, look how you've embarrassed the poor girl." Her words, and Elena obviously wanting to crawl under a rug, brought guffaws of laughter from the entire family.

At the table, Brad again showed his lack of manners. He looked from Cole to Clay. "Now, I'm gonna say this once. Ain't gonna bring it up agin'. Quint's an' Elena's baby, if they ever have one, is gonna be as much our grandchild as any you two might have—but reckon you gonna let 'im get ahead o' you."

Laura and Molly had their turn to blush, then Clay made it worse. "Hell, Pa, a man can only try so hard." He looked into Molly's arrowlike stare. "We doin' our best, Pa."

Molly followed her stare with "You keep talking like that, Clay Mason, an' I'll guarantee you we'll stop *doin' our best* for one heck of a long time." Clay seemed to shrink down into his chair, looking like a whipped puppy with his tail between his legs. Carmen, the longtime friend and servant of the Masons, saved the day. She brought trays of bacon, eggs, country fried potatoes, biscuits, gravy, and hot coffee.

Cantrell stayed another night, then, thinking he'd better not be out of sight too long in Presidio, he left. Cole and Clay left at the same time to join their men in the chaparral.

They rode until Cole told Clay he and Martinez were going to split off and head for their own bunch. He'd already reined his horse to the side when he stopped, pulled back, and, studying the trail ahead, said, "B'lieve I have a better idea." He looked at each of them. "You reckon all those men who ride for Soto stay in one place—one ranch, or one hideout?"

Quint quieted his horse a moment, then obviously thinking of Cole's question, he packed his pipe, lit it, studied the cloud of smoke, and asked, "What you got in mind, Cole?"

"Wonder if one o' us might go down there and take a look-see. We been hurtin' 'em pretty good. We need to know where they hole up, how many o' them they got left, have they got a permanent camp, are their womenfolk with 'em, what kind o' supplies they got, how they get 'em."

Cantrell grinned. "Hell, only one what knows all that'd be Santana." His grin widened. "An' I'll tell you one thing, I ain't gonna be the one what asks him them questions."

Cole gave Cantrell a head-on look. "Didn't figure to ask him; thought maybe since you already joined up with 'im, you could get the answers, an' come back to give us a report."

Cantrell squinted down the dusty trail, took a puff on his pipe, blew out the smoke, and shook his head. "I'm already workin' for Santana, but ain't nobody s'posed to know that but me an' him. That won't help me any with gettin' in with his men. 'Sides that, I might lose some of my ground on uncoverin' Soto."

A quiet voice cut into the conversation. "What about me, *señor*? I'm 'bout as good a Injun as you three, an' eef they catch me I can say I wanted to join up weeth them, but didn't know how to do it 'cept find them and ask."

Cole thought a moment, nodded, and said, "You thinkin' to try to sneak up on their camp—then if you get caught tell them that hogwash?"

Martinez studied his horse's ears a moment, then smiled and nodded. "*Sí.*" Then, his voice sounding hopeful, he added, "Eet might work."

Cole never took his eyes off the friend who'd sided him in one of the toughest ranch wars ever fought. "*Amigo,* I won't let you do it. I'll not lose a friend on the chance we might learn something. We need an idea a lot more sure than that one."

Quint, sitting his horse off to the side, cut in. "Martinez, you any good with that six-shooter?"

No longer smiling, Martinez gave Quint a straight-on look. "*Señor* Quint, I never make the beeg brag about how I handle the seex-shooter," he spread his hands, palms outward at his sides, "but you can see, *amigo,* I am steel heer."

"He's still here, Quint, and I've seen 'im in action. He may not be as fast as you, me, or Clay—but he's damned close to it." Cole shifted his glance to each of them, then settled his gaze on Cantrell. "What you got in mind, Quint?"

Cantrell frowned, packed his pipe, lit it, blew out a cloud of smoke, and nodded. "Yep, it might work. I got a idea I might be able to get Martinez a ridin' job with Santana." He puffed his pipe a couple of times, then looked at the slim, handsome Mexican. "You an' me leave this ornery, lazy bunch here. I'll tell you what I got in mind on the way to Presidio."

"Like hell, Cantrell." Cole's voice slipped between them, quiet and stubborn. "You're not takin' Martinez on one of your harum-scarum jaunts till I know what you figure on doin'. I know you too well. You think everything is even if all you have to face is three or four men. Now let's all hear what you have in mind."

Quint spent the next fifteen or twenty minutes laying out his plan to them. Several times one of them had a suggestion to enhance Cantrell's idea.

When they parted, Quint and Martinez rode side by side toward Presidio. When to the west of the town,

Cantrell turned his horse to enter from that direction, and Martinez continued on to the south.

Cantrell went directly to the hotel room he'd kept in his name before leaving for the ranch. He bathed, shaved, oiled his six-shooter and Winchester, honed his Bowie, buckled on his gun, and went out on the street, to head for Ojinaga.

In the wild Mexican town, he rode directly to the *cantina* where he'd first met Santana. He pushed through the batwings, moved to the side until his eyes adjusted to the dim light, then scanned those sitting at tables around the room. There were none here that he remembered. Then he flicked a glance along the bar. Martinez stood at the end closest to the back door.

Only a few feet from the bar, his voice slapped at Cantrell. "Cantello, *bastardo,* I tell you in Monterrey next time you see me—fill your hand."

Quint stopped, flicked the thong off his handgun, and turned to face the voice. Martinez had walked to stand several feet from the long hand-hewn bar. His hand hung only a fraction of an inch from the walnut grips of his six-shooter.

With the first words from Martinez's mouth, all noise in the room ceased, then loud crashes sounded as chairs, pushed back, fell to the side and feet scraped, rushing to get out of the way of stray bullets. Then silence again, so absolute that Cantrell could hear the small bubbles burst from the foam of the last poured *cervesas*.

"Ah, Martinez, you think it is a good day to die, eh, dog droppings."

Simultaneously each flashed his hand for his holster. To Quint's surprise, Martinez's gun appeared from leather almost at the same time as his own. Cantrell tilted his gun enough to miss the slim Mexican. Both fired—their bullets going into the ceiling. Through the cloud of powder smoke, both exploded in gales of laughter, choked on the acrid smell, and rushed to heartily pound each other on the back.

"Ah, *amigo,* ees long time I no see you." Martinez's voice carried to the far reaches of the room.

Cantrell took his friend's arm and steered him to the bar. "A bottle of your best tequila, Bartender. My *amigo* drinks only the best." His words were lost in the explosion of sound.

Men laughed, clapped each other on the back. Some growled, cursed in disappointment that they'd not seen a killing, but all were loud.

The words of several came to Cantrell. All sounded awed at the gun-quick of each man. The man now standing on the other side of Quint scanned each of them. "I never see two men so queek weeth the *pistolas.* I theenk you both be dead eef you not mees on the purpose."

Martinez looked around Cantrell at the man who'd spoken. "No, *señor,* my friend here is the *pistolero,* I'm just a *vaquero* looking for a job. You know anybody looking for a veree good rider who knows how to handle a gun?"

The stranger's brow puckered; he knocked back his drink, then his forehead smoothed. "*Sí, señor,* I theenk I know of a man who weel talk weeth you about theez theeng. I weel breeng heem here to see you." He stepped toward the door. "Only a few *minutos.* I'll be back *muy pronto.*"

Cantrell waited until the Mexican disappeared through the batwings, then turned his look on Martinez. "Wantta bet whether he brings Santana through those doors?"

Martinez smiled. "As you *Americanos* say, my friend, 'my mama didn't raise no fools.' No, I weel not bet on that theeng."

They each had another drink before the stranger came back into the room, and true to Cantrell's thinking, Santana walked with him. They came directly to the bar.

Santana flicked a glance at Cantrell, his face showing no recognition, and his words bore out that he didn't want Martinez, or any in the room, knowing he had anything to do with Quint. "My *amigo* here tells me you are both fast. I have already heard about *Señor* Cantello." His glance took them both in.

"Who the hell are you?" Martinez asked.

Santana pinned him with a hard look. He tapped his chest with his thumb. "I, *señor,* am Benito Santana, and I weesh to talk weeth you." He nodded toward a table at the rear, ordered a bottle of tequila and two glasses, and took them to the table.

When Santana ordered only two glasses, Cantrell took the hint that he wasn't wanted in that conversation. He ordered another drink, knocked it back, and waited while Santana and Martinez talked.

At the table, both men sat next to each other, their backs to the wall. Santana, using good Spanish grammar, leaned to say, "Where did you know this man Cantello?"

Martinez tightened inside, and felt as though his neck hairs stuck straight out. He was glad now that he and Cantrell had talked long on this subject. Without hesitation, he said, "I rode for his father. His *rancho* is south of Saltillo. Then I suppose we've ridden for five or six other ranches, and partnered all over southern *Mejico*." He nodded. "Yeah, we've been *compadres* for about fifteen years." He shook his head and let a sadness come to his eyes. "His father disowned him when he kept getting into gunfights. He goes by another name now, and I, *señor,* will not tell anyone the proud name he carried."

Santana filled their glasses again. "I hear he's very, very good with that *pistola* he carries."

"*Sí,* he is as good as you hear. He's better than me." Martinez smiled. "But maybe not so good with the cattle as me."

Santana shifted his chair to look directly into Martinez's eyes. "You ever swing a wide loop, as the *Americanos* say?"

Martinez shrugged. "What *vaquero,* at some time or the other, has not let his reata drop over the head of a stray cow?"

Santana's face hardened. "*Señor,* do not play with the words. I'm looking for men—men who do not care who owns the cattle, especially if the cows are on the *Americano* side of the river. And I want men who can shoot the *pistola* and the rifle, men who will not run when confronted with those who can also shoot."

Martinez, although pleased with the way the conversation was going, forced an angry look. "*Señor* Santana, I never ran from anything in my life, and as for the cows, if they're on the *norte* side of the river I think they will find a better home down here in *Mejico.*" He looked at Santana and smiled. "Who am I to deprive a poor cow of a good home?"

The big outlaw chieftain slapped Martinez on the back. "That's what I wanted to hear. I pay fighting wages— ninety *Americano* dollars a month, food, and a place to sleep."

"I didn't expect so much in *Americano.* I take the job."

8

SANTANA LEANED BACK in his chair with a satisfied look. "You start now. I take you to our *oficina principal* when we leave here tonight."

Martinez wanted to stand and shout to Cantrell that he'd find out pretty soon what they needed to know. Instead, he nodded and said, "Any chance I could have another drink with my *compadre* before we leave?"

"*Sí,* have your drink, then tell him I wish to have a few words with him."

Martinez walked to the bar, feeling every eye in the *cantina* staring at him, and knowing there were but few friendly looks.

He sidled up next to Cantrell, poured a drink from the bottle Quint had ordered, lifted it to hide his mouth, and said from behind the glass, "Got the job. Don't know how I'm gonna get back to the ranch to tell them what I discovered," he shrugged and smiled, "but I'll find a way. *Vaya con Dios.*"

He held his drink out for a toast. "*Amigo,* perhaps

someday we'll ride together again. Have your drink, then Santana wants to talk with you."

Cantrell knocked back his drink, put his glass on the bar, and walked to face Santana.

"Sit down. I wish to talk with you."

Cantrell spun the chair in which Martinez had sat around on one leg, straddled it, and spoke in Texan. " 'Fore you ask, I'll tell you: Ain't a damn soul up yonder who has ever seen Soto. Don't nobody have any idea who he is, or what he looks like. So startin' with that, I've checked out the banker, a young lawyer, the sheriff—they all seem to be what they claim.

"They's one man I talked with that the pieces don't fit very good. He's a preacher man—a preacher who practices with a single-action six-shooter enough he has calluses on his thumb. Ain't no parson I ever met has need for such. I figure to find out more 'bout 'im."

Santana stared at him a moment, smiled, and said, "You lay it out pretty plain, Cantello. That's what I wanted to know, but there's more. I'm supposed to meet Soto again tomorrow night, same place an' time as before. You be there like last time. This time—follow him and don't lose him."

"*Jefe,* if he's got any idea he's being followed, he's gonna know it's you who wants information. That ain't no safe ground to stand on."

"Cantello, you made a fool out of the man I sent to follow you. You're good, so good in fact, I think you can do what I ask without Soto having any idea he's being followed." He pinned Quint with a look that went through him like a stiletto. "And I might add, my *pistolero amigo,* you'd better be good enough or you're gonna have me *and* Soto out to kill you."

Cantrell, letting a slight smile break the corners of his mouth, and pushing words, soft yet hard as steel, between his slitted lips, said, "One thing you an' Soto better put 'tween yore ears, Santana, is I'm right hard to kill. An' don't ever threaten me, or try to scare me. It don't work."

The big outlaw chieftain gave a jerky nod. "That's why I hired you, *vaquero*. If I thought I could scare you, you'd already be dinner for the coyotes." He poured and knocked back a drink, coughed, and said, "Be there tomorrow night."

Cantrell had another drink with Martinez and left. He climbed aboard his horse, rode back to Presidio, stabled his horse, and went to his room. There, he checked his weapons, changed from boots to moccasins, and made certain he wore nothing that might make noise. Then he took a packet of jerky from his saddlebags, wrapped his canteen in soft cloth, and filled it.

He went out the back door of the hotel, making certain he was not seen, left his horse in the livery, and set out at a long, ground-eating pace for the *jacal* where he'd first listened in on the meeting between Soto and Santana.

This time, afoot, he figured to stay much closer to Soto. He'd be less likely to skyline himself, and with the moccasins he'd make no noise.

Again, he, the tarantulas, rattlesnakes, and scorpions spent a hot lonely night in the shack. His thoughts, as always, turned to Elena. The night they'd shared, already seeming to be months ago, had been like all the nights they shared—the giving and receiving of all they had to give each other, and the giving making the receiving even more complete.

He wondered how he'd ever gotten Elena to say yes to marrying him, then smiled into the dark heat of the shack. The fact was, he hadn't had much to say about it. Elena and her mother, Venicia, had both already agreed he was Elena's man, long before he ever thought he had a chance with the daughter of the owner of the largest ranch in Colorado. Lion McCord had been the first to endorse Quint as a prospective son-in-law, once he found that Cantrell wasn't wanted by the law.

"Sometimes a waddy jest flat gets lucky, whether he deserves it or not," Cantrell mumbled, still thinking of Elena as looking like a blond princess—tall, straight, fair, and spunky as any woman he'd ever seen.

He whiled away the afternoon, chewed a slice of jerky, drank a little water to soften it, and waited for the sun to sink below the horizon. From where he sat against the rough adobe wall, he watched the shadow of a tall yucca lengthen, then the edges got fuzzy, then the contrast between the shadow and the surrounding earth dimmed and disappeared. Dark set in, and with it his flesh tightened. He wished the idea of snakes and scorpions had gone along with the setting sun.

He pulled his pipe from his vest, put it in his mouth, and sucked on the fireless bowl. Sorry excuse for a smoke, but it would have to do until he got back to Presidio.

The hours dragged, as though time had an anchor tied to its backside. Finally, the muffled sounds of footsteps sounded, then the rough scraping of cloth down the side of the *jacal,* and silence. Santana had also selected to walk rather than ride.

The big outlaw leader had waited only a few moments when, almost silently, a horse stopped a few feet from him. "You here, Santana?" The question came as a hissing whisper.

"*Sí,* I have been here. What is it you want with me?"

Benito Santana answered. Quint wished Soto would just once talk a bit louder. It would give a little more with which to tie a face.

Soto continued, still using the sibilant whisper. "What I want is what you should be much concerned with: How bad are these gunmen Mason's brought in hurting us? Everything I hear is bad. You lose so many men here, so many there. Not once have I heard a report of your men winning one of the many gunfights."

"*Sí,* what you hear is true, *jefe*. Mason's men are fighting us with the tactics learned well in the *Americano* military academy. Cole Mason, old Brad Mason's son, went to school there. He is reported to lead the gunfighters his father has brought in."

Soto cleared his throat. "Can you not fight him in the same way? Perhaps I hired myself the wrong man. You have many men; why not take them all and attack the Mason headquarters?"

Santana felt blood rush to his face at Soto's words. "*Jefe,* you think you have the wrong man, you better find another. Don't ever push me." Sitting in the dark like he was, Santana banked on Soto not being able to see even the slightest movement of his hands. He eased his American-made Colt .44 from its holster and held it alongside his leg. He waited for the faceless man's reaction to his angry words.

"What will you do, Santana, go back to robbing old men and small ranchers? No, I don't think so. I pay you much *dinero,* and right now it is too much for what I'm getting. I want to hear very soon of Brad Mason being hurt—hurt bad. You understand?"

The big outlaw's thumb tightened to pull back the trigger, then relaxed. The sound of the hammer ratcheting back would warn Soto. He sucked in a deep breath and let it out slowly to let his anger cool a mite. "*Sí, jefe,* I understand. But I will not take all my men against him at once. That would be, as the *Americanos* say, putting all the eggs in one basket. I will not do that."

The outline of Soto's form shifted in the dim light. He chopped downward with his right hand. "Enough of this. This is not what I came over here for. What I want is for you to find out about this man Cantello. He is a very dangerous man, and from what I hear, he's asking questions across the river, questions that can be dangerous to us both." His whisper sharpened. "I want you to stop the questions. Send one of your best men with a six-gun to face him. If your best is not good enough—I want *you* to kill him, anyway you figure is the safest for us. *Comprende?*"

"*Sí,* I understand. We must get rid of those who oppose us." Even though not being able to smoke it, Santana pulled his tobacco sack from his shirt and fashioned a cigarillo. "I may have the man to do it. He will be expensive, I think. I've seen him pull a six-gun and he is very fast. He may not want to do it, but the way I figure it, money can buy anything. You bring any *dinero* with you?"

"Not a damned cent, and there won't be more until I see results. If this man of yours gets Cantello—then I'll bring money." He climbed back on his horse. "Next time we meet, I want Cantello dead, and Mason hurt—hurt so we can take his headquarters." He reined his horse toward Presidio. "I'll send word when I want to see you again."

Santana walked away at the same time Soto left, then turned back. "Cantello, you hear all that was said?"

Quint chuckled. "I heard. Now, 'less you want me to

lose the faceless bastard, I better get on his trail." He grinned, knowing Santana couldn't see him. "Better be a damned good man you send to gun me down—or you gonna lose another man." Without waiting for the outlaw's reply, he hit a long, soundless stride in the direction Soto had taken.

While headed toward Presidio, he wondered what the results would have been if he'd simply pulled his Colt and come out the door of the *jacal* shooting, killing them both. He had no doubt but what he could have got them that way, but that wouldn't have solved the problem. Santana's gang would have still been in place to rob and kill at will. All Soto's stolen land and money would be hard to find— and Cantrell wanted Brad Mason to recoup a goodly bit of that which had been taken from him. The only way to do that would be to take Soto alive, and get the information out of him.

With that thought, and thinking to take Soto before he got to Presidio, Cantrell lengthened his stride, but for some reason he heard Manuel Soto curse and kick his horse into a ground-eating lope. Cantrell fell behind.

He forgot caution. He'd made up his mind to get the supreme leader of the outlaws. He lengthened his stride into an all-out run, but still lost track of Soto.

Knowing it was futile to continue his chase, he slowed, crossed the river, and went directly to the livery stable. He went to each stall, felt the horses in each, and came up dry. He'd been sure he'd find one of the animals lathered with sweat, or perhaps breathing as from a run. He found neither. Now he pulled his pipe from his pocket, packed and lit it. Squinting through the cloud of smoke, his mind settled on only one thing: Soto probably had his own stable here in town.

That idea led him nowhere; there were several privately owned shelters in the town. He couldn't go plowing through them at night. Someone might take him for a horse thief and shoot him, or worse, hang him. Racking his memory, he remembered seeing a small lean-to in back of the parsonage. Maybe that's where the holy man's horse was stabled.

Only a couple of hundred yards beyond the stores and saloons the glow of a lantern lit the windows of the parson's house. Cantrell turned up the dirt path that served as the walkway. A glance showed that no one roamed the trail in front of the house. He went to the closest window and peered in.

The preacher sat, the lantern pulled close to him on a side table, reading a newspaper. A half-full water glass sat next to the lantern. Cantrell's shoulders slumped.

If Phillips was Soto, he'd have to have been mighty fast to get home, stable and take the gear from his horse, go in the house, pour himself a glass of water, drink half of it, and settle back to read the paper.

Still not convinced he was wrong about the man, Quint ghosted his way to the lean-to. Phillips's horse munched hay, and twisted his neck around to look when Cantrell rubbed his hand across the horse's withers—which were cool. The horse had not been ridden hard lately. Doubting himself now, Quint continued to worry the fact that the parson used a six-gun, often. Why?

While Cantrell puzzled over Phillips, Santana collected his horse at the livery in Ojinaga and rode toward his headquarters. His mind toyed with sending Martinez to carry out Soto's orders. But he didn't want to lose Cantello, and besides that, he wasn't sure Martinez would be fast enough. The fact was, he didn't want to lose either of the two men. They were the kind he would need desperately to fight Mason's men. Still, this might be the chance to find out how loyal his newly hired *vaquero* was. He pondered how to satisfy Soto, and not jeopardize any of his men. He'd have to give it some thought—but not too much. Soto had proven to have very little patience.

Having had a day to get acquainted with Santana's men, Martinez sat with a couple of them on the *portico* outside the bunkhouse. Each had a *cervesa*. They drank in silence.

While he toyed with his beer, Martinez's eyes constantly searched the area. This was not a hideout back in the hills with a few squalid shacks, as he'd thought it might be. It was a small town. The married men in Santana's gang had separate *jacals*. Santana had a house on a much grander scale, and although Martinez had no chance to get inside, he estimated the house had several bedrooms, a large living room, and a dining room and kitchen. Too, there was a large commissary from which the men bought the needs for their families and themselves.

The single men stayed in the bunkhouse, but they didn't lack for feminine company. The *cantina* had women, whiskey, gambling, and sported a floor show once a week. Santana had the show brought in from Saltillo.

The bandits had small reason to grumble, yet several times during the day Martinez had caught a word here, a word there that told him the outlaws were not happy with the way things went north of the border. Too many of their own were failing to come back.

He wondered how many men they'd started with,

before the Mason brothers and Cantrell started whittling them down to size.

Thinking that most of Santana's bunch were here, with maybe one or two groups of seven to ten men operating close to the Mason ranch, Martinez estimated the outlaw leader had about eighty men left.

With Brad Mason's riders, those Quint brought with him, and the twenty-seven or so the brothers brought, Martinez thought the odds too long for an all-out assault against the bandit stronghold—but with Cole's training at the academy he might have some ideas.

Martinez felt he had what he'd been sent down here to find out, but he wanted more. How did the small town get its supplies? How many men did Santana usually let leave his headquarters at any one time? How did the bandits get along with one another? And did the bandit leader rule through loyalty—or fear?

Even though he thought he had enough information to satisfy Cole, and knowing the longer he stayed the greater were his chances of being found out, he decided to stay a couple more days anyway. That night Santana rode into his "town."

The next morning the leader gathered his men about him. He stood on the gallery of his *casa*. Santana made an imposing figure—huge, handsome in a brutal sort of way—and the pair of bandoliers across his chest suggested he could be as brutal as his face implied. Martinez smiled to himself. Dangerous? Brutal? *Sí*, but a bullet would make him as dead as it would any other.

Santana called the names of twenty men, divided them into two groups, told them where they were to attack next, then pinned Martinez with an iron look. "You, Martinez, I will talk to you alone. I have a special job for you."

Martinez's gut tightened. He'd been hoping to be put in one of the raiding parties. That was about the only way he thought to get back across the border.

Santana motioned for Martinez to follow. The big outlaw leader spun and pushed through the door, Martinez following closely. Santana motioned him to be seated, while at the same time he yelled for *dos cervesas*. A young girl, eyes downcast, brought the two beers and put them on tables at their side.

A beautiful Mexican girl—skin the color of fresh cream, large brown eyes, hair pulled up in a bun—sat quietly in a corner of the room reading. With a careless flip of his hand toward her, Santana said, "*Mi puta,*" as though he pointed out a piece of furniture.

With the bandit's introduction of the girl as his whore, Martinez's heart went out to her. Treated as trash, he thought she was there against her will, and her body used in any way Santana wished. He wondered if there was a way to set her free, then abondoned the idea. His mission was to get information, not to get involved with any of Santana's people.

The bandit raised the beer to his mouth and drank half of it before again placing it on the table at his side. He turned cold eyes on Martinez. "How much you figure a friend is worth, *vaquero*?"

Martinez returned his look. "*Jefe,* I don't think a man can put a price on a real friend. Why do you ask this question, *señor*?"

Benito Santana drained his bottle of *cervesa*, rolled a cigarillo, lit it, and studied the dainty wisp of smoke rising toward the ceiling. "That answer is the one I thought you'd give to me, Martinez. An answer I wanted, and didn't want." He held up two fingers for the girl to bring a couple more bottles. "I've been told to have your friend Cantello killed. I thought you might, for a price, be the man to do it."

Martinez shook his head. "Not for any price, and I think you already knew I'd feel that way."

Santana nodded. "*Sí*, I knew it, and it makes my decision harder. You are a man I want with me for a long time. If your loyalty went only as deep as your pockets, I'd kill you myself." He shrugged. "But that doesn't give me a solution. I don't want Cantello dead any more than you do. He is valuable to me."

Martinez stared at the bandit, seeing a side of him he hadn't known existed; he was not only brutal, but smart, and would return loyalty with loyalty. The slim *vaquero* almost liked the bandit . . . almost. He took a swallow of his beer. "Do you not have someone else to send after Cantello? I know you don't have one who can match the gun skills of my *amigo,* but perhaps you have one who can make a good showing against him. That way you could convince Manuel Soto you did your best. It *is* Soto who gave you the order, is it not?"

Santana nodded. "*Sí*, he is the only man who gives me, Benito Santana, orders, and his money is the only reason he can do that."

Jaime smiled and shook his head. "If I agreed to face Cantello, it still would not get the job done; he is faster and more accurate than me. I would be the one to die, *jefe*, and I do not wish to die." He held his hands in front of him, palms outward. "No. Do not suggest that he be shot in the back. I do not do such a thing. Never have, never will."

Although Santana smiled, it was cold. His smile reminded Martinez of the open mouth of a rattlesnake about to strike.

Through his smile, the outlaw baron said, "No, I too have never shot a man in the back—but I have many men who will do such a thing." He spread his hands in front of him and shrugged. "I have had no need to do such, so I do not know whether, if it became necessary, I would do it or not."

Martinez had no doubt that, necessary or not, Santana would shoot a man any way he thought was certain to get him. A chill crawled up his spine. It had been *his* suggestion that the only way to get Cantrell was from behind, and he had no doubt that Santana would take that route after Cantrell had done all Santana asked.

9

FROM THE LEAN-TO behind Phillips's house, Cantrell went to the hotel. On his way through the lobby, he ordered hot bathwater.

Later, sitting on the edge of his bed cleaning his Colt, he pondered his strong belief that the preacher had a part in the B-bar-M troubles. He had only a strong hunch, but his hunches in the past had seldom been wrong.

After a long few moments he became aware that he'd run the cleaning patch through the barrel of his revolver more than necessary. He'd been staring unseeingly at the wall. He nodded, pushed an oily patch through the six-gun barrel, loaded the weapon, and dropped it gently into the holster hanging over the bedpost. Then he washed the smell of gun oil from his hands.

He admitted to himself that the preacher had not likely been the one to meet Santana that night. No. He had not had time, but suppose Manuel Sotos had a partner.

He sighed. He had enough trouble trying to sort out one identity. Now, if he was right, he'd doubled his problem. He stood, swung his gunbelt around his waist, and buckled it. A beer would taste good. He headed for the Cattleman's Rest Saloon.

He pushed through the batwings, scanned those sitting at tables, didn't see anyone he knew, or who he thought might know him, then turned toward the bar.

Ansel Rondell, the young lawyer, stood at the end of the long polished surface. A glance at the remaining men draped over the bar showed no other Cantrell recognized. He walked over, edged his way next to the wall, and grinned at the lawyer. "Didn't figure to see anyone I knew, but I'm glad for company. Buy you a drink?"

Rondell nodded. "If I'm to have another, reckon somebody better buy. I'm stone-cold broke."

Cantrell studied the man a moment. "That bad?" Then at the young man's nod he waved toward the bartender for two drinks, and turned his attention back to Rondell. "What you gonna do now?"

Ansel shrugged. "Reckon all that's left is go back to punchin' cows." Their drinks came before Cantrell could think of any encouraging words. They drank in silence a few moments.

While drinking, an idea worked its way around in Quint's head. "I figure they's a small job you could do for me. The pay won't be much, but it'll keep you goin' for a short while. Maybe till somethin' better comes along. You interested?"

Rondell smiled. "Hell, Cantello, I'll tell you if it's anything short of murder, or stealing, I'll take it. What you want me to do?"

"Let's get a table. Can't talk too much here." Quint motioned the bartender for two more beers, handed one to Rondell, walked to the back of the room, and sat with his back to the wall.

When they were seated and drinking their beer, Cantrell leaned across the table. "Rondell, you know most folks hereabouts. What I want you to do is make me a list of every man in town, how long they been here, what they do for a livin', do they seem to have much money, an'—if you can find out without askin' a bunch o' questions that might get you killed—where they come from." He eyed the lawyer a moment. "Think you can do that for me?"

Rondell studied Cantrell a few seconds. "You a ranger, Cantello?"

Quint chuckled. "Ansel, gonna tell you somethin' for a fact. I rode the outlaw trail for several years thinkin' I wuz wanted by ever' sheriff in Colorado and the New Mexico Territory, then come to find out it wuz some brothers what put the price on my head for killin' one o' them." He shook his head. "No, I ain't no ranger, but I also ain't no outlaw. You might say I'm just a cowboy with a lot o' curiosity."

Rondell sat back, took a couple swallows of his beer, then pinned Cantrell with a knowing look. "Cantello, that kind of curiosity gets men killed around here. You're determined to find out who this person Soto is, aren't you?"

Quint nodded. "Reckon I didn't fool you much—but yeah, for reasons o' my own, I need to find who he is."

Rondell took time to pack his pipe and light it. "Then what?"

"Then, Mr. Rondell, I'm gonna kill 'im deader'n last night's moonrise—an' they wuzn't no moon last night."

The lawyer's pipe had gone out. He lit it again, puffed a cloud of smoke toward the ceiling, then nodded. "I'll take the job you offered." He smiled. "Would do it for nothin', but I gotta eat. Sixty bucks for the job?"

"A hundred."

"Hell, man, I haven't made that much money in this town since I hung out my shingle."

Cantrell leaned closer. "How long you think it'll take you?"

"Two weeks fit your plans, Cantello?"

Quint dug his fist into his pocket and pulled out a handful of double eagles, counted out a hundred dollars, and placed them in front of the lawyer. "Two weeks'll be fine. If you finish sooner, let me know."

Cantrell downed the rest of his beer and stood. "I may be outta town for a spell, but I'll come callin' when you've had time to finish what I want."

With a couple of beers under his belt, he relaxed, only now feeling how heavy his arms and legs were. Tiredness seeped through every bone in his body. He went to the hotel and to bed, but not to sleep. He lay there staring at the ceiling, thinking of how he'd put the list to work. He went to sleep smiling to himself.

The next morning, he had a good breakfast of steak, eggs, fried potatoes, biscuits, and coffee. When he'd finished, he walked catty-corner across the street to the newspaper office. A slim young man sat on the veranda, tilted back, the chair sitting on its back two legs.

Cantrell, about to go into the office, glanced at the man, saw ink-smudged fingers, and stopped. "You b'long to this here newspaper?"

A nod, then a grin. "Yeah, reckon I b'long to it, or the other way around. I'm the owner, publisher, editor, and printer. Fact is, I'm the only one. What you need?"

Cantrell frowned. "Don't rightly know, but I'm

thinkin' if you keep a file of all yore papers, an' I study those from the last couple o' years, they might tell me of some of the big happenin's in these parts." He pushed his hat to the back of his head. "You mind me takin' a look at 'em?"

The newspaperman's grin widened. He nodded. "Yep, we keep a file of 'em. Hep yourself. They're right back yonder in those drawers at the back of the room—all filed by year." He stood. "I'll show you how to start lookin'. I'll want 'em back in those drawers in the same order you take 'em out."

Cantrell smiled. "Don't reckon that's too much to ask."

Cantrell followed the young man, wending his way around boxes, one old broken printing press, and wadded-up paper balls. The printer pulled open a bottom drawer, looked up at Cantrell, and nodded. "You're lucky we only put out a paper once a week; you won't have as many to scan that way." He frowned. "How far back you want to go?"

Quint thought a moment, started to say two years, then said, "How 'bout the last two and a half years?"

The newspaperman pushed the drawer closed and opened the one above it. "Work your way through this one, then take the one above, and so on. The top drawer'll be only half-full, and it'll bring you up to date."

Cantrell nodded. "Thanks, partner, I'll take care to leave 'em like I found 'em." With that, he fingered through those in the open drawer until he came to a satisfactory date, then changed his mind and went back another six months.

He scanned the headings, occasionally finding a piece that drew his attention enough to cause him to read the entire article. The writings covered everything from soaking rains to bank robberies—more bank robberies than rains—to new people in town.

Each time he came to a robbery, he jotted down the date, how much money the bandits got away with, and how many outlaws pulled the job.

He also wrote the name of each new resident, and the date they'd arrived in town. Then he came on a large headline: An Army paywagon, one carrying the payroll for several army posts, was held up close to Fort Stockton by about eight bandits. They'd killed nine men of the armed escort; one man survived. The bandits had got away with an estimated two million dollars.

The next week's paper carried another article on the holdup. Posses, combing the country for the outlaws, found six bodies dumped in a ravine. Four of the six had been knifed, the other two shot. Three of the bodies were positively identified as some of the bandits who'd participated in the holdup.

Cantrell sat back on his haunches frowning. It looked to him as though two of the outlaws wanted it all and, probably while the dead men slept, knifed four before the last two woke, and those two were then shot.

When Cantrell finally straightened and rolled his shoulders to take the stiffness from them, he had several sheets of paper full of unusual happenings, names of new arrivals in town, and everything dated. He looked at the open front door and, surprised, saw that the sun had gone down. He headed for the rectangle of dim light.

The young publisher sat in the same chair, tilted back. Feeling a sheepish smile break the corners of his lips, Cantrell said, "Aw hell, mister, I didn't mean to keep you here all day. What do I owe you for your kindness?"

The young man shook his head. "Don't owe me a

nickel. I ate two meals today while you poked through those papers—smoked two cigars, drank two pots of coffee. Geez!" He tilted his chair forward, back onto all four legs. "I wish this whole town found my paper as interesting as you seem to. You find what you want?"

Quint grinned. "I don't know. Reckon I'm jest hopin' it'll begin to make sense to me when I look at my notes." He stuck out his hand. "Shoulda done this before, but I'm Juan Cantello. If you ever need a favor, look me up. I'll be around town somewhere."

The young man gripped Cantrell's hand. "Price Waters. Don't know of anything I might want, but if I do, I'll look you up."

Cantrell hadn't realized how hungry a man could get just going through a bunch of newspapers. He headed for the café, changed course, and went to the Cattleman's Rest. A drink would be good before he ate.

He took his drink, went to a back table, sat, and studied those in the room. He'd not finished his drink when the banker came in and bellied up to the bar. Cantrell had found out his name was Nathaniel "Nat" Howley. Watching Howley, he saw none of the simpering businessman he'd seen in the bank. The man was a blustery, arrogant bastard, with a definite show of superiority. Quint still didn't like him.

Howley stood, his back to the bar, looking over the patrons. No one stood close or attempted to talk to him. His eyes swept the crowd, apparently spotted Cantrell, and walked to his table. "Mr. Cantello, how do you like our town? You've had a little while to evaluate it. Earlier, I noticed you come from the newspaper office. Still familiarizing yourself? I hope you've changed your mind about transferring your funds to my bank."

A guarded, tight feeling took hold in Quint's shoulder muscles. Howley was probing to see what business he might have had with the newspaper. He looked at the banker and smiled. "No, sir, I figured the paper could tell me how many banks had been robbed in this area." He nodded. "Yeah, I wuz thinkin' to move my money over this way, but after seein' how lawless some o' these towns are, reckon I'll keep it where it is till I find what I want in a small ranch. Don't want nothin' big, just a place I can build on an' not have a neighbor close enough to know my business." He shook his head. "Never did like nobody knowin' every time I went to the outhouse."

Howley, apparently satisfied about Cantrell's interest at the paper, nodded and went back to the bar. Cantrell knocked back his drink, left, and went to the café.

There, he shuffled through the notes he'd made during the day. Some he made a mark by to remind him to look into them further, others he thought to be of little significance, but he kept them in order to tie the information to Rondell's list.

Finally, too tired to continue to study his notes, he went to his room, turned the lamp down, and closed his eyes.

Early the next morning, he took a seat on the highly polished board bench in front of the general store. The board had been worn smooth by the trouser seats of the old-timers, the spit-and-whittle club, who took up their stations there every morning after having coffee, and commenced to chew their tobacco, spit, and whittle the same stick they'd worked on the day before. Cantrell brought his own stick, lit his pipe, and commenced to slice thin pieces from his own work of art.

Like most cattlemen, when a rider rode by he'd first

glance at the man in the saddle, then take a longer look at the brand on the horse he rode. After about an hour, Jarred Phillips rode by on a high-stepping line-back dun. He sat the saddle like a man born to it. Cantrell's eyes flicked to the dun's brand. He frowned. He'd been over much, most in fact, of the cattle country west of the Mississippi, and he'd not seen a brand like the one that marked the minister's horse.

The brand showed a horseshoe with an arrow cutting it in two. The crease between Quint's eyes deepened. There were several things about the man of the cloth that caused suspicion.

Then, Phillips reined in in front of the café, stepped down, and went in. A cowboy would get on his horse to ride to the place next door to where he lived, but a townsman would walk. The preacher's house stood less than seventy-five yards from the café. Cantrell allowed his lips to break at the corners. He was certain Phillips had put in a lot of time in the saddle—a helluva lot more than he'd put in behind the pulpit. Quint stood, and although not wanting a cup of coffee, he figured he might as well have one.

When he walked through the door, the minister sat at the table closest to it. Cantrell nodded and made as though to walk past, then stopped. "Want a little company, Preacher?"

Phillips glanced up and without a word motioned to the chair across from him. Cantrell smiled. "Already et breakfast, but figured another cup o' coffee'd be good." The preacher grunted an answer that Quint failed to understand, but it was obvious he wasn't welcome.

Cantrell made a motion to the waitress as though drinking from a cup. She brought a cup, poured, and waited for Phillips to order. He grunted that he wanted ham, eggs, biscuits, and gravy.

When she left the table, Quint glanced at the man across from him, then about the room. As he did so, he picked up a slight bulge under the preacher's left arm. Another glance and he was certain. The man of the cloth had a revolver of some kind in a shoulder holster. Why would a preacher feel he needed to carry a weapon?

When Phillips finished eating, and sat with a full cup of coffee in front of him, Cantrell frowned and looked at him. "When you feel the callin' to take up the good book, Phillips, or have you always been a man of God?"

Quint's words apparently brought Phillips back into the world of which he was a part. His smile, obviously forced, centered itself on Cantrell. "I believe I always wanted to carry the word, but I had to wait until I was eighteen years old before I left home back in Missouri with a Bible under one arm, and a bedroll under the other. I was a circuit preacher for a while, until I found a church in San Antonio. When I left there, I came on out here and set up in this church." He shook his head. "My church before was much larger than this one, but I believe I can do more good out here. These people need me."

Quint laughed. "Don't reckon I can disagree with you on that point, preacher man. These people out here're pretty rough around the edges." They talked about the weather, cattle, about which Phillips professed to know little or nothing, and after a while, Cantrell swallowed the rest of his coffee and stood. "Reckon I'll see you around town, Phillips. I'm lookin' for a small ranch I can settle in on, and let the world go by. Fact is, I'm figuring on takin' a ride around the country. Might see somethin' I'd like.

I've had 'bout all I can stand of workin' my tail off. Now, gonna sit back an' enjoy life."

Phillips pinned him with a look that said he didn't believe a word of it. "You're a mighty young man to be talkin' about quitting work."

Quint nodded. "Yeah, but by quittin' I might be keepin' myself young—and alive." He nodded and left. When he passed Phillips's horse, he again studied the broken horseshoe brand. He'd have to look into that.

Phillips watched Cantrell step out onto the boardwalk, pause, look at the line-back dun, then head for the hotel. His eyes squinted against the morning glare, and he watched as long as he could see the tall rider. He had the distinct feeling that the man he watched was trouble, and plenty of it.

Then he thought back on their conversation. He'd lied about having a church in San Antonio. He'd been there, but not in the church business. Too, it was not until after mentioning San Antonio that Cantello had said he'd be out of town a few days. Looking for a small ranch—hell, that cowboy's gonna head straight for San Antonio. With that thought, Phillips shoved back his chair, paid his bill, and headed home.

There, he rolled his bedroll, then cleaned and oiled both his shoulder gun and his Winchester. He decided while getting ready to take a packhorse with him. It was a long way to San Antonio.

Quint went to the hotel and flopped on the bed, hands clasped behind his head, thinking. There was one thing on which he'd bet a spotted pony: If Phillips really was a preacher, he'd not been one long, or he'd earned his living between sermons doing something that required a lot of horsebacking. There was only one way he could figure to find out. He'd have to go to San Antonio. But he couldn't go without leaving some word for those at the ranch. He stood, rolled his gear in his blankets, picked up his Winchester, and left.

Nothing out of the ordinary happened on his way to the ranch, and after having a few moments with Elena to tell her his plans, he sat at the kitchen table drinking coffee and eating a quarter of one of Laura's apple pies.

Quint told Brad and the women what he'd been doing, then said, "Twice I've had the chance to kill both Santana and Manuel Soto an' didn't do it. I had 'em within two, maybe three feet of each other, but was afraid that wouldn't solve our problem."

"Well, why the hell not!" Brad yelled, his face red enough to explode.

Cantrell looked at him straight-on. "Tell you why, Pa. If we kill Soto, we don't know where his money is, or what property he's bought under some other name— we'll have nothin'. When we get him, I want to know all that so we can get back what he's stolen from you. I want 'im alive so I can work on 'im a little until he squeals like a stuck hog; then, law or no law, I'm gettin' it all back."

Brad sat back and studied Quint a moment, and in that look there was no doubt he thought of Cantrell as his own son. "Quint, I don't want you doin' nothin' agin' the law. Too, I don't want you takin' any wild damned chances like I've been told you're of a mind to do more often than not."

"Pa," Elena cut in, "you're wasting your breath. I've seen my Quint when he sets his head to something. I don't believe anything, or anybody, could cause him to change." She turned her look on her husband. "You have something in mind—tell us about it."

Cantrell poured himself another cup of coffee, poured some for each of the others, and sat. He then told them of his idea that Soto was perhaps two men, partners, who had this grand scheme to take over the largest ranch in the Big Bend, as well as most of the smaller ones. "I b'lieve I know who one of the men is. I got no idea who the other is, but I think I can nail down right tight about the one I suspect. To do that I figure to ride over to SanTone an' do some checkin'. It'll take me 'bout ten days. Come to tell y'all my figurin' so's you could tell Cole an' Clay when you see 'em agin."

Elena stared at him a moment, her eyes showing fear. "You gonna keep your Colt in its holster while you're riding on this trip?"

He nodded. "Figure to do just that. Don't want nobody rememberin' me an' gettin' the word down here."

Elena sighed. "If that's all I can get, reckon it'll have to do." Then, her voice hopeful, she added, "You gonna stay with us overnight?"

Quint laughed. "You couldn't drag me away with a six-horse team before I held you close to me—all night."

Her face blossomed a bright pink.

,

The next morning, about a half hour from the ranch, Cantrell caught a flash of light, as though from a rifle barrel. The reflection came from a cluster of rocks about a hundred yards ahead. He jumped his horse into the brush at the side of the trail. A voice from the rocks hailed him. "It's all right, Cantrell, it's me, Cole."

Quint reined his horse back into the trail. Cole rode out

to meet him. "What you doing at the ranch? Thought you'd be too busy in Presidio."

Cantrell told Cole his plans. "Sounds good to me." Cole hooked a leg around the saddle horn. "An' your idea about there bein' two Sotos makes sense, but doubles our problem. We find one, we better find the other one right soon, or he might take the bulk of the money and take off."

Cantrell shook his head. "Don't think so, Cole. This game is so big, I figure wantin' it all would keep him here. Gonna play it that way anyhow."

Cole nodded. "You may be right. We've got Santana's bunch sliced down to where we can take on any of their war parties with one or two of our bunch. You need any help, let me know. Don't hog all the fun for yourself."

Quint let a tight grin take hold of his face. "Partner, I guarantee you, I'll squall like a wounded Comanche when that time comes." He stared at his old friend. "Reckon I'm gettin' old, or maybe smarter. I can do without all the hell-raisin' we used to do. 'Sides that, I got a whole bunch more days an' nights I want to spend with Elena."

Cole stared between his horse's ears a moment, then muttered, "Sure is unbelievable what gettin' married'll do to a man." He looked up and, with a caring look, said, "*Vaya con Dios,* old friend. Take care."

Cantrell, a knot in his throat, flung up a hand in farewell and kneed his horse up the trail.

He rode straight east, crossed the Rio Grande into Mexico, crossed Mexico to *Ciudad Acuna,* again crossed the river into Del Rio, then to Uvalde, and San Antonio. It took him four days of little water, few good meals, and no beer.

He rode into the town square, wondered why the citizens had let the Alamo go to ruin like they had since he saw it last, and looked at the hotel next to it. The sign above the door said "The Menger Hotel". He'd heard it was a first-class hostelry so he hitched his horse to the tie rail in front and went in. The Menger was in fact all he'd heard it to be. "Luxurious" was the word Elena would put to it. He registered, took his gear to his room, then went back outside to take care of his horse.

The liveryman promised to rub his horse down and grain feed it. Cantrell headed for the closest saloon. His throat felt like it had an inch of trail dust caked in it.

The saloon had lights, gas lights. Cantrell hadn't seen gas lights since the last time he and Elena went Christmas shopping in Santa Fe. A glance at those at the bar, and a look at the tables, showed no one he'd ever seen before. This time of day, suppertime, the saloon had but few customers. Quint took his place where he felt most comfortable—the end of the long polished surface where it butted against the wall.

He felt out of place in that most of the clientele were dressed in suits with string ties adorning their shirts. He still wore his trail garb, and ten days of dust. The bartender walked along, dispensing drinks as he came. When standing in front of Cantrell, he grinned. "Long ride?"

Quint slipped him a crooked grin. "Yeah. Draw me a couple of beers. I'll swallow 'em an' get the hell outta here. I ain't never felt like I didn't b'long in a place as much as I feel it now."

The bartender's face, so Irish it could have been the map of old Erin, carried a wider smile. "Cowboy, you take your time. B'lieve it or not, a couple hours ago half these people in here looked more trail-worn than you do, but they had time to go home, have a couple o' snorts there, clean up, an' come on down here where their wives wouldn't nag at their backsides 'bout drinkin' too much. When you get through with your two, I'll set you up a couple more on the house." He stuck out his hand. "Me name's O'Grady."

Cantrell gave his right name, and shook O'Grady's hand. The Irishman had made him feel comfortable despite his dress and lack of a bath.

When business slacked off a mite, O'Grady walked to stand in front of Quint. "Know you ain't from around here, or I'd've seen you before." He chuckled. " 'Sides that, it took a few days of travel to accumulate that many layers o' trail dust." He made a swipe with the bar cloth to wipe off the wet ring Cantrell's glass had made when he picked it up. "You figuring to settle here, or you just passin' through?"

Quint didn't think the Irishman was getting too nosey, so he answered him. "Neither one. I'm lookin' for a man who's been passin' hisself off as a preacher down Presidio way. Thought I might check the churches here an' see if anybody remembers 'im."

O'Grady grinned. "Well, Cantrell, gonna tell it like it is. I don't reckon we ever had a preacher man come in this establishment." He frowned. "But I believe you said 'passin' hisself off,' like maybe you don't think he really is a preacher?"

Cantrell studied the foam on top of his beer a moment, wondering how much to tell O'Grady, then decided to describe Phillips and see. He nodded. "There's something about the man that just flat don't ring true. Maybe if

I tell you what he looks like, you mighta seen 'im around town. That would help a bunch."

O'Grady glanced at Cantrell's tied-down holster. "You gunnin' for 'im?"

"If he's the man I'm lookin' for, I sure as hell am. He's 'bout to ruin a old man what always treated me like I was his own son." Cantrell nodded. "Don't never let it be said that Quinton Cantrell won't fight for his friends."

O'Grady stared at Quint a moment, frowning. "Thought I remembered the name. You're *that* Cantrell, the one from up Colorado way." He smiled and shook his head. "If I was that preacher, reckon I'd already be makin' tracks for California."

"O'Grady, if he's the one, he cain't run far enough. I'll track 'im to hell if I have to."

10

AFTER GETTING HIS trail gear put together and secured to his packhorse, Phillips went back to his house to await the coming of darkness. He couldn't leave town without letting his partner know what he suspected, and why he was headed for San Antonio. The wait for the sun to set seemed like the rest of his life. Every hour or so he'd step to the door and look at the sun.

Finally, the lengthening shadows blurred and faded to a soft velvety . . . nothing. Phillips stepped from his back door, went to an alley, down the backs of stores, past the last business, and stopped at the back of his partner's house. He tapped lightly.

A gruff voice answered.

"It's me, partner. Open up. Gotta see you."

"Thought we agreed we were never to meet each other here in town."

"Yeah, but somethin's come up I figure needs checkin' out." The door swung open and Phillips scooted inside.

His partner grasped his arm. "Stay here till I draw the shades. I'll light a lantern an' we can talk."

After a few minutes, sitting at the big man's kitchen table, Phillips leaned forward, took a swallow of the drink his partner had poured, then told him of all that had transpired. "I think he's dangerous. He's nosey, an' I don't think it's something we can let go. The man packs that sidegun like he knows how to use it—packs it like he's used it a whole helluva lot. I figure if we let him alone he can spoil all we've worked at for the last couple of years. We gotta make him dead."

His partner sat there staring into his glass, then he looked up. "Think you can beat 'im in a stand-up gunfight?"

Phillips grinned. "I don't figure him, or anybody else'll beat me that way, but I can't let anything like that happen here with me bein' a minister of the gospel. That's why I better go to San Antonio. There's no one there who'll associate me with a small town preacher. We can bury our troubles there. If I can't do it in a straight-on gunfight, I'll follow 'im outta town an' shoot 'im from behind once we get out on the trail."

His partner nodded. "We'll do it your way. I'll let the word drop here and there around town tomorrow that you had an uncle die and went to see if there was anything you could do for his family." He stood. "Be damned careful leaving here. Don't want anyone tying us together yet. After a while, after we get control of what we're after, it won't make any difference."

Phillips left as stealthily as he'd arrived, went to his lean-to, got his dun and packhorse, and left town in the middle of the night.

Cantrell spent his first full day in San Antonio going from one church to another, from mission to mission, and at each of them he found that the minister of that church had been there for many years, all except one, and that one had been a newcomer six years before. He visited the last church after the sun slid under the horizon.

Although it was dark, he showed the priest a list of the churches he'd visited that day. "You see any places I mighta missed, Father?"

The priest studied Cantrell's list a moment, went back over it, and shook his head. "I think you've been to them all, son. Why are you looking for this man?"

Cantrell took the list the priest extended to him and said, "Father, they's a man down where I come from posin' as a preacher. I figure he's a crook tryin' to steal all the good ranch land around there—all the time hidin' behind the good book. I got it in mind to stop 'im."

The priest stared at Cantrell a moment, then said, "Son, I hope I've not been made an instrument in getting a man killed."

Cantrell gave him a wintery smile. "No, sir, you ain't. He's gonna get what's comin' to 'im no matter who told me what." He nodded and left.

Although he'd not eaten since breakfast, Cantrell stopped in to see O'Grady. As soon as the big, redheaded bartender saw him, he smiled. "Dang it all, Cantrell, you clean up right well. Wouldn't've knowed you 'cept for the way you wear that there handgun." He reached for a glass. "Beer, or what?"

Cantrell put a coin on the bar. "Make it whiskey tonight, O'Grady." He leaned tiredly against the wall. "Found out one thing today. Tryin' to find a man what preached at one o' these churches is one helluva lot harder'n chousin' cow's outta the chaparral all day." He took a swallow of the drink O'Grady handed him, grimaced, and said, "Why didn't y'all call this here town the City of Churches?" He shook his head. "Damned if I woulda b'lieved they wuz this many churches in the whole state o' Texas."

Red O'Grady threw back his head and roared, then sobered. "You find out if the man you lookin' for wuz a preacher here?"

Cantrell nodded. "I found out."

Red leaned across the bar. "Well, tell me. Wuz he?"

Cantrell shook his head. "They never heard o' him in none o' those churches."

O'Grady went down the bar, drew a couple of drinks, and came back. "Cantrell, the man you described the other night fits a man who rode in today. He was in here less than a hour ago. When he bellied up to the bar, I took careful notice of 'im." He nodded. "Yeah, I'd say he was the same man you described—right down to wearin' a shoulder holster."

Quint's facial muscles tightened. His eyes went dead and cold. "O'Grady, knowin' where he keeps 'is handgun gives me a slight edge. I figure he knows how to use that weapon right well, judging by the callus I felt on his thumb." He pushed his hat to the back of his head and smiled. "You can bet one thing for sure. His hands get close to the lapels on his coat, he's gonna die right sudden."

The big redhead stared into Cantrell's eyes. Softly, very softly, he murmured, "Lookin' at your face, cowboy, I'm here to tell you I'm damned glad I ain't standin' in his boots." He reached under the bar, pulled the cork from a bottle of prime whiskey, and poured Quint's glass full again. "On the house."

Quint shook his head. "Nope, I'll pay for it. You keep on pourin' me free drinks, the owner might fire you."

O'Grady chuckled. "Now, wouldn't that be a helluva

note—me firin' me. I own this place, Cantrell. Me bein' different from most o' those Micks workin' for the Union Pacific, I saved my money, an' when the rails met at Promontory Point I quit buildin' railroads and come down here to get warm. Ain't never been sorry 'bout that decision."

Quint knocked back his drink, grinned at the big redhead, and said, "Hell, reckon we're two Irishmen what ain't so damned dumb, but I'm here to tell you they's times up there in Colorado, when snow's butt deep to a tall Indian, that I wish for some o' this Texas weather." He tipped his hat back down on his forehead and nodded. "See you 'bout this time tomorrow. Gonna go surround a good-sized steak an' potatoes right now."

Cantrell ate supper, went to his room, checked his handgun, put a shell in the empty cylinder he usually let the hammer rest on, then went to bed.

He lay there a long time staring at the ceiling. He had no doubt that Phillips had left Precidio with one purpose in mind, and that was to get him in front of his gun and get him out of the way. With that in mind, there was no question as to how he could get the preacher to draw on him, but he had to make it legal, keep it within the Code of the West. He rode the outlaw trail too long to have forgotten the long, cold, lonely days and nights. He wanted no more of that; besides, now he had Elena, and she was reason enough to play it straight.

Two doors down and one floor above Cantrell, Phillips sat on the edge of his bed wondering whether he got to San Antonio ahead of Cantello.

One thing of which he was certain: Cantello would not be hiding if he knew he was being hunted. Phillips knew a dangerous man when he saw one, and he thought the tall Spaniard would be one of the most dangerous he'd ever faced. Hmmm, maybe he'd better give a straight-on gunfight another thought.

He pondered the idea of following Cantrell when he left town, and ambushing him along the trail somewhere. He frowned. Hell, why was he thinking like that? He, himself, was the fastest man he'd ever known of—except maybe his partner. He hoped he would never have to face that problem.

He turned the wick down on his lantern and stretched out on the bed, fully dressed. He thought that after resting awhile he'd go to the saloon and play a few hands of poker. The austere style of living he was forced to observe while in Presidio went against the grain. He'd always lived high-wide-and-handsome. He smiled into the room's darkness and shrugged. Soon, maybe real soon, he could come out from behind the good book, and live like he was meant to.

The next morning, Quint stepped from the café, glanced around the square, and decided to shop for a nice gift for Elena. He figured to buy Laura, Molly, and Ma gifts also. He settled on getting them each a *mantilla:* Elena, one of an ice blue to go with her blond, silken hair; Laura a green one; Molly the same; and Ma a black one. The shopkeeper told him the lace was imported from Granada. He doubted the man's words, but bought them anyway.

Cantrell spent most of the morning wandering about the town buying gifts, careful to make certain they'd fit into his pack saddle without breaking.

All the while he shopped, he searched the face and build of each person his gaze fell upon. If Phillips was in town, Cantrell wanted to see him first. He didn't know enough about the man to determine whether he was a stand-up gunfighter, or a back-shooter—but he did believe the preacher was a gunfighter, and a good one.

At noon, he ate in the same café in which he'd had breakfast, then went back to his room. While there, he decided to go to the saloon for a drink before supper. If Phillips had been in the place the night before, Cantrell felt certain the man would return to the same watering hole. Most men were creatures of habit and preferred familiar surroundings. He would face the preacher, and take it outside if he could. If he couldn't, then at the risk of shooting up O'Grady's saloon, Cantrell figured to call the showdown.

Jaime Martinez worried for several days that Santana would send him to face Cantrell. Yeah, the big outlaw had use for both him and Cantrell, but would he openly go against Soto? Martinez had no intention of shooting Quint, under any circumstances—nor did he want to die at the end of Cantrell's gun. If it came down to having to ride to Presidio under that pretext, then he'd take the chance on getting to the Mason ranch without getting shot. But the worry proved to be in vain. Santana called him to the house.

The big outlaw sat in his huge, leather-covered chair and motioned Jaime to sit in the one next to him. Martinez, his guts churning, dreading the order he knew Santana was about to give, sat in the chair Santana indicated and accepted the tequila the maid brought.

Santana studied him a moment. "Martinez, is your friend Cantello a man of his word?"

Jaime nodded. "I never knew him to give his word and not keep it, *señor*. Why do you ask?"

The bandit studied the drink he held in his left hand a moment, then pinned Martinez with a look filled with both worry and anger. He nodded. "I will answer that. Our friend Cantello has disappeared. He has not been seen in Presidio in over five days. Either he has crossed me, and run off with my money, or Soto discovered he was working for me. As much as I like money, I hope it is that he has run off with it. If Manuel Soto knows Cantello works for me, it will be the end of the easy *dinero,* which is a lot more than that I gave to your friend."

He knocked back his drink, licked some salt from the back of his hand, and bit into a slice of lime. He shuddered. "Too, there is another thing which might have happened. Soto might have found someone across the river to kill Cantello." He shrugged. "If that is the case, then my money is gone, you've lost a friend, and I will not have the information that I hired Cantello to find for me."

He poured himself and Martinez each another drink. "But all that is not what I called you here for. While we wait to find out what might have happened to your friend, I want you to go with several of my best men to put a raid on the Mason ranch. Rinaldo Quantero will give you the instructions. You'll leave tonight to be there early *mañana.*"

Martinez gulped, swallowed his drink, and tried to keep relief from showing. This was the way he could get back to the ranch—if he didn't get killed while trying. He stood. "Is that what you wanted to tell me, *jefe*?"

Santana nodded, then smiled. "Ah, I see you are anxious to have a little action." He again nodded. "I knew you were that kind. You're a good man, *vaquero.*"

When Jaime left the house, it was all he could do to restrain himself from the yell bubbling in his chest. He didn't think for a minute that Soto, or anyone else, had been able to gun Cantrell down. Cole had told him too many times how good Quint was with a six-gun, and how good he was at staying out of situations where he could get back-shot.

As soon as he left Santana, Martinez looked for Quantero and found him in the *cantina*.

"*El jefe* tells me I'm to ride with you tonight to make the raid on the Mason ranchero, *sí*?"

Quantero nodded. "We leave here at two o'clock. We hit them just before daylight. If you get separated from the main bunch, you know the way back here."

Martinez smiled. "I have been waiting for this day. I'll be ready." He left to go back to the bunkhouse thinking that Quantero had no idea how much he'd been waiting for this day.

To make it appear he had really anticipated going on his first raid with them, he took out his Winchester and Colt and thoroughly cleaned and oiled them. He put them back in leather, then honed his Bowie knife and lay on his bunk fully dressed, thinking he'd never get to sleep. But he'd no more than put his head on the pillow before he drifted off.

When Quintero touched his shoulder to waken him, Martinez would have sworn he'd only that minute closed his eyes. He went to the pump, splashed water over his head, went to the stable, saddled his horse, and was mounted before the rest. He sat his saddle feeling the predawn coolness soak into him. The smell of the night air came to his nostrils fresh and pure. As men were wont to do upon waking before daylight, they talked in hushed tones.

Quintero mounted the horse next to Martinez. "Ah, the young *vaquero* is straining to get to the *Americanos*, eh?"

"*Sí*, I've been hoping for this day. Now it is here."

They rode from the armed compound in a tightly grouped, strangely silent bunch. Jaime figured they knew only too well from recent experience that many of them would not be riding back this way—perhaps none of them. He had a twinge of conscience; his throat tightened. There were many of these men he'd been growing to like.

He understood why most of them had turned to banditry. They had been raised dirt poor, with no chance to break from the squalid life to which they'd been born. Now the horses they rode were stolen, the guns they carried had all too often been taken from the bodies of the dead, and their clothes were of the poorest quality. He wondered, had circumstances been different, if he could have ended up much as these men.

He shook off those thoughts. His real friends were inside the walls of Brad Mason's ranch. Hopefully waiting for just such a raid as this one.

After crossing the Rio Grande, Jaime let his horse drop back into the bunch. He wanted to be as close to the rear as possible. If he had it figured right, either Clay or Cole would have a welcoming party waiting for them before they got to the ranch's wall.

The farther back he dropped, the heavier was the smell of dust. It clogged his nostrils, settled on his clothes, and even gave his teeth a gritty feel. The only sound now was the soft clopping of the many hooves in the powdery dirt.

Getting uncomfortably close to the *rancho,* Martinez's neck muscles pulled tight, knotted, gave him a headache.

When they were no more than three or four more minutes to the gate, the sharp report of a rifle split the early morning quiet, then rifle fire bloomed from each side of the trail. Saddles emptied. Martinez threw himself from his saddle, and at the same time felt a burning across the back of his shoulders. He hit the ground, gasped for breath, and lay still.

A rider pulled in close, reached to pull him up behind, and found death. Martinez had pulled his Colt when he fell, and now he fired straight up into the face of the rider trying to help him. His guts turned over. He vomited, and it had been a long time since he'd cried, but tears streaked his cheeks. Despite telling himself this was war, that these men were bent on destroying his best friend's father, he could not rid himself of the terrible guilt that threatened to gnaw his guts right out of his body.

Abruptly the sound of guns ceased. Quiet settled in on death's arena. His ears hurt from the lack of sound, then one by one crickets and cicadas began to sing their song. Light tinged the eastern sky. A bird trilled its song of territorial imperative, then men's voices joined in the awakening world.

Jaime lay sill, his cheek buried in the inches-thick dust. He tasted the dry earth next to his nose, afraid that if he moved, someone, thinking he was of the raiding party, would put a bullet in him to make sure he was dead.

He gathered his every bit of self-control and forced himself to stay as he was, curled up, his knees drawn against his stomach. He waited, waited, waited, for someone to come turn him over and discover who he was.

Among the voices, Jaime identified Cole's. He still waited, listening to them go from one of the raiders to the next, making certain they were no longer a threat. A trickle of warm blood spilled down his shoulders. He didn't think his wound was serious, but it burned enough to have been dipped in hell. Finally, footsteps padded through the deep dust and stopped at his side.

A boot toe slipped under Martinez's armpit and flipped

him to his back. The man, whoever he was, yelled, "Hey, Cole, Martinez is lyin' here. He's hit. Damn! Hope we ain't hurt 'im bad."

With those words, Jaime felt it safe to stand. He pulled his legs under him, pushed his hands against the ground, and stood. "Man, when you treat the friends like this, how you do to your enemies?"

The man Jaime now saw was Art King grinned, then laughed. "Cowboy, you done give me a scare. Cole told us soon's you left with Cantrell to be damned careful anytime we got raided to be sure we didn't shoot at you." He put his hands on Martinez's shoulder and twisted him so as to look at his back. "Hmm, don't look like it's anything but a crease. Thanks to the spirits of all my Apache ancestors you ain't hurt bad."

Cole ran to them. "Jaime, you all right?" Then without waiting for an answer, he yelled, "Damn, men, get 'im on a horse. Gotta get Laura to take care o' him." One of Cole's men brought Martinez's horse, and Art and Cole boosted him to the saddle. Jaime realized then that even if his wound was only a crease, it bled, and with the bleeding came weakness. He grasped the saddle horn with both hands until Cole rode alongside and helped to support him.

When they rode to the gate, it stood open; apparently those inside had heard them coming. Laura, Molly, Elena, and Ma were the first to reach the returning men. The young wives glanced at each rider, making sure none was hit bad. When Cole escorted Jaime through the gate, the three younger women caught him and eased him to the ground.

Sitting his horse to their side, Cole growled, "Hey, don't baby that man so much. First thing you know, he'll want to go to bed to get well an' I won't stand for that."

He looked down into Jaime's eyes, which had the crinkles of a smile trying to form.

Abruptly, Martinez squeezed his eyes tight shut and moaned. "Oh, *señor,* I theenk I am ver bad hit—I theenk I might die."

A deep line creased Cole's forehead, and quickly he swung from his horse and squatted at his friend's side. Maybe Jaime had taken another hit. "Where you hurt, *mi amigo?* You hit hard somewhere?"

Martinez's eyes opened wide. He laughed. "No you hard-nosed *bastardo,* I figured I might, as you *Norte Americanos* would say, feenagle a night's sleep in a soft bed, an' then take the next two or three days off to get well, despite you bein' such a slave driver."

He held up his arm to be helped to his feet. Cole sighed, feeling the tension flow from him. He grasped Jaime's hand and pulled him to his feet. He stared into his friend's eyes. "You pull that stunt on me, an' one day you might be hit hard. On that day I might not take you seriously."

"Aw, *amigo,* I was only funnin' you." Martinez frowned and stared at the ground. "But I tell you, Cole, I won't theenk eet ees funny anymore. I weel not do eet again."

Cole raised his hand to slap his friend on the back, then jerked it back. He'd forgotten the crease across Jaime's shoulders, and although not serious, he knew from experience how painful it could be. "Come, *amigo,* let's go have a drink of Pa's whiskey and get your shoulders patched while you tell me what you found out down in *Mejico.*"

An hour later, Martinez, dressed in a clean shirt, sat at the kitchen table along with the Mason clan, Art King, and Snake McClure. He told them that, in his opinion, Santana could be wiped out with the men at Cole's and

Clay's disposal, but—he shook his head—"Eet weel cost the lives of many of our men."

Clay took a sip of his coffee. "Why you b'lieve that?"

Martinez, drinking some of Pa Mason's whiskey, frowned. "Tell you, that *ranchero* ees built like a town. Eet has *jacals* for the married men an' their *esposas*, bunkhouses for the unmarried men, a store, a *cantina*, blacksmith shop." He shrugged. "Eet has everything a regular town has. Eet would be a bloody fight to try to take it with the men we have—or weeth twenty times as many."

Cole sat, a deep crease between his eyes. Finally he swept those at the table with a hard look. "We can take it without losin' very many men. Dynamite's the answer. We'll level the place, then we won't have to go house to house, building to building to get them."

Martinez sat back, took a swallow of his drink, and shook his head. "*Mi amigo,* I have sided with you in many a fight, but theez wan I weel not do."

Cole felt his face harden. "There must be a good reason, Martinez, there better be a good reason. Why you cuttin' out on me now?"

Jaime stared into the bottom of his now empty glass. "Because, *señor,* theez time we would keel women and children. That eez wan theeng I weel not do. Eef we can get them out from their *rancho,* I weel fight the men as long as there is one of them standing." He shook his head. "But I weel not keel the leetle babies—or the women."

Cole's face softened, and when he tried to say something, words caught in his throat. Finally he spoke. "Ah, Jaime, I just flat didn't think." He shook his head. "You know me well enough to know I won't attack them where even one woman or child can be hurt. No. We'll have to think of another way to get them."

Art King, as usual, hadn't had much to say, but now he leaned forward. "Tell you how I'd play it. The Apaches had a good thing goin' by showin' only a small bunch what wuz gonna attack them. We do the same, but we keep our main bunch hidden in a arroyo somewhere close, an' let the small bunch o' our men lure them into the trap. Then, by damn, we can use dynamite, or whatever we have at hand."

Cole, a slight smile crinkling the corners of his mouth, nodded. "Glad the Rebs didn't have many like you during the war, or we'd've been hard-pressed to win."

Art's face turned a bright red, and Elena swept them with a glance. "Tell y'all how it is, Art King seldom says anything, but when he does, it's a good idea to listen— listen hard."

Art's face reddened even more. He pushed back his chair and said, "Aw hell, knew I shoulda kept my mouth shut." He walked to the cupboard and poured himself a drink. He turned back to face the table. "Gonna tell y'all somethin', we better have a few more o' them there battles out here in the chaparral, cut 'em down a little more. Then we can talk 'bout gittin' them Mexes outta their town. Them're damned—'scuse me, ladies—them are good fightin' men."

Walking from bright sunlight into the dark saloon, Cantrell stepped to the side of the batwings long enough for his eyes to adjust, then went to the bar and asked O'Grady for a cold beer. He stood, holding it in his hand until he'd looked at every man in the room. No sign of Phillips, but he did spot a poker game at one of the back tables. He looked at Red. "Figure to play a few hands o' poker. If Phillips comes in, try to let me know so's I can get outside 'fore he sees me." He grinned. "Don't wantta shoot up yore place if I can help it."

O'Grady shrugged. "Hell, Cantrell, it's been shot up before. Don't you take any chances. You have to shoot it up, I'll bill you for the damages."

Cantrell nodded. He took a deep breath. "Funny how you get used to the smell o' stale beer an' cigar smoke after you been in a saloon for a while. Notice the odors when you first come in, then you forget 'em."

O'Grady shook his head. "Damned if you don't beat all. Here you are, maybe 'bout to have a gunfight, an' you talk 'bout smells." He shook his head again and went down the bar to serve another customer.

Quint watched the game awhile, waited until the player sitting with his back to the wall quit, then asked if they'd accept another player. They motioned to the empty chair and he sat.

He played carefully, and after about an hour his chips had grown only a bit. He figured he was about twenty dollars ahead. Every few moments his glance swept the room. Finally, over the tops of the batwings, he noticed the sun's late afternoon rays painting the adobe store-fronts across the street a golden tint. Soon be sundown. If Phillips was going to make a showing, Quint thought it would be soon.

He'd no sooner had the thought, than the doors pushed in, and Phillips stood inside them. Quint picked up his chips, cashed in, and told those at the table to gather their chips if they wanted to play later. He informed them there might be gunfire if he couldn't get it to move outside. They grabbed their chips and scattered about the room.

11

CANTRELL FLICKED THE thong off the hammer of his Colt
and circled the room, staying close to the wall. When the
preacher turned toward the bar, Quint came up behind
him. Then standing about ten feet away, Cantrell said, his
voice soft, "You lookin' for me, preacher man?"

Phillips spun and looked at Cantrell, his eyes register-
ing recognition. Quint waited, hoping he'd move his
hands to his lapels. He didn't. He stood there a moment,
then pushed a smile past tight lips. "Mr. Cantello, I didn't
expect to see you this far from home."

"The hell you didn't, you hypocritical bastard. You
come over here lookin' for me, figured I wuz gonna
check out that lie about you an' your church. Well, you
found me, an' I did check to see what church you'd
preached at." Cantrell shook his head. "Ain't nobody
connected with any church in this town ever heard o'
you."

Phillips continued to smile, a wintry smile at best.
Then he pulled a frown between his brows. "Did I say I'd

preached at San Antonio? Hmmm, musta got things con-fused. You see, I was thinkin' of taking this trip here even then. What I meant to say was that I'd had a church in Fort Worth." He let the smile come back to his thin lips. He nodded. "But I will say, despite your unfriendly greet-ing, I'm glad to see an acquaintance now that I'm here."

When he nodded, he raised his hands to grip his lapels. Cantrell went quiet inside. Phillips would make his move in a moment. Thinking to goad the gunfighter into mak-ing his move sooner than he wanted, Quint grinned and said, "Yeah, I'm one of the people you figured to sucker in down yonder, but you didn't think anyone had enough sense to unravel your an' your partner's land grabbing scheme." He nodded. "Yep, way I got it figured you're just half of the *Señor* Manuel Soto team." Cantrell's grin disappeared. He felt his eyes go hard and flat. "They's gonna be only one Soto left in a minute. Go ahead. Pull that six-shooter from under your coat."

Phillips's hand twitched, but he apparently wasn't ready. He shook his head. "Mr. Cantello, you are mis-taken. I have heard of this Soto, yes, but as for me being him, or having a partner, you are mistaken. Let's forget the whole thing." He turned as though to step toward the bar. That was when his hand slid under his coat.

All action slowed to about half speed. Cantrell waited until Phillips's hand moved from under his coat, grasping a short-barreled six-gun. Then, not even aware that his coiled muscles reacted, Quint swept his hand toward his holster. While drawing his Colt, he thumbed back the hammer and slipped his thumb from it when it pointed at Phillips.

The bullet hit Phillips's drawn weapon, flattened, and made a gory, bloody hole in his chest. Cantrell's second and third shots bracketed the larger hole, now gushing blood. Those two shots made nice neat, small, black punctures in the preacher's chest.

Phillips's eyes opened wide in wonder. Knocked backward a couple of steps by Cantrell's bullets, he struggled to step forward. His look shifted to his bloody right hand, then stared at the holes in his chest. His eyes turned toward Cantrell and he fell.

Quint walked to his side, squatted, and between clenched teeth, said, "I've seen several men faster'n you, but you wasn't bad for a damned lying preacher."

In a wheezy voice, blood bubbling between his frowning lips, Phillips said, "Who are you? Never seen anybody that fast."

Quint looked into the slitted eyes, now beginning to cloud over. He nodded. "Reckon a man's got the right to know who killed 'im. Those who know me call me Quinton Cantrell."

"The . . . the Colorado gunfighter." Phillips gave a great sigh; his eyes opened wide and did not close. His head fell limply to the side. O'Grady walked to Quint's side and stood there a moment before he said, "He get off a shot at you, Cantrell?"

Quint shook his head. "No. He only got his six-gun out but never had it leveled. Then I drew."

A crowd had gathered around, some looking at the body, but most staring at Cantrell. One of the onlookers said in awed tones, "All of you've heard tell of Quinton Cantrell, now you've seen 'im. Ain't a one o' us what won't be talkin' 'bout this gunfight long into our old age."

Cantrell stood, looked at O'Grady, and reached into his pocket. "Red, if I done any damage to yore place, I'll pay for it."

O'Grady clasped his arm around Quint's shoulders. "Like hell you will. First place, your shots didn't hit nothin' but him. Second place, you ain't even gonna pay for the drinks you an' me're gonna put away back in my office." He looked at one of the gawkers. "Stan, go round up the marshal. He's gonna have to get this story from several of us so as to clear Cantrell here. It was pure-dee self-defense far as any here would dare say." His gaze scanned them. "Right?"

The chorus shouted back at him—you bet, yeah, that's right—until he grinned and guided Cantrell toward his office.

They'd already knocked back two drinks when a light tap on the office door sounded. O'Grady yelled, "It's unlocked, come on in."

The marshal poked his head in the door. "Won't bother you. Just wanted to let you know I got the story from damned near eveybody in the room out here. Ain't no reason for you to worry none, Cantrell." His eyes shifted to the almost full bottle on O'Grady's desk. A grin cracked his weatherbeaten face. "On second thought, maybe I ought to talk to you too, Cantrell—but I don't talk very well with a dry throat." He faked a cough.

O'Grady chuckled. "Come on in, you old kidder. I just happen to have a spare glass here in my drawer." He poured a glass full for the marshal and sat back, then leaned forward. "Don't reckon you've met Quint Cantrell yet." He looked at Quint. "In spite of bein' a deadbeat, this here's Marshal Shaw, one o' the best, and straightest, lawmen west o' the Mississippi."

When they'd shaken hands, and the marshal had made himself at home, sitting on the corner of O'Grady's desk, he looked at Quint. "Wanted to talk to you anyway,

Cantrell. That dead body out yonder come in town a while back. He wuzn't alone. He had a partner. I'm tellin' you this so's you won't go blarin' outta here with blinders on. They might be somebody hangin' 'round a alley mouth waitin' to shoot you."

Cantrell nodded his thanks. " 'Preciate that, Marshal. I don't never go nowhere with blinders on, but I figure Phillips come over here alone. Probably left 'is partner back in Presidio to tend to business. But I gotta tell you, I don't have a clue as to who his partner is, or what he looks like. Figure you can help me there?"

Shaw nodded. "They wuz both smooth, well dressed. Neither one sported a gun out where anybody could see it, but I'd bet a painted pony the one you shot today wuzn't the only one o' the two who carries a pistol—an's pretty good at usin' it."

O'Grady laughed. "Pshaw, you ain't never seen nobody who was any better'n Cantrell." He went on to describe the gunfight.

When he finished, Cantrell eyed the marshal. "Can you tell me any more?"

Shaw described a man who could have been any one of a dozen men in the town of Presidio. When finished, he shook his head. "Know you done met hundreds like that, but that's the best I can do. I'll tell you another thing though, neither one of them, in spite of bein' dressed in town clothes, was a townsman. They were tough, range-broke critters to my way o' thinkin'. I watched 'em ride, an' they rode like cowboys. I looked at their faces, an' they wuz burnt by the sun much as any range rider would be. So don't you go lookin' for no smoothy desk-settin' man. The one left is just as tough as the one you eliminated."

Cantrell forced a tight smile. "Figured as much, Marshal." He stood. "Well, gentlemen, I come over here to kill a man if he wuzn't who he said he wuz. He wuzn't—an' I did." He pulled his hat down to shade his eyes when he went outside. Then, before pulling the door open, he said, "Don't reckon I ever set out to purposely kill a man but a couple times before, but the few I did needed it." He twisted the knob and pulled the door toward him, then nodded. "Sure good to meet two square shooters like y'all. Now I'm gonna go back to Presidio to hunt for a man I don't know. Good luck." He stepped through the door and headed toward the hotel to get his rifle and bedroll.

When Cantrell returned to Presidio, he went back to the newspaper office. Price Waters looked up from setting type, his face smudged with printer's ink, his hands black with it. "Mr. Cantello, what can I do for you?"

Quint nodded toward the back file cabinets. "Jest wanted to take another look at them papers I looked at the other day, if it's all right with you."

Waters shrugged. "Go ahead. You know where to look."

"Much obliged." Cantrell nodded and walked to the rear of the shop. He remembered which drawer held what he wanted to take another look at. He pulled the drawer open and it took only a moment to pull both papers that told about the Army post payroll holdup. This time he read the articles in detail. The first article had the specifics of the holdup; the second one was about the posse finding the bodies of the holdup men.

He studied them awhile. The more he read, the more

excited he became. He breathed a little harder, his heart pounded, he felt hot blood flush his face. Hell, he'd never gotten this excited when about to have a gunfight.

He wrote down some pertinent facts of the holdup that he'd missed before, as reported by the Fort Stockton paper, stuck his notes in his pocket, thanked Waters for his help, and set out to visit the young lawyer.

Rondell looked up from a stack of papers when Cantrell came through the doorway. "Shoulda charged you twice what you paid me for this job, Cantello. You got any idea how much work this is?"

Quint laughed. "Man, I finally got somethin' to tell my grandkids; I stuck it to a lawyer, 'stead o' the other way around."

Rondell grinned, stood, and came to shake hands with Cantrell. "Was gonna go lookin' for you, but from your appearance I wouldn'ta found you. You look like you just came off a trail drive."

Quint pushed his hat to the back of his head. "Feel like I mighta been on one all the way to Dodge City, but no, I been to SanTone, had a little business over there. How you comin' with the list?"

Rondell twisted to look at the stack of papers he'd left on his desk. "Just kiddin', Cantello, 'bout not chargin' you enough." He waved his hand toward his desk. "Way I figure it, I'm almost through. It wasn't hard to come up with names of the townfolk, an' not too much harder to set the date they came to this town, but I'm here to tell you, finding out where they came from was a different game altogether."

Cantrell picked up the sheaf of papers. He frowned. "Tell you what, it might not make much difference about where they came from. I got a idea that this, with some other information I dug up, is gonna be enough. When you think you gonna be finished with the job?"

"I'll have it all for you by noon tomorrow."

Cantrell handed the list back to the lawyer. "Good. If I don't pick it up then, hang onto it for me. I have a couple more things I need to do in the meantime."

Rondell scratched his head, a chagrined smile crinkling his eyes. "Tell you the truth, Cantello, I got to thinkin' it was a shame to take your money for doin' something that needed doin' anyway. I figure the tax rolls'll tell us about the property owners, but that won't even come close to listin' all the people in this town. I figure Price Waters, over at the newspaper, might want to buy this list from me, publish it, an' sell it to the folks around town, but since you paid for it to be done, I figure it's your right to sell it."

Cantrell frowned. Was there any harm in that? Would it cause the one for whom he looked to get suspicious? He studied Rondell a moment. "I'll make a deal with you. You don't tell anybody who wanted this list; make like it was your own idea, an' you can do what you want with it. Okay?"

The lawyer nodded. "You bet. Maybe I can get another month's eatin' money outta Waters. Isn't anyone's business why I came up with the list."

Cantrell turned toward the door. "See you tomorrow—maybe."

Outside the office, smelling dusty, and like old books, he took a deep breath. He didn't see how anyone could pen themselves up in an office when there was the whole outdoors in which to find something to do. He tilted his hat forward to shade his eyes from the late afternoon sun, rubbed his hand down his cheek, and thought he'd have a shave, haircut, and bath before doing anything else.

An hour and a half later, clean and clean shaven, he felt like a different man. He walked down the dusty street, stepping carefully to keep the dust off his freshly shined boots. He wanted to be seen. He wanted Phillips's partner, whoever he was, to see him and know his partner wouldn't be back. It might force him into making a move that would give Cantrell a clue as to who he was.

The other half of the Soto partnership had to be a pretty cagey character. He'd played his hand close to his vest, and let Phillips take the chances while he stayed in the background.

After a slow walk the length of the business district, only two blocks, Cantrell did it once more, then pushed through the batwings of the Cattleman's Rest. The first person he saw when he pushed his way into his corner spot at the bar was the banker, Nat Howley.

Howley's handsome, suntanned face showed only a bland smile. "Hello, Mr. Cantello. Did you find the property which might satisfy your wishes?"

Cantrell pushed a tired grin to his face. "Mr. Howley, I done rode the hoofs off'n my pony, an' I'm here to tell you there ain't no place like what I been lookin' for. I'm figurin' to stick around here another couple o' weeks, then maybe ride on. I'll find what I'm lookin' for somewhere."

Howley's face showed nothing but concern, he shook his head. "Now, that's a shame, Mr. Cantello. I thought with the money you have to invest there must be something here for you." He looked as though he really cared. He frowned. "But I'll tell you of some country I rode through several years ago. It was over against the mountains in New Mexico Territory, beautiful country. It might be just the place you're lookin' for."

Cantrell shook his head. "No. I'm thinkin' to take a look at east Texas. Over yonder in the piney woods country. Thanks for your suggestion, though."

He ordered a drink, knocked it back, and left. He thought to eliminate Howley from his list of suspects. If Howley had been in cahoots with Phillips, Cantrell felt certain he would have shown some emotion when he showed up back in Presidio instead of his partner.

Cantrell felt as though someone had let the air out of his balloon. Howley had the natural setup to run an outlaw operation, the respectability of a banker, the bank—an excellent place to keep stolen plunder, the smooth personality of a master salesman; hell, the man could probably sell cow manure to a rancher who owned three thousand head of cattle. Course, perhaps he was smooth enough to hide his emotion earlier.

Quint played a few hands of poker and, too restless to concentrate on the cards, stood and left. Damn! Soto must be one smart bastard to keep his identity a mystery and still control Santana's gang across the border. Of course he did it with money, and money could buy almost anything.

When he'd got to the front of the newspaper office, he stopped, stared at the front of the building, frowned, then nodded. Of course. Money! That money Soto was paying Santana must have left a trail behind it, but how could a man track it?

A few moment's thought didn't get him any closer to the answer. He kept staring at the door of the newspaper office. The feeling nagged him that the answer would be in those papers he'd scanned. But the office was now closed for the day.

Cantrell ambled on down the street, and the farther he walked, the stronger came the aroma of fried steaks, potatoes, and coffee. His stomach growled, reminding him he hadn't eaten for several hours. He came abreast of the café, pushed through the door, and went in.

There were several people eating with whom he had at least a nodding acquaintance. Bart Engstrom, the sheriff, sat at a back table. Cantrell walked back, pulled out a chair, and asked if he could join him.

Engstrom smiled. "Looks like you already have. Sit. I done et most o' my meal, but I'll have another cup o'coffee, or two, before I start my night rounds."

Trying for more information, Quint frowned and shook his head. "Don't you get tired of tryin' to keep a bunch o' drunk cowboys steadied down? How long you been doin' this, Sheriff?"

Engstrom frowned, obviously figuring, then nodded. "I was a Texas Ranger 'bout four years, then I seen this town needed a new sheriff, bein's the one they had had just got hisself killed. I ran for the office an' got it. That wuz eight years ago." His face hardened. "Nope, I don't get tired of it; fact is I welcome it a lot more'n I would tryin' to track down gunfighters, outlaws, an' such."

"Yeah, reckon if it was my job, I'd take the drunks ever' time." The waitress came and took his order. Engstrom finished his coffee and left Cantrell to eat alone.

Cantrell's thoughts kept getting in the way of his eating. He ate slowly, hardly tasting his food, but when he was finished, not feeling satisfied, he ordered a slice of apple pie, and mulled over what he knew about the Soto gang. He eliminated the sheriff from his suspects, then just as he'd done with Howley, he put him back on the list. All this was mental. He figured to get to his room and write down some of the names he knew Rondell would have on his list.

Back in the room, before he could get set to think about finding the identity of Soto, he sighed. He'd been on the trail over eight days, was tired, and needed sleep. He shoved a chair under the doorknob, placed his Colt ready to hand on the bed table, peeled off his clothes, lay down, and was soon asleep.

He wakened the next morning feeling drugged. He'd slept too hard; that was what being as tired as he'd been would do for a man. He shaved, brushed his teeth, combed his hair, and dressed. By then he felt like he could go for another couple of weeks without a good rest.

After breakfast, thinking to plant the idea further that he looked for a small ranch, he went to the land office. Able Princet sat poring over some topographical maps spread on his desk. He looked up. "May I help you?"

After introducing himself, and the land agent giving his name, Cantrell pushed his hat back. "Don't know whether you got anything like I want."

Princet smiled. "Well, don't reckon we'll ever know 'less you tell me what it is you want."

Cantrell chuckled. "Reckon that's a fact." He then gave the land officer a description of what he looked for; the same thing he'd told Howley. As soon as he mentioned the acreage desired, Princet shook his head. "Mr. Cantello, Austin don't allow me to deal in anything less than a quarter section of land." He sighed. "Although it'd make my job harder, I wish they'd let up on that. There're a lot o' people out here who'd like a little place to call home without goin' whole hog. The truth of the matter is that a quarter section's too much for most o' them to handle financially."

"Austin? Is that where your headquarters is located?"

Princet nodded. "State capital, where else? That's where all the desk polishers migrate to. I got outta there soon's I could. Reckon they were glad to send me out here, an' make room for some politician's friend."

"How long were you there?"

Princet pulled his mouth to the side in a grimace. "Three years. Seems like that was four years longer'n I wanted to stay with that bunch." He shrugged. "Reckon I'm just a country boy who refused to adapt to city ways."

Cantrell grinned. "Reckon I know how you feel. If I had to stay in a town very long, I think I'd go crazy as a rabid dog." He shrugged and tried to look disappointed. "Well, don't look like you can help me any. I'll get outta your way an' let you get back to work."

"Don't hurry, Mr. Cantello. I'm right pleased to have company."

Cantrell shook his head. "I 'preciate it, Mr. Princet, but I reckon I better be gettin' along. See you again maybe." He flung up his hand in a good-bye and left.

Outside, he grimaced. Another box canyon that didn't lead anywhere. Princet was another man he couldn't tell whether he could eliminate yet from Rondell's list. He roamed the town from one end to the other several times. Bored, by damn, that's what he was. He wondered if there was anyone he could visit, and came up dry. Hell, he'd rather be down in Ojinaga trying to cover his back-side, and maybe having to face some of those tough *vaqueros* of Santana's than stay up here doing nothing. He made up his mind then that, as soon as he got through with Rondell, he'd go to Ojinaga.

12

CANTRELL WENT BY Rondell's office and gathered him up to take him to lunch—with the promise he'd pay. The lawyer said he'd finished the list only a few minutes before Quint came through the door. He shuffled the stack of paper together and handed it to the tall cowboy.

"I took the liberty of copying each sheet of names as I went, so when you get through with yours you can do away with it."

Cantrell shook his head and smiled. "I'll bet you won't have to wait for Waters to make you an offer. I figure he'll jump at the chance to publish a roster of everybody in this town. Probably ain't no other town in Texas what has a listing like we got here."

Rondell nodded. "Figure you're right. Come on, let's go get that lunch you promised to pay for."

Lunch finished, and the list Rondell had given him stacked in his room, Cantrell forded the Rio Grande, and rode into Ojinaga. His back muscles tight, his hair feeling as though it stood out from his neck, he wondered why at a time like this he felt more alive than at any other—except when he held Elena in his arms. He'd have to make it a habit to pull her close to him more often. He chuckled to himself. She already swore that was all he cared about—but she always came readily to his embrace. No, all the love and desire he felt wasn't one-sided. She loved and wanted him as much as he did her.

He brought his mind back to earth. His horse walked down the dusty, stinking, garbage-laden street of the small Mexican town. Now his thoughts were only on the town itself. He searched every nook and cranny—alleyways, second-story windows, inset doorways—anywhere there might be a sniper.

He'd made enemies in this town, those who had lost a friend to his gun. Even though they'd brought the trouble to him, when revenge was the issue, the fault of the killing made no difference. He reined his horse in in front of the same *cantina* where he first met Santana. There was no chance he'd be bored in there.

When he stepped through the batwings, the smell of tobacco smoke—pipe, cigarettes, and cigars—along with the stench of stale beer and whiskey hit him. As soon as his eyes adjusted to the darkened room, he swept it with a glance, and met only stares of dislike—hatred in most cases.

He ran his thumb along the serrated edge of his Colt's hammer, making sure he had the thong off, and stepped to the bar. The entire end of the polished surface where it curved up against the wall stood empty. He went to the wall, put his back against it, and ordered a beer. He continued to search the room for anyone he might know. Then he let a smile break the corners of his lips. The same slim Mexican who'd tried to shadow him into Presidio, at Santana's orders, pushed away from the table at which he sat and hurried from the room.

Cantrell nodded. Santana's spy had headed out to tell the outlaw leader who was in town. He figured it would be only a short while until the big bandit showed up. He was right.

Santana pushed himself through the batwings as though he was the emperor of Mexico, glanced at those at the bar, sighted Cantrell, and moved his head, signaling for Cantrell to join him at the back table, which had four men seated around it. A flick of the big bandit's wrist caused the four to scatter from the table as though it had caught fire.

Cantrell picked up his beer and worked his way to the table at which Santana had already seated himself. While getting to the table, Quint kept close to the wall, and continued to watch the men in the room. Arriving at the table, he pulled out a chair next to the bandit king and seated himself.

"Why for you so careful, Cantello? You among friends here."

Cantrell gazed into Santana's eyes a moment. "*Señor,* if those in here are my friends, I better take another look at them folks I done eliminated along the way."

Switching to English, Santana grunted, "Why for you speak the Texan, *señor*?"

"Reckon it don't hurt to keep them what's in earshot guessin' 'bout me." He leaned closer to the outlaw. "Come down here to ask you a question."

"Ask. I don' need to answer."

Before answering Santana, Cantrell noticed he hadn't gotten a drink. A girl stood at his shoulder waiting to take the order. "What you drinkin', Benito?" This was the first time he'd used the bandit's first name. He wanted to see how it floated. It apparently set well with Santana.

He smiled. "Ah, we are friends, eh? Not many call me by my first name." He looked at the waitress. "Tequila, *muchacha*."

She looked at Quint. "Beer," he said. Then to the bandit, "Got somethin' I want to try on you; see what you think."

Santana nodded. "Talk."

Treading carefully, not wanting to upset him, Cantrell fingered his money belt through his shirt, then said, "Notice the *dinero* you gave me to find who Soto is wuz all in gold coin. Noticed too that ever' time you pay for anythin' it's the same."

Santana nodded. "That ees the way Soto pays me to geev to the men." Santana fingered his huge, drooping *mustachios*. " 'Fore you go on, gonna ask a question." He leaned forward, his face stiff, jaw muscles knotted. "Where you been the last two weeks?"

Cantrell had been waiting for that question. He grinned, and changed to Spanish. "Ah, *señor,* you have been checking on me, eh?" He leaned closer to Santana. "What I have to say is going to surprise you, *amigo*."

Santana nodded. "Eet better be good. I doan like surprises." He sat erect, his eyes hard.

Cantrell grinned. "*Amigo,* what would you say if I told you Soto is not one but two *hombres*?"

The big bandit's head jerked around to look hard at Cantrell. At his reaction, Quint nodded. "It is true, Benito. At least it was true until I disappeared, as you called it."

"If eet was true then, why ees it not now, Cantello?"

Cantrell pinned Santana with a hard look of his own.

"Because, Santana, I suspected who one of them was, went to San Antonio to check out my suspicion, an' he apparently figured what I left town for and followed me. I shot 'im in a *cantina* while I was there. He's dead." He sat back and smiled. "An' if I'm right 'bout Soto bein' two men, I've solved only half our problem. That's what I came over here to talk to you about."

"What has theez payment in gold got to do with it?"

Cantrell shook his head. "Don't rightly know yet, but if all he's usin' is gold to pay you with, he had to get it from somewhere—an' he's gotta be keepin' it somewhere."

"Doan tek no real smart *hombre* to figure things out that far, *amigo*."

Quint finished his beer and signaled for another and a couple more limes and salt. He leaned forward and put his elbows on the table, feeling a little uncomfortable with his hands that far from his Colt, but he wanted to appear relaxed and innocent of trying to run a sandy on Benito Santana. "I've gathered some stuff that might lead me to find where he mighta got the money—where he's keepin' it is where you come in."

"How so, *mi amigo*?"

Cantrell allowed himself a sly grin. "You ever rob a bank, *mi grande amigo*?"

Santana's eyelids drooped almost closed, enough that Quint couldn't read his reaction. "No. Cattle, stagecoaches, men on horseback, mercantile stores—but never a bank. Why you ask that question?"

He thought about it a moment. "Well, way I figure it he mighta put it in the bank; if not, he's got it buried someplace.

"If it's in the bank, a robbery might be just the thing to bring Soto out of hiding." He grinned. "Not to mention, if you take the money from the bank, you'll have a bunch more *dinero*."

"Ah, but, *señor,* I weel get some of my *vaqueros* keeled eef I rob the bank."

Cantrell shook his head. "Maybe not. It's something you an' me gotta study on. I better git back to Presidio. In the meantime, you give what I done suggested a lot o' thought. I'll try to figure a way for you to do it without gittin' any men shot." He downed the rest of his beer and stood. "I'll see you in 'bout a week, tell you what I come up with, an' you can tell me what you think of the idea. Okay?"

At Santana's nod, Cantrell again worked his way around the wall to the batwings, pushed through them, and left. He toed the stirrup, and left Ojinaga behind.

About the time Cantrell forded the river, Cole sat across the table from his father. They were the only ones in the kitchen. "Pa, I'm tellin' you Quint's gonna be all right. Hell, he and I have been in a lot tougher spots than he's in now."

"Yeah, but this's different. You an' Quint always knew who you were facin'. That boy's down yonder gropin' in the dark. He don't know who his enemy is. Why hell, it could be anybody; the man he has breakfast with, the hostler, the lawyer—anybody."

Cole nodded. "That's true, but I'm tellin' you right now, if I go down there and we're seen together, there're men who'll shoot him on sight."

Cole took their cups, went to the stove, filled them, and again sat across from his father. "Pa, people know me, know I'm in the game to beat them. Quint's been there talkin' to people, people who might tell 'im something they wouldn't tell me." He shook his head. "Nope, I'm not going to interfere with what he's doing. Besides, my men need me here."

Cole emptied his cup, stood, and looked longingly toward the hallway. "Sure wish I could stay here with Laura. Fact is, I wish all of us could just stay here and be a normal family." He shook his head. "Well, reckon the best way to make that happen is to find Soto, eliminate 'im, get some o' your money and cattle back, and only then can we begin to get back to normal. We came down here to do a job. We'll get it done."

He clamped his hat on his head, pulled it down to shade his eyes, and before going out the door, looked at his father. "Pa, tell Laura I'll see 'er when I see 'er. Hope the next time it'll be for good."

Brad watched his tall son toe the stirrup and ride out, then he went to the bunkhouse. All of his men, along with Jaime Martinez and Snake McClure, sat around a table, each with a stack of spent brass in front of him, and all were reloading the old shell casings. Brad started to say that it looked like they were expecting a war, then clamped his jaws tight. These men didn't need that sort of dumb joke; they not only expected a war, but were in the middle of one.

He nodded. "Howdy, men, just come down here for company. The womenfolks didn't come downstairs yet for supper, so thought y'all could bring me up to date on how you figure we've hurt Soto." He looked at Martinez. "Jaime, couldn't we end this by going down to Santana's place an' hittin' 'im hard?"

Jaime finished packing powder into the shell he worked on, frowned, and nodded. "Maybe, *señor,* but maybe not. Seems Cantrell's got some idea he can find where most o' your cows, an' even some o' your *dinero,* is. Eef we go bustin' down yonder an' hit Santana's bunch, we might lose all that." He shook his head. "Quint and Cole figure all we've done would be for nothing eef we don't play the whole hand out." He placed the cartridge he'd finished loading on the table with a stack of others. "Those two, *señor,* are smart in the ways of fighting. I trust them. Let's let them do it their way."

Brad wiped his hand across his face, and unconsciously his shoulders slumped. He nodded. "You're right. Reckon a old man oughtta leave things alone and let you young'uns take care of it." He turned on his heel to leave, and said, "Only thing y'all let me do is protect the ranch."

"Ah but, *señor,* that ees the most important job of all. You are protecting the womenfolk, which lets us free to fight Soto."

Brad grumbled a bit then left to go back to the *hacienda.* When he went into the dining room, the ladies stood by their chairs about to be seated for supper. Laura looked over his shoulder, obviously searching for Cole. He shook his head. "Cole left. Said to look for him when you saw 'im." That set them all to talking at once, until Elena held up her hand for silence.

She pulled her chair back. "Let's sit an' eat. Don't want none o' them men comin' home to a bunch o' pale, sickly women."

Back in his room at the hotel, Cantrell took out the notes he'd made at the newspaper office and placed them on the bedside table, along with the list Rondell had prepared for him. He stared from one stack of paper to the other.

After scanning them, he decided that the only thing that made sense was that whoever Soto was, he had a lot of money to throw around, especially if he intended to keep the Mexican bandits happy. Then, with the idea in mind that few people with honest, or dishonest, intent had as much money to operate with as the Mexican bandits were costing, he wondered where the Soto partners got that kind of money. Holdups?

Now he took a pencil and, studying the notes from the papers, underlined every holdup, where it had taken place, and the dates. Then he pulled the Rondell list in front of him, squinted at it, trimmed the lamp for a brighter light, and carefully went down the list looking for dates of arrivals in town, especially those dates when persons came to town on the same day, or were only separated by a few days.

From there he looked to see if any had shown a degree of affluence upon arriving, or had suddenly seemed to come into a fortune. That got him nowhere.

Tired, he stood and poured a glass of water from the white pitcher on the comode. He sipped at the water, all the while staring at the two lists.

After a half hour of this, he put his glass on the comode, stood, buckled on his gunbelt, tucked the lists and notes under the mattress, and headed for the Cattleman's. A drink would be good.

Cantrell walked straight to the bar on entering, and although not expecting trouble, he swept the room with a glance as soon as he settled his back against the wall at the end of the smooth surface. When Spike Barron got to him, after pouring several drinks along the way, Quint asked for Barron's special brand from under the bar.

While the bartender poured, he leaned toward Cantrell. "Man was in here askin' for you a while ago. Didn't look like anybody you'd want ridin' at your back."

"What'd he look like?"

Barron frowned. "Well, he was clean shaven, neat shirt and trousers, but shifty, never looked me in the eye while we talked, an' he never had his hand far from his holstered six-gun.

"He wore his six-shooter much the same as you." Spike passed the bar towel across a wet spot. "Tell you what. I noticed soon's he come through the door, he flipped the thong off the hammer of his sidegun. Don't know why he'd do that then ask 'bout you."

Cantrell smiled, knowing it showed little humor. "The hell you don't, Spike. What'd you tell 'im?"

Barron shrugged. "Told 'im I hadn't seen you for several days, but that when you were in town you usually come in for a drink."

The batwings swung open, then shut. Barron glanced that way, then said, "Speak o' the devil."

Cantrell dropped his hand to his side, flicked the thong off the hammer of his Colt, and watched the man as he walked directly toward him.

The rangey, cold-eyed man stopped about five feet in front of Quint. "From the description I have, you're Quinton Cantrell." He said it loud enough for those standing close by to hear. The words caused everyone to look straight at Cantrell. They knew him as Juan Cantello.

Cantrell held his glass in his left hand and pinned the man with a hard look. "You got the wrong man, mister. I go by the name of Juan Cantello. What you want with this man?"

"What I want with him's my business, but," he reached

for his shirt pocket, "I got a wanted notice on 'im, they's money on his head, an' I aim to collect it."

Cantrell slanted the man a wintry smile. "Reckon you done carved yoreself out a chunk of work, if what I hear 'bout Cantrell's true."

"What you mean?"

Cantrell's voice hardened. "First place, I wantta know your name, an' second place I wantta see by what authority you're lookin' for Cantrell. I knew 'im up in Colorado. They wasn't no money on his head up there, an' far as I know he's still up there."

"My name's Biggs. I got nothin' but my Colt that gives me the authority to take 'im in. I figger you're Cantrell. You can come to the sheriff with me—or I'll drag you."

"Bounty hunter, huh?" Cantrell spit the words out as though they were poison. "Now, gonna tell you somethin', sonny, ain't nobody ever dragged me nowhere. I may fit yore description of Cantrell—we been mistaken for each other before, but I ain't him. Now you wantta make good yore brag 'bout draggin' me to the sheriff—get with it."

Quint's words, and obvious lack of fear in forcing a showdown, caused Biggs to hesitate. "If . . . if you ain't Cantrell, you shouldn't oughtta be afraid to go to the sheriff with me."

"Gonna tell you again, sonny, I ain't goin' nowhere with you. You want the law to look me over, go get 'im an' bring 'im here." Then, never taking his eyes off Biggs, he brought his glass to his lips to take a sip. It was then that the bounty hunter went for his gun.

Cantrell's Colt came to his hand as if by magic. He stepped close to Biggs, chopped down with the barrel making contact with the bounty hunter's wrist, and heard a snap.

Biggs stared at his gun laying on the floor at his feet, then at his hand, dangling as though only flesh held it to his arm. Then he swung fear-filled eyes to look at Cantrell. "You broke my arm—bad."

Quint nodded. "Figured to do just that. You're damned lucky yore gut ain't surroundin' a couple chunks o' lead." Then he grabbed Biggs by the shirtfront and pulled him toward the door. "C'mon. Now we gonna go see the sheriff. He's gonna tell you I ain't Cantrell, then I'm gonna run you outta town."

"I gotta see a doctor—get my arm fixed."

Cantrell jerked the man's shirt. "You ain't gonna get yore arm fixed. This way you won't be able to ever again handle a gun. Course, you wasn't worth a damn at handlin' one 'fore I broke that arm for you." He shot the bounty hunter a cold grin. "You oughtta be thankin' me for savin' yore life. The next man you tried to pull a gun on mighta shot you." He jerked Biggs through the batwings, pushed him off the edge of the boardwalk, and angled across the street to the sheriff's office.

When he opened the door, Sheriff Engstrom swung his feet off the scarred old wooden desk, looked at the man Cantrell had in tow, then back to Cantrell. "What you got here, Cantello?"

Cantrell locked gazes with the lawman. "Case of mistaken identity. This man pulled a gun on me an' I had to break his arm to keep 'im from shootin' me." Then, never letting his eyes leave Engstrom's, he said, "He tried to get me to come over here with him so he could collect the bounty on my head. He figured I wuz Quinton Cantrell." He pushed his hat to the back of his head. "Sheriff, I know Cantrell, an' I happen to know they ain't no reward out for his arrest."

Engstrom stared at Biggs a moment. "Shows how wrong a man can be. You were wrong on two counts. This ain't Cantrell, an' Cantrell's got no price on his head."

Cantrell let go a gusty sigh. He had no doubt that the sheriff, after having his memory jogged, knew he was in fact Cantrell. Quint pulled Biggs's handgun from its holster where he'd stuck it after picking it up from the saloon floor. "You ain't gonna have a need for this no more." He tossed the revolver to Engstrom's desk. "Now, I'm gonna say this only once. Get on yore horse an' make tracks outta town. I see you again, I ain't gonna be nice enough to break your arm."

"I gotta git my arm fixed, Mr. Cantello. Let me do it, please."

"You ain't outta town in five minutes after I kick you outta the door—I'll kill you. Now git."

As soon as the bounty hunter cleared the door, Quint looked at Engstrom, and caught him with an awed look on his face. "Damn, *Cantrell,* I always heard you were a hard man—now I know the truth of it."

13

CANTRELL STARED AT the sheriff a long moment. "You don't act surprised."

Engstrom shook his head. "Knew who you were the first time you came to see me. Wondered what kind o' game you were playin'. Wantta tell me about it?"

Quint nodded. "Yeah, Sheriff. You might even be able to help with the danged puzzle I done come up with." Without being asked, he went to the coffeepot and poured himself a cup full.

A slight smile broke the corners of Engstrom's lips. "Why don't you hep yourself to a cup o' my coffee, Cantrell?"

Quint returned his smile, and nodded. "Thanks. Wuz just thinkin' to do that." Again without being asked, he took a chair across from the sheriff. "Engstrom, you knowin' I'm Cantrell, you know I was raised by Brad Mason. Now he's in a heap o' trouble, his boys an' me figure to get 'im outta it."

The sheriff nodded. "Figured as much. Tell me 'bout your puzzle."

"Gonna take a while."

Again Engstrom nodded. "I got all sorts o' time. Go ahead."

Quint started at the beginning, told him about Soto, and his suspicion as to there being two of them, told him about shooting one of them in San Antonio, told him about Santana—the whole story.

When he finished, the sheriff frowned, stared at the wall, then said, "So you think there're two Sotos, eh?" He shook his head. "I'm here to tell you, Cantrell, I ain't no further ahead on figurin' it out than you are. I been suspectin' that preacher man o' bein' him, but I figured he was in it all alone." He drained his cup, frowned, said "Cold," stood, and poured himself a hot cup full. "What you got in mind? Any way I can help unravel the puzzle in an official capacity?"

Cantrell pushed his hat back, stared into his cup a moment, then nodded. "Maybe so. I thought o' findin' a way to see where Phillips wuz keepin' his money. He shore had a lot of it to throw around. I figured to go dig around his horse shed, maybe dig up the boards in his house, check to see if he had it in the bank. Hell, anywhere a man might keep money he didn't want nobody to know about."

"I can probably help you there. As the law around here I have a right to search a dead man's property."

Before he finished, Quint shook his head. "I wuz figurin' to ask you about that, but on second thought, it would let the other half of the partnership know the law was workin' with me.

"You see, whoever he is, he thinks I'm the only one

who got wise to Phillips, an' if you start lookin' around the preacher's house, the other Soto will know that you know Phillips is dead, an' he'll most likely figure that you know I killed 'im."

Engstrom nodded. "You're probably right." He spread his hands palms up. "But what can I do?"

Quint drained his cup, stood, and tipped his hat forward to shade his eyes. "I'm workin' on findin' out somethin'. When I get it straight in my head, I got a idea there's a lot you can do. Let me think on it awhile. Soon's I figure I'm on solid ground, I'll let you know what might let the last piece of this puzzle fall into place."

Engstrom stood and stuck his hand out. "I'll keep my ear to the ground while you work on your end of it. This is somethin' that's been diggin' at my worry spot for some time." He nodded as Cantrell pulled the door open. "See yuh."

On leaving the lawman's office, Cantrell ambled slowly along the street. He thought of his suggestion to Santana about holding up the bank. That idea would hurt a lot of little people, people whose entire savings were kept in Howley's bank. The banker might try to make it good for them, but Quint didn't think he would—or could, unless he had a lot of his own money somewhere else.

On impulse, he walked across to the bank, took out a hundred-dollar bill, and asked for gold coins in its place. The teller looked at the bill, held it up to the light, studied Cantrell a moment, then counted out gold coins to replace the paper money. "Don't you trust our government's money, Mr. Cantello?"

Quint eyed him a long few seconds. "Mister, I don't

trust no paper of any kind. I know what gold's worth—
an' I know paper don't come to anywhere near that
much." He tipped his hat, grinned, and left.

While walking along, he inspected the coins. All of
them had obviously been in circulation a long time, judging by how worn they were. He shoved them in his
pocket and muttered, "Didn't find out a damned thing by
doin' that."

He looked up and down the street, then went to his
room and pulled out the sack of coins Santana had given
him as half payment to determine who Soto was. He
inspected every coin in the bag. They were all in mint con-
dition, uncirculated, and all from the Philadelphia Mint.
He took out the notes he'd made while at the newspaper
office, and again read them.

Long before he finished reading, his head bobbed up
and down several times. "Yep, it fits. Looks like that
Army payroll ended up down here, an' Soto is using it for
his banditry expenses south of the border." He stared
unseeingly at the wall. That money, spent in Mexico, had
little chance of being traced to anyone in the States, especially since it was all in the hands of a Mexican bandit.
He dropped the coins back in the bag, stuffed the bag
inside his belt, and sat on the edge of the bed.

He shook his head. He'd been thinking along those
lines for quite a spell now, but what had it gotten him? He
wasn't any closer to finding out who Soto was than
before—even if he did figure that, whoever he was, he
and his partner, Phillips, had pulled the Army holdup.
Heck, he wasn't even sure of Phillips's true identity.

His shoulders slumped. Hell. Every time he thought he
took a step forward, another problem jumped up to stand

in his way. He pulled his boots off and stretched out on the bed.

Clay nudged Snake McClure. "You gittin' bored just sittin' around fightin' a few o' Santana's bunch ever so often?"

Snake groaned. "Oh, Lord, why'd you partner me up with Clay Mason? I know he's 'bout to suggest some damn fool thing we oughtta be doin'." He groaned louder. "An' to top it off, I know I'm gonna agree with 'im an' then we gonna be in more trouble."

"Aw, c'mon, Snake, we ain't been doin' nothin' to help Pa lately. I got a idear what'll make life more int'restin'."

Snake shook his head and said, "Nope, we ain't done nothin' but get ourselves shot at on a continuing basis, an' now I know you're gonna tell me we can have some fun by goin' down to Ojinaga an' take on some o' Santana's gun hawks—jest for fun, o' course."

Clay stared at him, his eyes wide in mock surprise. "Snake, we been partnered up too long. Why hell, now it's gotten to where you can read my mind."

Snake lifted his face from his hands. An ear-to-ear grin stretched his mouth. "When we start, partner? I been 'bout ready to ask you 'bout doin' the same thing."

Clay cuffed Snake on the shoulder. "Reckon we better let Cole know what we're 'bout to do?"

Snake shook his head. "If we do, he might have some other ideas. Nope, we better jest git outta here. We can be back by sunrise tomorrow. Better tell Martinez, though, so he'll know where to place the men in case another raid comes along."

Fifteen minutes later they were on their way to the border. They forded the river and soon rode down the trash-laden street between the *cantinas y tiendas* lining each side.

"Clay, we cain't jest go in one o' these *cantinas,* pick a fight, an' start shootin'."

"Didn't figure on doin' nothin' of the kind. Way I got it figured, we won't finish even one drink 'fore one o' them'll find some way to start a fight with us—then we start shootin'. One thing we don't want to do is get in a fistfight or knife fight with any o' that bunch."

"Why not a fistfight? You an' me can take on a whole passel o' Mexes."

"Damn, McClure, don't you never use yore head for nothin' 'cept to hang yore hat on? We get in a fistfight with 'em, they'll pull knives, then we got a whole bunch o' trouble."

McClure pushed his hand down into his saddlebags and pulled out an extra Colt .44. "Might need more'n six shots." With those words he opened the loading gates and pushed a shell into the empty chamber of each handgun. Clay did the same.

They tied their horses to the hitching rail in front of the nearest *cantina* and pushed through the batwings. Inside, they selected a table closest to the door for a quick exit, and told the waitress to bring a couple of *cervesas*.

As soon as he sat, Clay felt the animosity push against him like something physical. "Won't be long, partner. Maybe we can thin down some o' Santana's bunch without waitin' for 'em to come north of the river."

"Yeah, less'n they thin down some of the Mason bunch by two dumb cowboys."

"Ah, hell, McClure, you always gotta look on the bad side. Think how happy Cole's gonna be when we tell 'im what we done."

McClure slanted Clay a sour look. "Two things wrong with what you jest said. He ain't gonna be happy—he'll probably whip yore butt. Second thing is, we might not git back to tell him anything."

Before Clay could think up a good answer to McClure's voice of doom, a squat, brawny *vaquero* walked to stand at the side of their table. "You *Americanos* lost or something?"

Clay glanced around the room. "We ain't the only *Americanos* in here. Why you ask us? 'Sides that, we might have business with Santana."

The squat Mexican flicked his thumb toward the room. "Them're our friends. An' they're Santana's friends. You ain't."

"Yeah, but we might get to be, if you'd give us a chance."

"Them others ain't part o' the Mason crew. Ain't no Masons our friends. That's why we gonna take you apart right now, *Señor* Mason." With those words, the Mexican dropped his hand to his holster.

Clay didn't wait. His Colt jumped to his hand. He fired into the *vaquero,* then swung his gun to point into the room, at the same time every man there stood, or ducked behind a table he'd overturned. Figuring there wasn't a man in the room who wouldn't be shooting as soon as his weapon cleared leather, Clay wasn't particular who he shot. By now McClure's .44 was also talking.

The room came alive with orange blossoming gunfire, smoke, breaking glass, and yelling men, most of whom coughed from the acrid smell of cordite. Feeling

McClure at his shoulder, Clay stood fast, braced against the expected jarring, flesh-tearing slam of a revolver slug. He deliberately emptied his right handgun, then made a border shift and fired three shots from the fully loaded .44 now in his right hand. He backed toward the door, holding his left arm out to sweep Snake along with him.

Outside, people ran toward the sound of gunfire, some apparently curious as to what was going on, others wanting to get into the fight regardless of what the shooting was about. And it didn't seem to make a difference which side they helped—they simply began firing.

Clay saved his three unfired shells in case he needed them for close-up work, toed the stirrup, and swung his horse toward the river, McClure at his side.

They headed straight for Presidio, rode into the main street, and pulled between two stores. McClure clasped his left hand tightly to his thigh. In the dim light, Clay looked from Snake's hand to his face. "You hit, partner?"

Through clenched lips, McClure said, "If I ain't, I don't know what that warm, wet feel I got flowin' over my fingers is." He groaned. "Reckon I better see a sawbones 'fore we leave here."

"Better wait a few minutes, see if any o' that bunch follered us 'cross the river."

They had waited only a few seconds before Snake said, "To hell with 'em. I gotta git this bleedin' stopped." He nudged his horse from between the buildings, stopped the first person he saw, and asked to be pointed toward the doctor's office.

"Doc ain't gonna be in his office this time o' night." The man pointed toward a small white house down the street. "He lives right down yonder. Should be there 'less somebody called 'im into the country to deliver a baby or somethin'."

Snake nodded his thanks and headed in the direction the stranger had pointed.

Clay pounded on the door and in only a moment it swung open. A white-haired, tired-looking man stared at Clay. "C'mon in, Cole. Reckon I'll patch you up again so' you can go out an' get another chunk of lead in you."

With McClure leaning hard on his shoulder, Clay stepped through the doorway. "I ain't Cole, I'm Cole's brother Clay, an' you never had to dig any lead outta me. 'Sides, I ain't hit, it's my partner here."

The doctor helped Clay lead Snake to a table, pushed him flat onto it, and slit his trousers down the side to expose the still bleeding hole in his thigh. "I didn't hear any shootin', son. How'd you get this?"

McClure stared at the doctor through pain-filled eyes. He poked a thumb toward Clay. "I let this crazy bastard talk me into goin' over to Ojinaga for a beer—an' maybe a fight. We found both."

The sawbones frowned, then nodded. "Yep, sounds like something one of the Mason boys would do. Cole and Quint Cantrell kept me in business when they were growin' up." He shook his head. "Things've been right dull 'round here since they left." He talked while he worked. He sponged the blood from around the hole, picked up something that looked like long-nosed pliers to Clay, then told Snake to grit his teeth. He had to dig the slug from his leg.

While he probed for the bullet, McClure turned the color of biscuit dough, then groaned, then turned even whiter, and finally passed out. The doctor looked at Clay.

"He lasted longer'n I figured. B'lieve I'da passed out 'fore now."

A worried frown creased Clay's brow. "Most men would have, Doc. That's one tough cowboy."

The doctor grunted in satisfaction, tightened his hand on the forceps, and pulled. He held up the slug so Clay could see it. "Now I'll put some linament in the hole, dress it, an' he'll be good as new in a few days. He's gotta stay off that leg though, give it a chance to heal."

Clay shook his head. "You better tell that to him— when he wakes up."

The doctor frowned. "Now, tell me just why the hell you crazy bastards went across the border lookin' for trouble."

Clay snorted the odor of the strong-smelling linament from his nose, looked at his partner, then back to the doctor. "Tell you, Doc, it wasn't as crazy as it sounds. Them Mexes been bringin' the fight to us for quite a spell. They been gettin' the worst of it, but still they been comin' to us."

He sniffed again, then said, "I figgered it might cause 'em to sit back an' take notice if only a couple of us went over there and eliminated a few o' them. We did just that." He grinned. "I figger the hell we raised wasn't nothin' to what Cole's gonna do when we tell 'im how Snake got shot. Whooeee. That brother o' mine is right good at tellin' folks how the cow ate the cabbage."

The doctor nodded. "I understand why you did it, but it wasn't the smartest thing a man could do."

Clay shook his head. "Doc, I ain't never been known for bein' the smartest cowpoke around." He reached in his pocket. "How much I owe you?"

"Two dollars, but you better let your partner rest awhile 'fore you get 'im offa that table."

Snake stirred, opened his eyes, stared at the ceiling a moment, obviously getting his bearings, then turned his eyes on Clay. "You say anything 'bout me passin' out to Cole and our bunch, I'll whip yore butt." He shifted his weight to the side, and winced.

Clay smiled. "You feel like walkin' far as the hotel?"

"Yeah. Ain't nothin' wrong with me now the danged hole's done stopped leakin'."

Clay helped McClure to his feet, helped him take one step at a time down the outside stairs, helped him around the corner to the boardwalk, and came face-to-face with one of the *vaqueros* they'd faced in the *cantina*. Snake leaned hard against Clay's right shoulder. The Mexican cowboy, obviously surprised, but quick to comprehend his advantage, dug for his handgun.

Clay threw McClure to the side, swept his hand down and up. The two antagonists fired at the same time. A hammering blow hit Clay in the left shoulder. Knocked back against the wooden front of the store, he eared back his Colt's hammer for a second shot. The only thing in front of him was a heavy cloud of smoke.

He coughed, swung his .44 from side to side, eyes swinging with the motion of his handgun, searching for the *vaquero*. He snorted to clear the acrid smell of gunpowder from his nostrils, then turned his look groundward. The Mexican cowboy lay stretched out on his back, shoulders hanging off the edge of the boardwalk.

Men were only now erupting through the batwings of the nearby saloons. He then searched for McClure. The tall, lean, cowboy sat on the edge of the walk holding his wounded leg in both hands, rocking back and forth, moaning and cursing.

Apparently having run out of curse words, he turned his look toward the storefront. "Damn you, Clay, why you push me down like that? You had that Colt stuck down in yore belt you coulda used 'stead o' usin' yore sidegun."

Clay, only now feeling pain wash over him, slid down the storefront to sit on the boardwalk. The men he'd seen rush from the saloons seemed to weave, stretch, shrink, divide into two or three shapes, then come together again so he could see them plainly. He sat as still as the pain would allow. He was damned if he'd give McClure the satisfaction of watching him pass out.

Remembering that Snake had asked a question, he shifted his eyes to him. "Ain't used to havin' a gun tucked behind my belt. Did what I had to do." Before he could say more, a couple of men pulled him to his feet, then one of them supported him under his right shoulder and half dragged him back to the doctor's office.

Doc Burns opened the door, stared at Clay, sighed, and said, "Just like old times. Don't reckon it makes any difference which Mason it is, anytime one o' them's in town, hell's gonna pop. Bring 'im in, boys."

A couple of punchers helped Snake to the chair Clay had sat on only a few minutes before. He grinned through his pain. "Wanta watch you dig that slug outta his shoulder, Doc. Hope he don't do no better with it than I did."

McClure had no more than gotten the words out of his mouth when Engstrom pulled the door open and stepped in. He looked from McClure to Clay. "Which one o' you shot that man at the bottom of the stairs?"

One of the men who had helped Clay up the stairs nodded toward the younger Mason brother. "Reckon you'll have to talk to him, Sheriff. I seen it all. That Mex downstairs pulled iron first, then Mason threw his friend there aside and drew. The Mex an' young Mason here fired about the same time, only the *vaquero*'s bullet didn't go straight as Mason's."

Engstrom pinned McClure with a look. "Why'd he wantta shoot Mason?"

McClure shook his head. "Don't know, Sheriff, 'less'n he wuz some teed off 'cause we had a little fracas over in Ojinaga a little while ago. Mason shot 'bout five o' the Mex's friends. Reckon the *vaquero* didn't have much sense o' humor."

Engstrom pinned McClure with a hard look. "Why'd y'all go over to Ojinaga? You mighta knowed damned well you were gonna get in trouble."

Snake nodded. "Yep, Marshal, we knowed it, that's why we went down yonder. They been bringin' it to us for quite a spell now. Clay figgered we'd had enough, figgered it wuz time we took it to *them* for a change. We did. I got four of 'em. Clay got five." He winced and straightened his leg. "Gonna tell you somethin'; this ain't the end of it. Soon's my leg gets better, I'm goin' back down yonder, with or without Mason, an' get me some more of 'em."

What's this fight of the Masons' to you, McClure?"

Snake scratched his head, looked toward the table they'd put Clay on, then back to Engstrom. "Well, Marshal, Clay an' me done partnered up for some time now. We been in several gunfights together. He backs me, I back him."

The marshal only shook his head, and said, "Try to stay outta trouble, at least on this side o' the river." He walked out.

After Burns patched Clay's shoulder, the two invalids bedded down in a room at the hotel. They'd not been alone over an hour when a light tap brought Clay upright in the bed. He pulled his Colt from its holster, lying at his head, cocked it, and said, "Yeah? Who is it?"

14

CLAY TRAINED THE revolver about where he figured a man would stand to tap on the door. He repeated, "Who's there?"

This time he heard a loud whisper. "Cantrell. Open the damned door."

Clay looked at McClure, but the slim cowboy only grinned and rubbed his bandaged leg. Mason groaned. "You bastard, I bet I pay for takin' you across the border for six months."

When he stood, Snake grunted, "Longer'n that, *mi amigo.*"

Clay pulled the door toward him only enough to let Quint slip through. "What you doin' here, Cantrell? Thought you wuz out yonder somewhere makin' like a detective—or sittin' on yore lazy bottom."

Quint cast each of them a sour look. "The point is, what are you two doin' here? Thought Cole had enough trouble out at the ranch without you two goin' lookin' for more." He shook his head. "Yeah, Engstrom came lookin' for me soon's he left the doc's office. Told me what happened. Said y'all shot up a *cantina* in Ojinaga, then come over here to finish the fight off."

Clay massaged his wounded shoulder. "Wasn't our idea to bring the fight back to the States." He eased the hammer of his Colt down on the empty chamber. "The cold fact of the matter, Cantrell, is we got tired o' waitin' for them night-raidin', cow-stealin', slimy bastards to hit us first." He nodded. "Paid off too. 'Tween me an' Snake we sent nine of 'em to hell. That's as many as we usually get during one o' their raids."

Cantrell had been holding his left hand behind his back; now he brought it to the front. He grinned. "Figured with each o' you surroundin' a chunk o' lead you'd not feel like goin' to the saloon for a bottle, so I brung you one."

This time, Snake swung his legs off the bed and grabbed one of the two glasses. "You take one, Cantrell; Clay can wait fer us to finish. He's the one got us into all this trouble in the first place."

Mason stared at his partner a long moment. "Notice you didn't have much trouble gettin' around on that leg when a jolt o' whiskey wuz at stake."

Snake grinned. "You gotta make up yore mind what's important, good friend. I jest put pain at the back o' the fire for now."

After Quint poured the glass full, he handed it to Clay. He sat at Mason's side on the edge of the bed and told them what he'd been doing, and that now he felt at a dead end. His jaw hardened. "But that's only for now. I'll uncover who this damned Soto is, an' when I do, if I gotta fight the whole Santana bunch alone, I'll do it."

Mason looked at Snake, then nodded. "See there. I told

you what kind o' ranny Cantrell is. Here he figgers to hog all the fun to hisself."

Snake shook his head. "You know what, Clay—you're crazy as a skunk. I done had 'bout all yore kind o' fun I b'lieve I can stand for a long while."

Clay knocked his drink back, then handed the empty glass to Cantrell, who poured himself one, knocked it back, and said, "Want you rannies to remember somethin'. Ain't but a couple folks in this town know I'm Cantrell, so don't any o' 'em know I got any interest in the B-bar-M's affairs. Leave it like that."

Clay took a swallow of his drink, gazed at the wall a moment, and said, his voice cracking, "Wonder how our womenfolk are doin'."

Cantrell and Clay were lucky they didn't know what their womenfolk were doing at that moment. Every one of them was spitting mad. Each, in her own way, scolded her man with the most salty language she knew. Martinez had come to the ranch for supplies, and had told Brad Mason what Clay and McClure had decided to do—all by their lonesome.

Laura, showing that her temper fit her auburn hair, berated Cole for not keeping closer watch on the men. Molly, her eyes spitting fire, only shook her head, saying that nothing anyone could have done would have prevented her husband, Clay, from doing exactly as he'd done.

Elena moved close to them both, wrapping her arms around their shoulders. "Laura, Molly, all our men are cut from the same mold—they're *men*. That's why we love them. I reckon all of us have good reason to worry ourselves sick about them, but we all know if we had to pick men to fight for us, or for anything we believed in, we'd never find men any more fit for the job than those men of ours."

Laura smiled through her tears, and said, "Well, reckon it's gonna be a long night. I'll put the coffee on. Elena, see if you can find one of Brad's bottles of special stock. Someone'll come tell us what happened, maybe in time for breakfast." Her estimate proved correct.

They'd all settled into their places at the table when hoofbeats sounded outside, a man yelled for someone to tend his horse, and Art King came stomping into the house. A stomp for King was a soft padding of boots across the wooden floor.

At Brad's motion for him to take a chair at the table, Art pulled out a chair and sat. His hawklike gaze swept them. He nodded. "All here. Got somethin' to tell you. Cantrell sent me." At their half-scared looks, he shook his head. "Now, don't y'all git yoreselves in a tizzy, ain't nothin' bad."

He saw them braced for the worst, yet half taking his word for it that he brought no bad news. He helped himself to a plate before saying anything more, then he took a sip of the hot coffee offered him by the maid. "Y'all prob'ly know by now that Clay an' McClure took off for Mexico last night. They had a gunfight. Killed nine o' Santana's bunch. McClure took a slug in his leg, then when they got to Presidio, an' after the doc took care o' Snake's leg, one o' Santana's men put some lead in Clay's shoulder. Doc took care of him, an' they're both all right, restin' in the hotel. Cantrell's watchin' to make sure ain't nothin' more gonna happen to 'em."

Molly started to speak, then at King's head shake she quieted. "Done told you ladies yore men are all right.

Don't worry 'bout it. Cantrell's takin' care o' them. Ain't nobody gonna git within shootin' distance o' their room."

Elena, a half smile breaking the corners of her lips, and as usual trying to make King as uncomfortable as possible, said, "Tell us all about it, Art. We might nota heard the straight of it."

King slanted her a sour look. "Elena, I done said all I'm gonna say. 'Sides that, you jest wantta git me to talkin'." He put a whole *frijole* in his mouth and grinned, then pointed to his mouth and chewed.

Elena giggled. As sparing with words as King was, anytime she could get him to say more than a dozen, she counted as a victory, but she'd accomplished her goal. Kidding Art had broken the tension. They all began to talk about more mundane things.

During the meal Elena noticed that none of the women except her and Ma Mason ate much. Every one of them picked at her food, and in the middle of the meal, each of them found an excuse to leave the table. Must have a touch of chilblains, or maybe the grippe had gotten ahold of them.

Three days later, Elena got the same malady.

Ma frowned. It seemed that all of them had caught something that might be contagious. If only one of them had had the same symptoms, she thought she might have taken a good guess at the problem, but all of them? She shook her head. Not likely that could happen to all of them at the same time.

Outside the thick adobe walls of ranch headquarters, deep in the chaparral, Cole pulled his men around him. "I got an idea Santana's gonna make another strike at headquarters soon. We been hurtin' him bad every time he's taken a notion to steal more cattle. Besides, stealin' cows now is too much trouble. They've thinned down the herd, so now they have to chouse them outta the brush. They aren't gonna take that much of a chance here on our side of the border."

He studied the grounds in the bottom of his cup, then glanced around the group, his eyes settling on Slim Matthews. "Slim, want you to find Clay's men, an' those who were ridin' with Art King. Neither Clay nor King will be with them, but send them all to this camp. Tell 'em it's important that they get here soon as possible." Matthews left while Cole talked.

All through the afternoon, and on into the night, men straggled into Cole's camp. By three in the morning, Cole estimated they were all gathered, except for Cantrell, Clay, McClure, and Art King.

Cole noticed that few of the men slept during the long night. They rolled up in their blankets, but every time a rider came in, each of them raised up for a look, groaned, then pushed back under his blankets. With all the men on site, Cole set the coffeepot to the side, smothered the fire, and pulled his blankets around his shoulders.

He rolled out before sunrise, dumped out the thick overnight coffee, and poured fresh water into the pot from canteens. By the time the aroma of fresh coffee had awakened the last man, Cole had splashed cool water into the pot to settle the grounds and poured the first cup, then had the cook prepare breakfast.

When the last man had eaten and cleaned his gear, Cole stood. "Men, while we been cuttin' Santana's bunch down to size, they been runnin' enough of our cattle across the border so they're so scarce in this brush it won't pay them to try and round up a herd of any size.

The best way for 'em to hurt Pa now is to attack the ranch. Here's what we're gonna do to stop 'em."

When he'd laid out his plan, he looked at Red Benson. "All right, Red, you've heard it all. Now I want you to ride to the ranch and tell Pa what we're gonna do. Tell 'im to post a watch around the ranch day and night. Tell 'im to have all the men sleep on the wall, or right close to it, with plenty of rifle and revolver shells." He nodded. "All right, get movin'."

He again looked at the men. "We'll get in position soon's we can. We might have to sit there one day, two, three." He shrugged. "Hell, we might spend a week waitin' for them to come—but come they will. I figure they'll bring every man they have with them this time."

Fat Stuff Meaders, rail-thin, who had to stand in the same place twice to cast a shadow, shook his head. "Cole, we been hurtin' them *vaqueros* with surprise ambushes right steady. What makes you think they gonna fall for the same thing this time? It's jest I always heard you can go to the well once too often, then you gonna find it dry. Seems like we're 'bout to do that."

Cole stood there a moment, stared at the ground, then shook his head. "Don't know, Fats. You got a better idea?"

"Well, I got one; whether it's better or not reckon you'll have to decide. Let me toss it in the ring an' see what you think."

"Let's hear it."

Fats pushed his hat back, scratched his forehead, grimaced, then said, "I got to thinkin' them *hombres* gonna be ridin' all bunched up from the time they leave their hideout. They gonna ride to the river, cross it, an' head for the B-bar-M 'bout as straight as they can get to it."

Now obviously having gathered his courage after challenging Cole's idea, Fats's voice took on a deeper and more positive tone. "If we can figger where they gonna cross the river, set our men up along the bank on this side o' the Rio Grande, we can shoot 'em like ducks sittin' on the water 'fore they can get across."

Cole thought about Fats's words a moment. He nodded. "I like the idea." He shook his head. "Only problem I can see is findin' out where they're gonna cross."

Fats rolled a quirley, lit it, and sucked smoke into his lungs, then let it trickle out of his mouth and up his nose. "Got a idea 'bout that too, Boss. I figger them Mexes been crossin' 'bout the same place ever' time they made a raid on us. They gonna have a big bunch o' riders, an' I think they ain't gonna be lookin' fer a different place to cross. Figger they gonna take the place they know best." He frowned. "Been my experience that people, even after doin' somethin' one time, will most likely not change, 'less'n o' course they're forced to."

"How do you propose we find where they been crossin'?"

"Let me take a ride down yonder, scout the bank, an' I bet I'll find where they been comin' across."

Cole frowned. He liked the idea—but if they were wrong, and Santana got across without being caught in Fats's trap, then they'd have a clear route to attack the ranch. He pondered the idea so long he noticed Fats begin to squirm. He shook his head. "No, Fats, I believe you have a good scheme. I was just wonderin' how much of a gamble we'll be taking in leaving the ranch to protect itself in case we don't hook up with Santana at the river."

One of the other men spoke up. "Why don't we warn your pa, let 'im know he's on his own if we miss our bet?

Fact is, if we scatter a few men along the riverfront as scouts, they can get back to us if we miss their crossin' then we can dog Santana's flanks all the way to the ranch. Yore pa ain't gonna be fightin' alone for a very long while, only long enough for us to get there on Santana's heels."

A slow smile broke across Cole's somber features. "Reckon like they say, boys, two heads are better than one." He looked at Fats. "We'll do it your way. I b'lieve you've got a real winner here." He walked to his horse, threw the hull on him, and while tightening the cinches, said over his shoulder, "Let's all head for the ranch, tell Pa what we've decided, get a good meal, an' maybe drink a little of his whiskey, then we'll wait for Fats to come tell us where we better set up to wait for the Mexes."

Cantrell looked out the window of his hotel room. Barely daylight, people were stirring out on the street, some taking advantage of the morning cool before the sun again baked the dusty little town on the banks of the Rio Grande, others starting what would be a long, hot day of drudgery. Quint went back to the bed and readied his weapons. He wanted to be ready for whatever the day would bring.

He went to the hotel dining room for breakfast. Even though it was early, almost every table was full. Nat Howley, the banker, sat at a back table. Cantrell looked for a place closer to the door. He didn't want to sit with Howley. He'd almost decided to wipe him off his list of suspects, but the fact remained he just flat didn't like the slippery bastard.

After breakfast, Quint went back to the hotel to see how Clay and McClure were getting along. When he tapped on the door, McClure growled that the door was unlocked and for him to come in.

Cantrell raised his eyebrows. After being shot, they sure seemed trusting. He pushed the door open and found himself staring down the barrels of two .44s, one in the hand of each of them. He chuckled. "Now you cowpokes look like what I expected. I was thinkin' y'all was mighty trustin' invitin' me in like you did."

"Naw, we wuz both hopin' you wuz another one o' them Mexes come to visit us." While talking, McClure shoved his Colt back in leather.

Cantrell studied them a moment. They were both dressed, and had their gunbelts buckled around their middles. "Where the hell you men think you're goin'? You wantta start those holes in your sorry hides to bleedin' again?" He pushed the door closed behind him. "Now y'all get undressed an' back in bed. I'll go have the clerk bring you some breakfast up here."

"Ain't goin' back to bed. Ain't goin' nowhere 'cept back to the ranch. They might need another two guns out there. 'Sides that, I wantta see Molly. We can eat when we get home."

Cantrell studied both of them long enough to determine that an argument would be futile. He nodded. "All right, I got better things to do than play nursemaid to a couple o' hardheads. See you out at Pa's one o' these days." He pulled the door open, peered down the hallway, saw no one in sight, and slipped out.

He went directly to his room, collected his Winchester, filled his pocket with shells, went to the livery, saddled his horse, and took up a watch where he could see Clay and Snake when they came from the hotel and also have a good view of the street.

Not more than five minutes had passed when Clay and McClure came through the hotel doorway, each helping the other as much as his wound would permit. They had the hostler saddle their horses and, after a couple of attempts, climbed into leather and rode out.

Cantrell watched them a moment, then scanned the street, noticed no one following them, toed the stirrup, and rode to the backs of the stores. There, two men rode, and each time they passed an alley, they gazed down the length of it.

Quint hung back as far as he dared in order to stay hid from their sight, but he made certain he didn't lose them. He thought on their behavior a moment and decided that if he wanted to know what progress someone on the main street was making, but didn't want to be seen, he'd do it exactly as the Mex and the *Americano* were doing.

He felt a surge of satisfaction. He'd been right. He'd bet his bottom dollar the two had been waiting for just such a chance to even the score with Mason and McClure. Cantrell pulled his Colt and shoved another cartridge into the chamber. Now with his .44 and Winchester fully loaded, he figured to have something to say about the way his friends were treated.

When the *banditos* got to the end of the business district, they held their horses out of sight from those on the main street and waited. Cantrell pulled his horse into the back end of an alley and waited for them to ride on. But they would stay there long enough for Clay and McClure to get around a bend in the trail, and with heavy brush to hide them, they'd follow until far enough out of town to escape attention. That satisfied Cantrell. He didn't want to advertise that he was friendly to the Mason forces, or knew them for that matter.

He watched for a good two minutes, anxious for them to get gone. The stench of garbage in the alley caused him to breathe in shallow gulps. Damn, but he was glad he didn't have to live in a stinking town.

The Mex and the *Americano* urged their horses from behind the store and rode to the trail. Cantrell rode through the alley and pulled onto the main street a good two hundred yards behind where the two adversaries trailed Snake and Clay. He noticed the Mex look back a couple of times, obviously to see if they were followed, but Quint and his horse were lost in the traffic at the end of the street.

When Cantrell lost them around the bend, he urged his horse to a lope, drew closer to where the trail took the lazy curve out of town, then slowed his horse and eased far enough around the curve to bring the two back under his gaze. Now they were about a hundred yards ahead, but not more than a hundred fifty yards in front of them rode Mason and McClure in easy rifle range.

The *Americano* pulled his horse in, drew his rifle from its scabbard, and dismounted. The Mexican followed suit. As soon as they reached for their rifles, Cantrell did the same. He touched solid ground when they did.

When the two leveled their weapons, pointed toward his friends, Cantrell centered his sights between the *gringo*'s shoulders, squeezed the trigger, jacked a shell into the chamber, and fired at the *vaquero*. He missed. The *Americano* lay sprawled at the side of his horse. The Mexican had disappeared into the chaparral at the side of the trail.

Cantrell's nerves tightened; his stomach felt like a big hollow under his ribs. This was the kind of fighting he liked. He melted into the brush, but only far enough to keep the assailants' horses in sight. He banked that he had more patience than the Mexican, and that the *vaquero* would wait awhile then try to get back to his horse. He hunkered down to wait, placed his rifle on the ground, pulled his Colt, and eared the hammer back. When he and Mex saw each other again, Quint figured they'd be in six-gun range. He'd played this game with the Apache and knew what to expect. The Mexican's first move would be his last.

He still had Clay and McClure in sight, although they'd slipped from their horses and were hunkered in the brush at the side of the dusty road. Now Quint could wait out the *vaquero*.

His mind pulled him strongly toward the deeper brush. He wanted to circle, try to get the Mexican between him and the bandits' horses. But—common sense, and years of experience, kept the *vaquero* hunkered in the same spot where he'd gone to ground.

After what seemed hours, Cantrell's legs cramped. Sweat ran from under his hat brim, down his forehead into his eyes. He squeezed his lids together to rid himself of the burning fluid against his eyeballs. Rivulets of salty liquid flowed down his back, from under his arms, and down his chest in maddening trickles, causing him to itch. To move enough to scratch might give his position away and draw a rifle slug in a hurry.

An hour dragged by. Cantrell couldn't help but admire the Mexican for his patience. Not many Apache could equal it. A few minutes later, a rattlesnake slithered its way along, within a foot of Quint's right knee. He didn't flinch, though every nerve in his body screamed for him to jump to his feet and get away from the reptile.

The rattler stopped, moved its head from side to side as

though looking for something, anything, to strike—then it pulled itself into a tight series of curves, straightened, and moved on out of Cantrell's sight. Suddenly, he heard the branches of a mesquite bush bend slightly. There was no wind, not even a whisper of a breeze.

Cantrell held his Colt steady, pointed toward the base of the bush. The few moments it took for the Mexican to come into sight seemed to stretch into days.

The bandit pushed his head through a thick tangle of brush surounding the mesquite. His eyes stared directly into Cantrell's. Quint read death in the Mexican's face. Knowing he was going to die, the *vaquero* whipped his rifle barrel toward Cantrell, squeezed off a round, and then tried to jack another shell into the magazine. But Cantrell's one shot had already put a small, black hole in the *vaquero*'s throat. The hole remained black only a fraction of a second, then great spurts of blood turned his neck and shirt crimson.

Cantrell stood, walked to the dead man, stripped him of weapons, then walked to the middle of the sun-baked trail. "All right, come on out. I done yore fightin' for you."

Clay, holding his wounded shoulder rigid, and McClure, hobbling on his gunshot leg, came out of the brush. Before they could utter a word, Cantrell blistered them up one side and down the other with every means he had at hand to tell them what a couple of stupid bastards he figured they were.

Finished with his first outburst, he pulled his bandana from around his neck and swabbed at his face. "How the hell you two have stayed alive is beyond me. Neither of you seemed to have the first inklin' you'd be followed. After last night, I reckon you thought them Mexes was

gonna kiss you an' make up." He pushed his hat to the
back of his head and again swabbed his forehead. "I don't
believe I seen either o' you glance behind, even once, to
see was you followed."

He turned to go fetch the horse he'd ground reined
when he left the saddle, then turned back. "You figure
you got 'nuff sense to get to the ranch by yoreselves?"

Both Clay and McClure looked like little boys who'd
just gotten a paddling. Clay looked into Cantrell's eyes.
"Aw, Quint, quit rawhidin' us." He nodded. "Yeah, reckon
we deserve what you been sayin'," he shook his head
along with a chagrined smile, "but damn, man, I didn't
know you could chew a man out like that."

Snake mumbled, "Jest turn us loose, Quint. Reckon we
can get along home without pullin' anything else as dumb
as we jest done."

Cantrell nodded. "Git along then. I got things to do in
town." This time he made it to his horse, toed the stirrup,
and rode back toward Presidio.

15

CANTRELL RODE DIRECTLY to the livery, took care of his horse, then walked to the wide double doors and studied the main street. Midday traffic glutted the boardwalk and hot dusty street. He stepped up on the boardwalk, then slowed. A couple steps ahead stood Howley, who was being approached by a lanky cowboy.

"Charley Butts. What you doin' down here in this acre of hell? Thought you might still be up in Dodge skinnin' cowpokes like me outta their trail wages."

Howley slowed, eyed the puncher, and coldly stated, "You got the wrong man. I've never been in Dodge City." He didn't bother to take the extended hand of the puncher, then nodded and walked on.

Cantrell slanted his course toward the nearest store-front, leaned against the wall, and watched to see where the cowboy went. He tried to keep a look on Howley also. The banker walked about twenty paces, then twisted to look at the departing puncher. Quint had never seen both fear and rage so vividly stamped on a man's face. Howley turned and headed for the bank.

Cantrell waited until the banker had taken out his keys, unlocked the front door of the bank, and stepped inside before looking around again for the cowboy. The puncher had only just pushed at the batwing doors of the Cattleman's Rest. Quint turned his steps in that direction.

Inside, he let his eyes adjust to the dim light, then looked around. His man leaned on the bar, a beer in front of him. A small space showed beside the puncher. Cantrell pushed his way into it, getting a couple of dirty looks.

He stood there a moment, and waited for Spike Barron to work his way down the bar to him. When Spike looked a question at him, he said, "Two beers—one for me, one for this young fella next to me."

The cowboy grinned with a surprised look and said, "First friendly thing been said to me in this town." He stuck out his hand. "Name's Stover, Hank Stover."

"Howdy, Stover, I go by Juan Cantello. Seen yuh out yonder on the boardwalk try to shake hands with our banker. Didn't get a friendly reception there, did yuh?"

Stover frowned. "I sure as hell didn't. But you know what? I ain't never been that wrong before, an' I ain't now. That crooked bastard sat right across the table from me in the Long Branch Saloon in Dodge an' rooked me outta sixty-five bucks. I knowed he wuz cheatin' but didn't know how to catch him at it." He nodded. "Yep, in spite o' what he says he's Charley Butts—at least that's the handle he wuz usin' up yonder."

"How long ago was that?"

"Oooh, I'd say 'bout two an' a half years ago." He nodded. "Yep, that'd jest 'bout hit the nail on the head 'cause we'd delivered our herd to the buyer, been paid off, an' were lettin' the wolf howl a little 'fore we headed back to Texas."

"This Butts have a partner when you knew him in Dodge?"

Stover twisted to look him in the eye. "Now, how'd you know that? You know him from somewhere?"

Cantrell grinned and shook his head. "Nope. Never saw 'im before I landed in this godforsaken hole, but usually a crooked gambler has a partner. I wuz jest guessin'."

Stover knocked back the rest of his beer and frowned into the empty glass. "Damned good guess, cowboy. Yeah, he had a partner, tall, good-lookin' gent, well built, went by the name of Bart McCandless. He was a gambler, but he musta done a lot o' ridin'. He wuz 'bout as sun-cured as most o' us who make a livin' outta pushin' steers up the trail."

Cantrell picked up the full glass of suds Stover had ordered, took a swallow, and tried to keep his satisfaction from showing. He felt like a kid with a new pony. He'd bet everything he owned that Howley was Butts the gambler, and that Jarred Phillips was Bart McCandless. He rolled the two names over and over in his mind. He didn't want to forget them.

He and Stover had a couple more beers, before Cantrell put his glass on the bar with a thud. " 'Nuff. I got enough, or I might spend the rest o' the day in here." He shook his head. "Can't do that. Promised my wife I'd get a few things for her before I came home." They shook hands and Cantrell left. He angled across the street to the sheriff's office, went in, and found the office empty.

Disappointed, he pulled a scrap of paper from the sher-

iff's desk and wrote the names of both McCandless and
Butts on it, then crammed it into his shirt pocket.

He went to the café and ordered steak, eggs, biscuits,
and gravy, and then he noticed they had corn on the cob.
He had an order of that also.

It might as well have been cardboard for all the attention he paid to the taste of what he chewed. He studied
the notes he was carrying with him. Now he wanted to get
back to his room and make comparisons. He pushed the
notes into a pile, folded them, stuffed them in his pocket,
and gave what was left of his meal his full attention.

After eating, he again looked in the sheriff's office.
Still not in. He went to his room, hid his notes behind a
piece of loose wall plaster, checked his guns, went back
to the livery, got his horse, and rode down to Ojinaga. He
thought to see Santana, find out what his latest orders
from Soto were.

He had sat in the *cantina* about an hour nursing his first
beer, when the big bandit leader came through the doors.
His head swung from one side to the other. Then, apparently seeing Cantrell, he headed straight for the back table
to join him.

He pinned Quint with a look that was as hard as the
twin bores of a twelve-gauge shotgun. "You feenish the
theeng you do for me, *señor*?"

Cantrell shook his head. "Not yet, *amigo,* but I think
very soon. I got some information today that may lead me
to the man you seek." He spoke Spanish with Santana.
"I'm not in a position yet to tell you what I think I have,
but as soon as I know for certain, if it's in your best inter-
ests to do so, we'll take care of him."

"Why you do not tell me now, Cantello? I may be able
to sweat it out of thees man you suspect."

Cantrell shook his head. "He might not be the one. We might tip our hands and give the real Soto some ideas about getting rid of us."

"You theenk he ees more dangerous than me, *señor*?"

He shook his head. "*Amigo,* if we tip our hand, and don't know for certain who he is, he'll have the edge. I don't think we want to give him any extra chances at us."

Santana nodded. "You theenk well, *mi compadre*. We'll wait till we know for certain, then I'll take care of heem."

Cantrell pushed a slight smile through tight lips. "Santana, I have a hunch. When I find him, if he has any idea I have uncovered his secret, I'll never get back to you with what I've found. I'll have to kill him. He'll force me to it."

Santana took a swallow of his drink. He shrugged. "I theenk I would like to do eet to heem myself after I get all the *Americano* gold from heem." Then with an ear-to-ear grin, he said, "But, as you say eet, I have the hunch there ees not much of the gold left. He has spent much to keep me an' my men doing hees work for heem."

"What you reckon he's gonna get outta all this, Santana?"

"Land, *mi amigo,* land. He wants all the land the *Señor* Mason has. He has found that Mason, unlike most ranchers in the *Americano* West, has clear title to the land and water he grazes his cattle on. He ees not telling me to breeng the cattle back once thees ees all over. I have maybe seex thousand head of Mason's cattle in a small valley southwest of my headquarters." He spread his hands as if to say, *What more could a man want? I have the gold, an' I have the cattle. He can have the land.*

Blood surged to Quint's chest. He wanted to jump up and down and yell with joy. He'd found where Pa Mason's cattle were, and he suspected they were mostly intact.

When this thing ended. When Soto and Santana were both dead, and the outlaw leader's gang broken up, the B-bar-M crew, along with Cole's, Clay's, and his men, would ride into Mexico and drive the cattle back where they belonged.

He looked at the bandit a long moment. "Soto been down here to see you since the last meeting I listened in on?"

"*Sí*. He has tell me to keep my men close to my head-quarters. He ees think of making one beeg raid on the Mason *ranchero* headquarters." Santana spread his hands, palms up. "He knows I have lost many men. He wants me to not lose more until the beeg raid."

Cantrell frowned. "He give you any notion when he wants to pull the big raid?"

Santana shook his head. "No. He just say that maybe two, maybe three weeks he weel come back down to see me, an tell me when to do eet."

"You want me to listen in on what he has to tell you next time?"

"*Sí*, I need you to hear every word he has to say. Eet may help us to know who he ees." He hesitated a moment. "Also, I tell you he has not pay me the last two times we make raids. I don't like that."

Cantrell stood. "Let me know when, an' where, an' I'll be there. I better get back to Presidio. Need to follow up on somethin' I found in the last day or two." Santana nod-ded and poured himself another glass of tequila.

McClure and Clay rode through the gates of the ranch headquarters. They hadn't cleared their saddles before

Molly landed in the middle of them with the most acid tongue Clay had ever heard. He looked at Snake. "You feel like a scalded cat, Snake? Hell. I thought Cantrell had given as much what-for as I ever heard, but my woman sure done topped his chewin' out." He slid from the hull with a sheepish grin, which he couldn't get wiped from his face.

Molly gave him hell for perhaps another minute, then, tears streaming down her cheeks, she threw herself into his arms. "Oh, Clay, why do you do these foolish things?" She grasped him tightly to her, and all the while he grimaced with the pain she pushed through his gunshot shoulder. "Oh! Now I've hurt you again. Come in the house."

After leaving Santana, Cantrell rode back across the river, went to his room, and pulled the papers from behind the cracked wall plaster. He wrote down the date Stover told him he saw Howley in Dodge City. He now thought of Howley as Butts. In a column to the side, he wrote down the names of the towns in which they'd had a bank holdup, stagecoach robbery, any kind of outlawery, and the date. He continued this until he'd gone through his latest notes, then he studied the results.

Finished with that task, he shuffled the papers together, stuffed them into his pocket, buckled his gunbelt around his waist, and went out. The sheriff should still be making his nightly rounds of the watering holes to keep down trouble.

Quint went directly to Engstrom's office, and poured out the pot of coffee that had probably been simmering on the stove for two days, judging by the smell of it. It smelled like dirty socks. He made a fresh pot. Then, finished with that chore, he walked around the sheriff's desk, sat, and put his feet on the desktop to wait.

He tamped his pipe bowl full of fresh tobacco, lit it, let it go out, then nodded. Footsteps sounded outside the door. He straightened in the chair and relit his pipe. Engstrom came through the doorway, stopped, glanced at Cantrell's feet on his desk, poured himself and Quint a cup of coffee, then said, "Make yourself to home, Cantrell." He looked at his watch. "To what do I owe this midnight visit?"

Cantrell grinned. "Got a little somethin' I been studyin'. I done come up with some answers I want to pass by you—see if my idea makes sense to you." His grin widened. "An' 'fore you ask if it couldn't wait till mornin', I b'lieve you gonna be just as sure as I am that it's worth losin' a few minutes' sleep over."

Engstrom groaned. "Don't reckon anything I could say would make you wait'll mornin'. I'm tired. Been on my feet most of twelve hours now."

Cantrell passed his cup of coffee under his nose, breathed in the rich aroma, put fire to his pipe, and ignored the sheriff's complaint.

He sat forward and dug in his pocket for the sheaf of papers he'd crammed into it. He spread the papers out, took the paper he'd made comparison dates on, and pointing to each entry, explained his reasoning to the lawman. By now, Engstrom had apparently forgotten his fatigue. He leaned over the scarred wooden surface and studied the writing.

Quint looked up from the papers. "You got a map o' all

this country west of the Mississippi here in yore office, Engstrom?"

"Reckon if I look hard enough I can find one." He walked around his desk to the wall behind it and pulled a drawer out. He fingered several folded sheets to the fore end of the drawer, then pulled a sheet out that looked to be thicker than the rest.

"B'lieve this is what you were askin' for, Cantrell." He spread it on his desk, pulled the lantern closer, and followed Quint's finger down the map in almost a direct line from Dodge City to Presidio.

"Engstrom, it wouldn't take much more'n a day's ride to either side o' this line for a man to reach every one o' these towns. You beginnin' to see why I stayed up, an' kept you from gittin' in bed too? Hell, man, we may have somethin' here."

"Yeah, but what do we have?"

Cantrell leaned back in the chair. "Way I got it figured, Sheriff, the same man, or men, could have pulled every one o' these holdups. An' I think I know who the man is."

"Well then, tell me who you think he might be. I admit what you say makes a lot o' sense to me. Tell me, an' we'll go bring him down here an' sweat the truth outta him."

Cantrell shook his head. "That's what I thought you'd say, but if the man is who I think, we're dealin' with a damned smooth, cold cow paddy. I want you to get more facts before I tell you who I believe he is."

Engstrom nodded. "All right. You don't need to say it. You gonna want me to write letters to the law in all these towns. Have them send me descriptions of the outlaws, what name they used when in their town, how many of 'em they were—oh hell, any information they got that we could use."

All the while Engstrom talked, Cantrell nodded. When the lawman finished, Quint sat forward. "When's the northbound stage due in?"

"Noon, an' you ain't gonna get me to do what I think you gonna ask. I'm gonna git some sleep, then I'll do it."

"What you think I'm gonna ask you to do, Sheriff?"

Engstrom took a swallow of his coffee. He squinted at Cantrell. "You gonna say if we start writin' them letters now we might get finished in time to put 'em on the stage 'fore it pulls out."

Quint feined a look of astonishment. Eyebrows raised, his mouth hanging open a moment, he shook his head. "Man! I didn't know you could read my mind." He nodded. "Yep. That wuz 'zactly what I wuz gonna suggest."

Engstrom sighed, reached in his top left-hand drawer, and pulled out an extra pen and an inkwell, then he reached into the middle drawer and pulled out a stack of paper. "Reckon we might as well get started." He looked at the Regulator Clock hanging to the side of the door. "We get started now, we oughtta git 'em all done time for the stage."

They'd each written about five brief letters when Engstrom looked up. "Reckon you know you're gonna take my rounds for me tonight?"

Cantrell's eyes widened. "Sheriff, I ain't got no authority to do that. If I had to bust a drunk's head, or shoot somebody, I'd be outside the law."

Engstrom gave Quint a cold smile. "Naw. No such. Stand, an' hold yore right hand up."

"What the hell for? You ain't gonna make no lawman outta me."

With a nod, the sheriff stood. "Yep. That's exactly what I'm gonna do. Now hold up your right hand and repeat after me."

Cantrell opened his mouth to protest further, then thought about some ways he could use the badge to his advantage. He grinned and raised his hand.

Engstrom finished administering the oath before he apparently saw the look on Quint's face. He studied Cantrell a moment. "Wish I knew what you're thinkin' right now. Bet if I knew what it was, I'd take that badge and put it back in the drawer."

The grin not leaving his face, Cantrell said, "You don't wantta know, Engstrom, but I'll tell you this much, I might be able to do some snoopin' 'round where I couldn't 'less'n I had a badge. Let me tell you, though, I ain't gonna do nothin' to get you in trouble. I like the way you operate."

The lawman grumped a moment, then looked at the papers spread on his desk. "Go do rounds and I'll get the rest o' these letters written."

They finished the last letter at quarter past eight, stuffed them in envelopes, and stacked them on the desk. Engstrom looked at them a moment, put them in his desk drawer, and said, "Let's go get some breakfast. Ain't et since 'fore sundown last night."

On the way to the café, Quint asked, "How long 'fore you figure we'll get an' answer to them letters?"

Engstrom thought a moment before looking at Cantrell. "Reckon, allowin' for them to go both ways, an' the law in the different towns to check out the answers, we gonna be four, maybe five weeks gettin' answers to all o' them."

Now in front of the café, Quint pulled the door open. He shook his head. "I could get the answers faster just by takin' the slime I suspect, and showin' 'im how the Apache get the answers they want." He fingered the badge pinned to his shirt pocket. "Don't know how I got rooked into takin' this here badge. Reckon wearin' it, I cain't do everythin' like I want to."

Engstrom grinned. "Now you beginning to get the real idea why I put it on you. Figured you for an honorable man, a man who'd keep his sworn word to uphold the law."

"I'll just give it back to you."

"No you won't. You can only be released from that oath you took when I say I'm through with you."

Quint frowned. "You knowed all along you wuz trappin' me, didn't you?"

Engstrom smirked and stepped into the café.

16

HOWLEY SAT AT his desk by the front window of the bank. He'd been there all night. He'd seen Cantello go into the sheriff's office and not come out. The man had worried him for quite some time. He had given up on his partner Jarred Phillips ever showing up again, and he was certain that Cantello had something to do with that. He cursed Santana for not doing his part in eliminating the smooth gunfighter.

Where had this Cantello come from? Why hadn't he heard of him? Many gunfighters not nearly as good as Cantello were legend. They were talked of around every campfire in the West, and Howley had sat at many a campfire; still he'd never heard the name Cantello mentioned.

He gritted his teeth. Damn! He was too close to achieving his goal to have some gunslick come along and ruin everything. He sat back in his chair and studied the tip of a pen which he'd shoved back and forth across his desk during the long night.

He ran every option he could think of through his

mind. He could brace Cantello himself, or he could put more pressure on Santana. Pressure on the big Mexican *bandido* would be withholding gold.

To call Cantello out and have a gunfight would draw suspicion from the town, and he'd worked too hard and long to build his image after taking over the bank. He wanted Brad Mason's B-bar-M, and he wanted to keep the bank.

Why had this gunslick taken an interest in his affairs? Everything Cantello did seemed aimed at uncovering the past. Howley shook his head. His part in events that had occurred in every bank between here and Dodge City was close to exposure. He and Jarred Phillips had not been careful enough in covering their trail from the time they left Dodge City. And then along comes that puncher, Hank Stover, who recognized him, and bellowed out his name for all to hear.

Howley pulled a cigar from the humidor at the back of his desk, bit the end off, and lit it. Cantello had passed soon after Stover had said his name out there on the street. Howley wondered if the gunslick heard the name the Dodge City cowboy had used when greeting him.

The gunfighter had been busy visiting the newspaper office, the sheriff's office, and people around town. How could a gunfighter have that much business in a town where he'd only a few weeks ago made his first appearance? Maybe he was a United States Marshal.

The banker smoked his cigar until a long ash hung off its end. He tapped it into an ashtray and pondered the possibility of Cantello being a federal lawman. Finally he shook his head. The shoot-outs the gunfighter had had since coming to town didn't fit the behavior a federal marshal.

He finished his cigar and headed for the cafe.

Howley took a seat as far back toward the kitchen as he could find. At the front table sat the sheriff and Cantello, wearing a deputy's badge. That gave the banker more cause for worry. Another man came in, hesitated, looked around, apparently spotted Cantello and Engstrom, then went to their table and pulled out a chair. Doc Burns.

The sheriff nodded. Cantrell looked up from his coffee and said, "Howdy, Doc. You look mighty tired. Have a lot o' night doctorin' to do?"

Burns slumped into the chair he'd pulled out, sniffed, and told the waitress to bring him a cup of coffee. "If it's as good as it smells, keep it comin'." He looked at Cantrell, and nodded. "Yep. Babies don't seem to want to come into the light of the world. They wait until night sets in." His coffee came, and he took a sip and shook his head. "This'n was a breech birth, had a helluva time gettin' 'im outta his mother, but when he got here he was a squallin', healthy boy." He sighed, and his face crumpled as though he would cry. He squeezed his eyes tightly shut a moment, opened them, then glanced at the sheriff and Cantrell. "I lost his mother. She'd been havin' a helluva tough time of it since a horse fell on her husband during roundup and branding last fall. It killed him. She tried to run their small ranch by herself all during her pregnancy." He shrugged. "It was too much for her."

Cantrell shook his head. "Weren' nobody to help, nobody who could've took care o' her?"

The doctor shook his head. "No family I ever heard of. Just those two kids trying to make a go of it." His lips tightened; he blinked his eyes hard. "Don't know what's gonna happen to the baby. I'm gonna take care o' him long's I can, maybe hire a woman to stay with him while I work."

Engstrom lit his pipe, took a swallow of coffee, and leaned forward. "That'll only be a stopgap sort o' thing, Doc. Ain't there no family hereabouts what might want a baby?"

Burns shook his head. "Not one I'd give a baby to. When I turn loose that young'un, it's gonna be to a family I know can care for him."

Cantrell shuffled his feet under the table, reached in his pocket, and put a couple of double eagles on the table.

Doc Burns placed a finger on top of the two coins. "What're those for?"

Cantrell looked Burns in the eye. "Tell you what's a fact, Doc. That there baby's gonna have a nurse—a good nurse, a woman who'll look after him like he's her own. I'm here to tell you right now, you ain't footin' the bill for her all by yoreself; I'm payin' part, or all of it."

Engstrom fished in his pocket a moment and pulled out a like amount. "Deal me in. Reckon 'tween the three o' us we oughtta get the best woman they is in this here country."

Burns stared at the two of them a moment. Now there was no doubt that tears flooded his eyes. "Bless you, men. I reckon with us pullin' for 'im, he's gonna make it real well. Soon's we finish our breakfast, reckon we oughtta go see the young'un."

They ate in silence. Each of them seemed to want the quiet. With breakfast finished, Quint asked where the girl's ranch lay. Doc told him and asked why. "Well, I figured to ride out yonder, hitch up their buckboard, bring 'er into town, an' get 'er a fittin' burial. Bein's we ain't got a preacher no more, I figure Engstrom here could say a few words over her at the funeral. You an' me, Doc, can scare up a few people to see 'er on her way."

Burns stared at Cantrell. "Don't know whoever said you were a hard man, Quint, but I'm here to tell 'em you've got a heart big as Texas."

Cantrell felt his face turn hot. "Don't spread that word around, Doc. You'll ruin my reputation."

They laughed, stood, and all three departed at once. Howley scowled at their backs. What could the three of them have in common? That gunfighter was getting in too solid with the influential people of the town. In only a few weeks Cantello had made friends with people he, Howley, had tried to cultivate for over two years, and with whom he still remained nothing more than a slight acquaintance.

The morning after Molly took her husband to their room, the two of them came down to breakfast, both smiling, both looking as though there had never been a cross word between them. Brad Mason looked up from his coffee, looked at Ma Mason, and grinned. "Them young'uns have many more spats like they had last night, reckon we ain't gonna have to wait too long fer 'em to git us some gran'babies."

Molly's face flamed, Clay shuffled his feet a couple of times and stared at the floor, and Ma stood by the stove turning flapjacks. She stopped in the middle of flipping a golden brown cake to the other side and pinned Brad with a look sharp as a saber. "Mr. Mason, if I hear one more word outta you about gran'babies, *you're* gonna be the one to sleep in the bunkhouse." She dropped the hotcake to the griddle, and turned her back to her husband.

Brad laughed, a deep rumble coming from his belly.

"Hell, Ma, that ain't gonna do the trick. Reckon you an' me lost the pattern when we made Cole an' Clay. Only babies I want 'round here is them I can give back to their ma when they start squallin' or mess their diaper."

Ma raised her shoulders high around her neck, and a long "Ooooh" came from her throat. She swept the young people with a look. "Y'all pull out a chair an' set. I'll have enough of these flapjacks to fill the whole crew in a few minutes." She cast a reproachful look at Brad, then turned back to the young'uns. "Don't pay no nevermind to Mr. Mason. When y'all bring your grandbabies to see us, I'm thinkin' I'll have to push my husband aside just get a look at 'em. An' don't you worry none, when the good Lord wants you to be havin' babies, I reckon he'll just up an' give you one."

Clay took a swallow of his coffee, then blew into the cup, hoping to cool the contents a bit. "The way it stacks up, Ma, is that when Molly an' me got married we figured on waitin' a year or two 'fore we had any young'uns. We jest flat wanted to enjoy each other awhile." He grinned. "An' I guarantee you that's what we been doin'." Molly's face flamed again.

Cantrell and Engstrom followed Doc Burns across the trail and up the outside stairs to his office. They tiptoed across the room to a desk drawer where Doc had placed towels around the sides and bottom to cushion the baby.

Cantrell stared at the little boy a moment. He had a strange feeling in his chest. Everything inside felt made of mush. The baby boy stirred, pursed his lips, and made a sucking noise as though dreaming he was at his mother's breast. "Doc, that boy's hungry. We got any way o' feedin' 'im?"

Doc eyed Cantrell, a look of wonder molding his face. "Quint, babies make those sucking sounds all the time in their sleep." He leaned over the drawer serving as a crib. "That boy's already been fed as much as he'd eat. I know of a young Mexican woman who has a baby only three months old. She has enough milk for him and two more babies if she needs it. I got her to come around several times a day and feed this little one."

He straightened, took a step to the opposite side of his desk, pulled out another drawer, and removed a bottle of whiskey. "Been savin' this bottle for a special occasion. Brought it from Tennessee when I came out here years ago. I figure this is the special occasion I been savin' it for."

He took three glasses from a cabinet and poured each over half full, then handed one to Engstrom. He held the other toward Cantrell, but Quint was too busy to notice. He'd placed one of his big fingers in the baby's tiny fist and the infant had clamped down on it.

Cantrell looked from the baby to the doc. "You ever see anything like it, Burns? Hell, that baby's already takin' hold o' things. Bet in a couple o' months he'll be grabbin' for a set o' reins, wantin' to ride the first horse we put 'im on."

His mouth twisted off to the side in a look of disgust, Doc shook his head. "Cantrell, don't you know anything about babies? That's only a natural reaction. I've never seen a baby who didn't do that."

Quint knew his face flushed from the heat of it. He stared at Doc. "Well, dammit, this here baby just flat has a better grip than most. I know 'cause it wuz my finger he wuz squeezin' "

Burns's lips crinkled at the corners. "Oh, c'mon,

Quint, I was just joshin' you." Then he laughed. "But I'll say one thing in all seriousness, I have a feeling that baby's gonna be well loved and well cared for."

Engstrom gently nudged Cantrell aside, then held the backs of his rough, work-hardened fingers to the baby's cheek, and looked up into the eyes of his two friends. "You ever feel anything as soft as this little one's cheek? Why, I'll bet they ain't no other baby what has the feel o' this one."

The words hardly out of his mouth, he cocked his head to listen. "Somebody's comin' up the stairs, Doc."

Burns pulled his pocket watch out, glanced at it, and nodded. "Figured she'd be showin' up soon." As soon as he spoke, the door opened and a pretty, large-breasted girl came in and walked directly to the drawer.

She picked the baby up, looked at Cantrell and the sheriff, and pointed toward the door. "*Vamanos, señores.* I feed the baby now. I don't need no help from the likes of you."

Quint and Engstrom, holding hats in hand and semi-bowing and nodding, headed for the door. When outside and standing at the top of the stairs, both sweated profusely. "Damn, Cantrell, you don't s'pose she thought we wuz wantin' to stay in there an' gawk at 'er, do you?"

Quint grimaced. "Don't know what she thought, but I'm here to tell you I ain't never been so mortified in my life. Jest thinkin' she mighta figured we wanted to stay makes me right down ashamed."

Engstrom stepped toward the top step. "C'mon over to the office. I'll fix a pot o' Arbuckle, then we gotta do some talkin'."

A half hour later, the two sat at either side of Engstrom's desk, neither talking, just sipping their hot drink and puffing their pipes between swallows. The sheriff finally frowned and looked at Quint. "Been thinkin', Cantrell. That there baby's gotta have a name."

Quint nodded. "Thinkin' 'bout the same thing. I figure we oughtta give him a first name, then let whoever gets him for good hang their own handle on 'im." He jerked his head in another nod. "Course I don't figure to let jest any old folks have that boy. Don't figure Doc would stand still for such neither, an' I'll bet a painted pony you feel the same way."

Engstrom grinned. "Reckon we got that settled. Now, let's you an' me write down every boy's name we can think of, then we can take what we come up with to Doc an' let him add some. The three of us can study them names an' maybe decide on one."

Cantrell's brow creased. "Bet we gonna have a helluva time gettin' any agreement 'tween us." He shrugged. "But if we don't git busy writin' them names down, we ain't gonna have nothin' to argue 'bout. Hand me that piece o' paper an' a pen."

They sat there for over an hour, compared their lists, crossed off names they had duplicated, drank another cup of coffee, and agreed the Mexican girl had had ample time to feed the boy. They stood, ready to go back to Burns's office, when the door swung open and Price Waters came in. "What's all the confab about? Y'all stayed in Doc's office a good while, then come over here, and spend another while. If anything's happening in this town, I figure the people have a right to know what it is. I'll put it in the paper."

"Not this time, Price." Quint looked at Engstrom for confirmation.

The sheriff's face hardened. "Cantrell's done said it. If

you print what we know an' are 'bout to tell you, we could be doin' a little baby a great wrong—an' that I ain't gonna be guilty of."

Waters pinned them each with a straightforward look. "I'll tell you right now, gentlemen. You ask me not to print somethin', an' I guaran-damn-tee you I won't print it."

Cantrell and the sheriff looked at each other, nodded, and told the newspaperman what they knew.

While they talked, an awed expression came on Waters's face. When they finished, he lifted his shoulders in an exaggerated shrug. "I don't see why you don't want me to print the story. How could it hurt the baby?"

Engstrom again sat and leaned forward. "Tell you why. They's many o' married folk who ain't got no children, nobody to help with the chores, an' that's all they'd want with a young'un after he got old enough. Probably take 'im to a one-horse ranch, feed 'im porely, dress 'im worse, an' work hell outta him. I ain't gonna stand for that a'tall."

A slight crinkle broke the corners of the newspaperman's lips. "Sounds like the little feller's got two danged good friends to start 'im on his way in this world. Can I get in on helping the little tyke? I had five brothers and sisters, all younger'n me, so I know about babies."

Cantrell stood. "We're goin' back to the doc's office. You might as well come along an' get to know the little feller." He clamped his hat on his head and turned toward the door. "Now, when we git up there, don't make no noise. He's prob'ly asleep."

When they walked from the sheriff's office, Howley watched from the window at the side of his desk. He frowned. His gut tightened. His mouth dried. What the hell was going on? He'd never seen the newspaperman and the sheriff spend so much time together. And that Juan Cantello seemed to be right in the middle of whatever was happening.

A chill ran up his spine. When he was a kid, there'd been a saying that when a man got that tingling feeling up and down his backbone it meant someone had stepped on his grave. He sat forward, his stomach churning. He watched until the three men climbed the stairs to Doc's office. The only thing he couldn't imagine was why the doc had anything to do with whatever those three were cooking up.

He thought about that a long while, and couldn't come up with anything except that it must involve him somehow. Maybe they were on to what he was doing. Maybe they knew who was behind trying to take over the B-bar-M. Maybe they were about to stumble onto who Manuel Soto was. He studied that idea, and decided he'd better make preparations to get out of the game if it became necessary—but the fact remained, he wanted the B-bar-M, *and* he wanted the bank. But most of all, he wanted Cantello dead. His problems had all started when that Mexican gunfighter showed up.

He opened the humidor at the back of his desk, took out a cigar, bit off the end, spit it in the spittoon on the floor at his side, and lit the cigar. He thought to try to see Santana, prod him into getting rid of Cantello as soon as possible, then decided he'd better give the whole situation more thought—a great deal more. He needed to examine his plan, see where there might be weak spots in it, and at the same time devise an alternative in the event the first one failed. But he damned sure wouldn't admit the failure of the first until staging a last-ditch fight.

In Doc Burns's office, Cantrell, Engstrom, and Waters

stood around the baby's drawer\crib. Each had taken a turn at touching the little fellow's cheek, making kissing motions toward the sleeping child, and looking at Doc with each action to see if he disapproved, then Burns came over, felt the boy's bottom, nodded, and said he needed changing.

The only one of the doc's visitors who seemed to know what to do with a baby was the young newspaperman. The other two, hard men by most accounts, quick and accurate with a gun, men who would not hesitate to kill you if it were called for, were the ones who amazed him. Hell, they were soft as jelly inside.

Finished with pinning the diaper in place, Doc held the little bundle toward Cantrell. "Here, Quint, hold the boy. From the way you've been touching him, and cooing over his crib, I'd say you'd like to hold him."

Cantrell backed off a step, a terrified look blanching his face to a putty color. "No—uh no, Doc. I might break 'im." He held his hands in the air, afraid if he lowered them Burns would place the fragile little tyke in his arms.

Doc chuckled. "Cantrell, this baby is tougher'n you and those two men who came in here with you. All you have to do is hold your hand under his head to support his neck so he won't hurt his spine. He'll get to where he can hold his head up in a few weeks, then we can all stop supporting him in that fashion. C'mon, I'll show you how."

Quint, more scared than he'd ever been in a gunfight, lowered his hands and stepped toward Doc. "Keep yore hold on 'im, Doc, till I see if I'm gonna hurt 'im."

Burns nodded. "All right, but you're not gonna hurt 'im. Just be gentle with him, then put him to your shoulder. Bet you a double eagle he'll nuzzle right into your neck." He held the little bundle toward Quint, who gingerly took the baby in his big work-hardened hands. Then, gaining a little confidence, he brought the soft little thing to his shoulder, and damned if the doc wasn't right. The baby turned his face into Cantrell's neck and made little mewling sounds accompanied by grunts.

"Well, I'll be damned." Quint looked at Doc. "You were right." He held the infant close, crooning to him as though night-riding a bedded herd of steers. He had taken a couple of turns around the office when, apparently, Engstrom decided that if Cantrell could do it, so could he.

"You done had 'im enough, Quint. Let me take my turn now."

With proper instruction from Cantrell, the new expert, Engstrom, took his turn, then Waters had his try.

Cantrell, Engstrom, and Waters offered to take turns caring for the baby while Doc went about his business. Doc agreed, and promptly set about showing them how to change a diaper, give the baby water, bathe him, and calm him in case he got grumpy.

Each of the three men made a point of arranging his activities to fit the schedule they'd made out. Then the problem of naming the baby inserted itself into their routine. Doc suggested they name him Quinton Price Bartholomew after the three friends in his office, and wait for a last name until they knew who would raise the little fellow.

Engstrom raised hell about the Bartholomew. He twisted the brim of his hat in his hands a couple of times, then eyed them. "Gonna tell y'all what that name done to me. Ever time some dude would call me Bartholomew 'stead of Bart, I had a fistfight. Fact is when I joined the Rangers, I told 'em my name wuz Bart—nothin' else. I shore as hell don't wantta saddle the little guy with a everyday fistfight all through school." He looked at Doc. "What's yore name, Doc?"

Doc grinned. "Wors'n yours, Engstrom. Mine's Ezekiel, and I'll guaran-damn-tee you we won't saddle him with that." He went to the crib, took the baby into his arms, looked at the three friends, and said, "Y'all have had your say, now I'm gonna have mine. We'll call this little one after some mighty fine Texians. How 'bout Austin Travis, an' I'll leave the last name blank till we know who's gonna raise 'im. And I'm tellin' you right now, we won't let anyone have this child unless all four of us agree. It's gonna have to be a married couple, financially able to give him a good start in life." He pinned them with the look of a dagger. "Any of you take exception to that?"

The three "foster" fathers looked at one another, each looking somewhat relieved that the name situation had been settled. Cantrell finally nodded. "Don't take no exception, Doc. Only thing I been thinkin' is that part o' Austin's schoolin's gotta be learnin' 'bout runnin' a ranch, cowboyin', you know, ropin', ridin'—all that sort o' stuff."

Waters frowned. "You gonna set up a right tough life for him from the start." He smiled. "But I'll tell you I've never seen a cowboy who'd swap places with anyone. I agree with what you're sayin', Quint."

Engstrom grinned. "Yeah? Wait'll he's out clearin' ice outta the nostrils of froze-up cows in below-zero weather so's they can breathe, or ridin' into the face of a duststorm, or ridin' night herd in a thunderstorm, then he's gonna wonder if his folks love him at all."

"Men, even though I chose to be a doctor, I can't think of a life that's more free—or healthy—than the one you've chosen." He nodded. "We'll make danged sure he gets proper parents, ones who'll give him schooling, and a shot at a free life."

The Mexican girl came in to feed the baby, and this time the three men hurriedly made their exit without prodding.

They went from Doc's office to Waters's newspaper office. There, they discussed the things they had to do, and when they had to do them. Finally they came up with a schedule for watching the baby around the clock.

Clay and Snake McClure ate enough of the pancakes Ma Mason cooked that she had to go back to the mixing bowl to make more. Finally, Molly shook her head and told Clay to stop eating. "You'll work your poor mother to death, Clay. Besides that, you never had an ounce of fat on you when I married you. You keep on eating like you just have, and I'll have me a man who's fat an' only good for sittin' on the veranda soaking up the sun."

Clay leaned over, put his mouth close to her ear, and whispered. Her face turned a bright red. "If you want to sleep with the crew, try another remark like that."

"Aw hell, Molly, can't you take a little funning?" He patted his stomach. "Reckon I did eat a little too much. I shoulda stopped when I ate the first half of that last cake."

Molly looked at her plate a moment, then, as though afraid to ask, said softly, "When are you and Snake gonna get back with Cole? I think you both should stay here a few days and let your wounds heal."

Snake shook his head. "I figger we gonna be well enough to ride come day after tomorrow."

Her eyes holding more than a little fear, Molly said, "That's not enough time. You'll break those wounds open and they'll start bleedin' again."

Clay put his hand over hers. "Molly, Cole needs us now as much as he ever has. I got a hunch we gonna wrap this thing up in a week or ten days. I figure we gonna have Santana's bunch cut down to size before Cantrell finds out who Soto is, an' if we do, we're goin' after Pa's cattle, bring 'em home, and then go to Presidio to help Quint."

Cole had sent six men to the river with orders to ride it upstream and downstream, find where heavy traffic crossed it leaving a well-worn trail, and report back to him. He looked up from pouring a cup of coffee. The six he'd sent out were riding back into camp.

Fats was the first to dismount. "We found what I reckon is the right place. All of us agree. They's several places where one or two riders been crossin' the river, but we come up on only one place where many riders been crossin'. From the tracks, an' the way the bank's wore off on each side, I figure they been usin' that same crossin' ever since they been raidin' yore pa's ranch."

"The other men agree with you?"

Fats nodded. "Ever' danged one o' us took a look at it an' all come to the same answer. That's where Santana's men been comin' across."

Cole frowned, studied his boot toe a moment, then swept the six men with a glance. "What's the land like along our side of the river?" Are there trees close to the bank, or if no trees, how about dry washes? We need a place to hide our men until the *bandidos* are in solid rifle range. Is there that kind of cover?"

Fats thought a moment, then shook his head. "Not none I'd wantta count on for safety." He pushed his hat to the back of his head, scratched his temple, then looking like he had an idea but hesitated to say it, he looked into Cole's eyes. "Reckon I got another idee if you're agreeable to hearin' it."

"Spit it out, *amigo*."

"Well, back durin' the war, when we couldn't find natural cover, we made our own." He nodded. "You know, we dug holes in the ground, threw the dirt up in front toward where we figured the Yanks wuz comin' from, an' hid behind them piles. I figure with the small chance anybody'd see us we could dig in an' be waitin' fer 'em."

Cole liked that idea. He'd used the same strategy several times during the war. Frowning, he stared at the ground a few moments, then noticed Fats squirming. He nodded. "Good idea, Fats." He looked to the side, his glance sweeping four or five men, and told them to ride to the ranch, get all the shovels they could muster, and get back to the river as soon as possible.

He again looked at Fats. "Send one of the men who rode to the river with you back with them so he can lead them to the crossing. Meanwhile, you take the lead. We'll figure the best place to dig our cover while we wait for the shovels."

A couple of hours later, his men gathered around him, Cole scanned the place Fats had told him about. Not that he'd disagreed with Fats and his men's evaluation, but he wanted to study it for himself. Finally, he nodded. There was no doubt this was the place Santana's men had been using. He rode to the river, urged his horse to the middle of the stream, reined him around, and faced the American side. He sat there a long while, perhaps fifteen or twenty minutes, studying the bank, the tree line, the stretch of beach unbroken by gullies or land swells. There were five blown-down trees lying along the bank, three of them large old cottonwoods, the other two too small for his needs. He rode back to the bank and called his men around.

"Men, when the shovels get here, I want you, Smalley, and you, Bennie, to bank dirt under the trunks of those three large trees. Don't want to chance a bullet passing between the trunk and the ground. I'll assign about three men to each tree. Now, the rest of you walk this bank for about two hundred yards each side, and pick spots that'll give us a good field of fire toward the crossing. We'll dig in at each spot we find."

He grinned. "When you pick a spot to dig a hole, pick it like you're the one who's gonna be risking your tail in it." He tipped his hat back over his forehead to shade his eyes. "All right, let's get at it."

Howley studied every move Cantrell, Engstrom, and Waters made. He could see their faces clearly from his chair by the bank's window. They were about serious business. Their expressions were as solemn as a bereaved widow's. What the hell were they so serious about? He began to sweat. Maybe they had spent all that time together to hatch a plan that would force him to reveal himself.

Maybe they'd figured out who led the gangs that held up the banks, stagecoaches, and Army pay wagons from here to Dodge City.

The longer he gave his imagination free rein, the harder he sweated. His shirt stuck to him. He had three cigars burning at once, and the full quart of whiskey he'd pulled from his desk drawer now held only a water glass of the fiery liquid.

The more he drank, the more convinced he became that he had to get rid of Cantello—soon.

He'd first heard of the Mexican outlaw Santana after having already formulated his plan to take over the B-bar-M. Figuring greed controlled most people, he thought the outlaw might be the tool he needed to break the Mason ranch. But, he had wanted no one, not even the *bandido,* to know who he was. That was when he decided to adopt the name Soto.

He'd figured that any contact with the outlaw would have to be by the written word, but how was he to accomplish that without letting the messenger know his identity? Then, on arriving in Presidio, he'd met the mute. And again banking on human greed, he had sent a small amount of gold with the deaf old man when he sent the first note to Santana. From that time, he'd had Santana hooked.

More than a little drunk, he placed his hat on his head, slipped his hand under his coat to the shoulder holster, and touched the walnut grip of his Colt 45. A flow of confidence flooded his chest and throat. He took a blank piece of paper from his desk and wrote five words on it: "Tonight, same place, same time."

He left the bank. The mute worked for the hostler down at the livery. Howley reflected on his stroke of genius—and luck—when, soon after arriving in Presidio, he'd shown the man a slip of paper with writing on it, and found the man could read only a few words. He knew he had his messenger to contact Santana. This one factor had been a problem he'd spent many worried hours pondering. With a slippery, crooked, drunken grin, he reflected on how brilliantly his mind worked when he set out to solve a problem.

Under the pretense of taking a short ride, he had the mute saddle his horse, at which time he slipped the old man the note and a cartwheel. The dollar disappeared into the dirty trousers of the wrinkled, stooped man, then he finished tightening the girth, held the stirrup for Howley to mount, and nodded. He pointed his thumb to his chest, then gestured toward the river, and made a motion of his right hand sliding past his left.

Howley had received the same gesture before. The man was telling him he'd leave right away to find the *bandido* leader.

When Howley had ridden for only a half hour, he reined his horse back toward the livery. His mouth tasted sour, and his head ached. He needed another drink—then a short *siesta*. Santana would take care of Cantello this time. He would make the bandit a proposition he couldn't turn down.

After having three turns taking care of little Austin, Cantrell realized how attached he was to the small, soft bundle. With that realization came anger. He'd be damned if he'd allow just any old body to take the baby. The boy must have the best. He must be loved. He must have folks who had a reasonably good home.

Now he finished pinning a dry diaper on the little fellow, studied the job he'd done, shook his head, and thought he'd better get Doc to show him how again. Every time he picked Austin up after changing him, the damned diaper slipped down over the chubby little bottom and fell off.

He looked at the child lying in the desk drawer, frowned, and decided to hunt a carpenter when Waters relieved him, which turned out to be only two minutes later.

Cantrell left Austin with the newspaperman, went to the general mercantile store, and asked Happy Knowles, the proprietor, if he knew of a carpenter, one who could make a good piece of furniture.

The store owner frowned through a solid grin. He nodded. "Yeah, reckon I do." He shook his head as though in disbelief and said, "There seems to be a rash of folks hereabouts wantin' furniture built all of a sudden."

"Don't reckon I find that so outlandish, Happy. They's a whole bunch o' new folks movin' into this town. Reckon I must've met six or seven couples in the last two weeks lookin' fer a place to put down roots."

Knowles nodded. "Yeah, s'pose you're right. Town's growin' mighty fast. I notice it in the amount o' business I'm doin'."

After passing the time of day for a few minutes, he told Cantrell where to find the carpenter.

The man to whom Knowles steered him stood at the site of a new home in the early stages of building. He held up a two-by-four with one hand while he pounded a nail to hold it in place. Quint studied the workmanship of the frame house the man was building, decided he was pretty good at his job, and explained what he wanted.

The carpenter cast him a strange look, then said, "Must be a rash of babies comin' all at once around here. This is the third baby bed I been asked to build in the last two days."

The two men discussed the size, the price, and how long it would take before Cantrell could pick it up.

Quint left the carpenter thinking of Austin. A soft, jelly-like feeling invaded his chest and stomach. Well, dammit, a young'un deserved something better than an old desk drawer. Besides, it wouldn't be very long before he'd be too big to stretch out in it. Feeling self-satisfied, he decided to treat himself to a cold beer.

After letting his eyes adjust to the darkened room, he recognized the broad shoulders and slim, long-legged form of Art King leaning against the long shiny bar of the Cattleman's Rest. He walked to King's side and said out of the corner of his mouth, "Anybody in town know you're with the B-bar-M bunch?"

"Nope. Ain't never set eyes on them or them on me."

Cantrell nodded. "Good. We can make like we're old friends from down in Mexico. I'm known by most in this town as Juan Cantello." He looked at the bartender, asked for two beers, then picked them up and walked to a back table. "What you doin' in town?"

"Cole sent me to tell you what we got planned." King took a swallow of his beer then twisted to look Cantrell in the eye. He spiked out the operation Mason had planned, then leaned closer. "Soon's we git them Mexes taken care of, he figures to send a couple o' us in to cover yore back." King's thin-lipped mouth straightened and widened. Cantrell knew from past experience that this was as close as King ever got to a smile. "I tried to tell 'im that I'd seen you in action, an' anybody he sent in would only be in the way."

Quint gave him a half nod. "You're right, Art, but this time I got a idee I'm gonna need men at my back. Whoever Soto is, he wants me dead, out of his way. He's already tried to hire someone to gun me down, but my friend across the border keeps puttin' him off, sayin' he don't know anybody fast enough. Soon though, I figure he's gonna find a back-shooter. Maybe he's already found one."

Art rolled a quirly, stuck it in his mouth, and lit it before he said, "If you're right, you want me to stay here in town an' watch yore back?"

"No. I think Cole's gonna need every gun he can muster down there on the river. You go back to him. I'll play it safe as I know how, then by the time you get back to me, I believe I'll pretty well have Mr. Soto identified." He pulled his hat down tighter, tilted his head back to drain his beer, and signaled for two more.

"What you gonna do when you find out who he is?"

Cantrell grinned. "Well, if I wuz a generous cuss, I'd prob'ly let you help me, but bein' a stingy type I think I'll hog all the fun."

King gave him that straight-lipped smile again, and nodded. "Yes, sir, I knowed all along how tight you wuz with keepin' all the fun to yoreself." He built another cigarette, took a swallow of beer, then lit the quirly. "This time I'm gonna hep you. Remember, I told you my ma wuz a Apache. Reckon I know things to do to a man you ain't never heered 'bout." He looked at Quint's beer. "Want 'nother'n?"

Cantrell shook his head. "Ain't got time. Gotta go see Doc Burns. You got no time either. You better get back to Cole. No tellin' when Santana's gonna decide to pull his all-out raid on the ranch."

King pinched the fire from the end of his quirly, then scrubbed it out in the sawdust on the floor. He stood, cast Quint a dry grin, said for him to watch his back, and left.

Cantrell went to his room, unbuckled his gunbelt, hung it over the bedpost at his head, and stretched out on the bed. Damn! He didn't know whether he could wait for Engstrom to get a reply to the letters they'd spent the night writing. He was certain the description of one of the bandits would match Jarred Phillips, and he had some ideas on the other half of Mr. Soto too.

The longer he lay there thinking, the sleepier he got. His eyes got heavy, drooped—then a light tap sounded at the door. He pulled his Colt, walked to the side of the door, unlatched it, and said, "Come on in."

The same Mexican youth who'd brought him messages before opened the door only wide enough to slip in and close the door behind him. He looked at Cantrell's .44 pointed at his stomach, grinned, shook his head, and looked Quint in the eye. "Ah, *señor,* you are steel ver' careful, *sí*?" Then, obviously not expecting an answer, he said, "*Señor* Santana, he say he has a friend gonna visit weeth heem tonight, same place. He say he want you there like before."

Cantrell nodded, withdrew a cartwheel from his pocket, and handed it to the messenger. "Get yourself a *cervesa,* and tell the *señor* I'll be there. Check the hall before you step out into it."

The youth cracked the door only an inch, peeked out, pulled it wide, and left.

Quint latched the door and went back to bed. He wondered if he might get some idea as to when the big *bandido* would take his forces across the Rio Grande to attack the B-bar-M headquarters. And every time he crossed the river to listen in on one of the Soto/Santana meetings, he wondered if he was walking into a trap.

He took a couple-hour *siesta,* cleaned up, and went to the café. He wasn't hungry, but it was a way to kill time. Engstrom sat at the front table. Cantrell sat with him.

After Quint had learned that no answers to their letters had come in, they talked about Baby Austin throughout the meal.

Cantrell frowned. "You know what, Sheriff? Ever' damned one o' us, includin' Doc, is gettin' too tied up with that baby. It's gonna be pure-dee hell when we have to give him up."

Engstrom, his face somber, stared into his coffee cup. "I done give that a lot o' thought, Cantrell. I'd like to keep 'im myself, but bein' single, an' the business I'm in, it jest flat wouldn't make for bein' a good parent."

Quint nodded. "I give that considerable thought too." He shook his head, then told the sheriff he was going to spy on Santana's visitor that night. He grinned. "Reckon ain't neither one o' us cut out to be longtime daddies." He stood, went to the counter, and paid for his meal. When he left, Engstrom's words, "Be careful," followed him out the door.

Although it was now only a little after sunset, he wouldn't sit in that *jacal* through the heat of the day again. He checked his weapons, stuck a couple sticks of jerky in his shirt pocket, went to the livery, got his horse, and rode to Ojinaga. He put his horse in the stable there, walked into the chaparral, and on to the *jacal*.

17

DESPITE HAVING WAITED until after dark to come, he still
had a three-hour wait before he heard a man approach the
front of the falling-down old adobe. Quint assumed that
the first to arrive was Santana. Now, in a few moments,
Soto would get here, if he followed the same pattern as in
the past. Before he had the thought firmly in mind, the
soft sounds of a horse's hooves broke the stillness.

As before, Santana slid down the outside wall to hunker against it while the rider slipped from the saddle.
Without preamble, Soto's voice cut through the dark
night. He spoke Spanish. "Santana, I have two things I
want you to do. First, and most important, even if you
have to bring your entire outfit to Presidio to get the job
done, I want Juan Cantello disposed of. I don't care how,
when, or where you do it. I want him dead. He's been
poking around in my business.

"He's quite thick with the sheriff, the newspaperman,
and even the young lawyer. And now, I notice him wear-

ing a deputy sheriff's badge. I don't know how he fina-
gled that, but he did."

Sitting in his dark hiding place, Cantrell could picture
the cold smile breaking Santana's lips—no humor, just
the smile not reaching his eyes. In a soft Spanish drawl,
Santana said, "Ah but, *Señor* Soto, I have already given
my men orders to attack the Mason *ranchero*. They are
even now getting their weapons in shape; cleaning, oil-
ing, and firing them for accuracy. They are all out to
destroy everything the Masons own. We've lost a lot of
men, and those of us left want revenge. I'll take care of
Cantello as soon as we have taken care of the rest of your
business—breaking the power of the B-bar-M."

Cantrell held his breath during Santana's speech, hoping he'd say when his men would attack the ranch.

"*Señor,* you said there were two things you wanted me
to do. What is the second one?"

"I'll tell you that little thing in a moment. How bad
would it upset your plans to attack the ranch *after* getting
rid of Cantello?"

"It would appear to my men that I cared more for one
man than I did for those who gave their lives for our main
job. I must not do it your way, *señor.*"

A long silence followed the *bandido*'s words. Cantrell
could picture Soto trying to squelch his anger at running
into an obstacle. Then, apparently accepting Santana's
reason, he said, "It makes no difference. The B-bar-M
has been my objective all along. I don't see that it'll put
a barrier to my plans as long as you bring your men
from Mason's *ranchero* straight to Presidio and get rid
of Cantello."

Despite the smells of dust, animal dung, and snakes in

the *jacal,* Cantrell smiled. It was strange to squat within easy hearing and listen to his own death being plotted.

Again Santana prompted Soto. "What is the second request?"

Soto coughed, then coughed again. "*Amigo,* I've made a friend of the banker in Presidio—well, not a friend exactly, let's call him an acquaintance. He brags to me about how much money is being brought in for some of the large ranches hereabouts to pay their crews. My second goal when I came here was to gain control of the bank.

"To do that I must break the man running it, destroy the townfolks' trust in him—I want you to rob the bank."

"How will I know when there is enough money in that bank to make it worth losing some of my men?"

"That's where I can help. I can pump the information outta him, then I'll send word to you. The mute will bring you a note. All it'll say is the day the most money will be in the vault."

Santana cleared his throat, rolled a quirly, and was apparently groping for a match when Soto spoke up, his voice cold as the wind off a snow-laden mountain. "Do not strike that match, *amigo.* One look at my face and I'll have to kill you."

"I 'ave tell you before." Santana's voice grated harshly in the night, and he now spoke English. "Don't you ever threaten me. *Sí,* I know you 'ave the gun pointed at me, but if you can see into this shadow where I sit, I also 'ave my *pistolo* pointed at you. Besides, my friend, you need me more than I need you, so let's make this a friendly meeting, eh?"

"Yes, my bandit friend," Soto replied, his voice obviously holding a volcanic temper under tight control, "friendly it'll be. You have any questions about the bank job?"

"*Sí.* I wan' to know when the law eez gone home for the night. Too, I weel need dynamite. Can you get theez thing for me?"

"I'll get it. I'll send it across the river with the mute. Okay?"

"*Sí.* I weel do the bank job for you. I keep what I get out of the bank, *sí*?"

"Yes. Clean it out and it's all yours." With those words, Cantrell heard the creak of saddle leather as Soto climbed aboard and settled himself in the hull. The soft clop of the horse's hooves disappeared into the night.

A rasping whisper came through the doorway. "You hear all that, Cantello?"

"Yeah. Reckon *Señor* Soto figures I'm a right dangerous man to ask you to bring yore whole outfit to wipe out one pore defenseless *vaquero*. You gonna try it, *amigo*?"

Santana chuckled. "Don't know. Maybe he geev me whole bunch of *dinero* to keel you. I weel 'ave to think whether I want you in my gang more than the *dinero*."

"You thinkin' 'bout me joinin' up with you?"

"*Sí,* I 'ave theenk about it *mucho*. You ever theenk of riding with a pack?"

"Don't cotton to it much, Santana, but I ain't never had a chance to ride with a bunch like you got. You think 'bout it, an' I'll do the same. Right now I'm headin' back to Presidio. Gonna get me a good night's sleep."

Not long after leaving the big *bandido,* Quint stowed his horse in the livery and walked down the boardwalk toward the hotel. He passed the bank, then turned and retraced his steps. A dim light cast a momentary flash toward the window.

Cantrell frowned. Now, who would be in the bank this time of night? Could someone be trying to beat Santana to the money? He thought about that for a moment, then walked across the street, found a doorway in deep shadow, and stood there hoping to see who came out. The bank had no back door; the only way out was through the front.

He waited about fifteen minutes. The door opened and Howley came out carrying a canvas bag. From the way Howley favored the side he carried the bag on, it looked heavy. Now, what do you suppose Howley was doing in the bank at night? Cantrell decided to follow him and see.

As quiet as smoke, and about as invisible as air, Cantrell shadowed from one doorway to another until he reached the last store. With long strides, Howley stayed ahead of him about a hundred feet. He never looked back but once. Catching the twist of the banker's shoulders, Cantrell dropped to the ground just as Howley's head turned enough to look back.

Cantrell stayed on the ground until the banker opened the door to his house and entered. Soon, a match flared, then a steady light brightened a window toward the rear of the house. Quint stood and ran bent over, stopping only inches below the window from which the light showed.

Even though the shades were drawn, about a two-inch space remained at the bottom. Cantrell peered through the crack. Howley stood on a chair, reached up to a cabinet door high above the cabinet one would use for dishes, utensils, and the like. Looking as though the content of the bag he lifted over his head was quite heavy, he shoved the bag into the space and closed the top door. Then he opened a lower door and withdrew a full bottle of whiskey.

Cantrell had seen all he figured he'd see for one night, but the drink Howley poured for himself decided Cantrell to head for his room, have himself a belt, and go to bed.

Later, sitting on the edge of his bed sipping a drink, Cantrell pondered what he'd seen. There was no reason the banker should have been in the bank at this hour, and even a lesser reason to be carrying a heavy bag from the security of the building. Quint wondered if this was the only time Howley had visited his place of business at night like this, or did he make a habit of it? He decided to keep closer tabs on the man. He'd find out what was in the bag if he had to sneak his way in to take a good look.

Cole threw the last shovel of dirt up in front of his bunker, patted it smooth, wiped sweat from his eyes and off his brow, then scanned the bank upon which his men were also busy digging themselves a place of safety. A safe place for them all—he hoped. So far he'd had men catch lead, but none of them had bought the farm. He hoped they could be that lucky when Santana crossed the Rio Grande.

He'd had them dig their bunkers close to the river to ensure that when the bandits had their horses belly-deep in the water, unable to make a run for the bank, his men could open fire. With the bandits at that disadvantage, it should be like shooting ducks on the water.

The setting sun signaled the approach of suppertime. A few of Cole's men had completed the construction of their trench and now gathered around him. He detailed a couple of them to go a distance from the riverbank, build a fire, and start cooking their evening meal. "Make sure it's a smokeless fire, and shielded from view across the river."

The next morning, as soon as they finished breakfast, Cole had every man gather dead brush and toss it in piles every hundred feet, then he dispatched a couple of men to Presidio to buy four cans of coal oil. "Get back as soon as you can. Don't even stop for a beer. When this is over, I'll take every one of you to town and buy you all the beer you can drink, but first we have a job to do."

He looked at Jaime Martinez. "Got a job for you. Want you to ride like your tail was on fire to the Vasco Fernandez *rancho,* tell 'im what's about to come off here, and see if he's got any men he'll send with you."

When the sun stood directly overhead, the two men he'd sent to Presidio returned with the coal oil. "Good job. Now put one can by each brush pile. The rest of you men find a place to get out of the sun, get as comfortable as you can, and relax. We may be here as long as a week, but when Santana makes his move, I want to be ready."

Cole took his station at the highest point along the top of the bank. He'd spend the day, or days, there. From where he elected to watch, he figured he could see a large body of riders approaching for as much as a mile. Well, he might not see them, but he was sure to see the dust cloud they'd raise. He'd have ample time to get his men in their bunkers. At night he'd put out a couple of men afoot on the other side of the river. At the sound of horses, they could get back to him in time also. He settled down to wait. He stretched his mouth into a grim smile. Hell, this wasn't so different from the Army, where "hurry up and wait" was a way of life.

• • •

When the day came that the carpenter said he'd have the crib ready, Cantrell camped on his doorstep soon after daylight. Listening to the rattle of pans from the kitchen reminded him he'd not eaten breakfast. He shrugged. He'd have breakfast after he took the crib to Doc's office. Then came the smell of fresh coffee brewing, the pungent aroma of bacon, and the sizzling of eggs frying. His stomach growled. He wished he'd gone to the café first.

Before he could think on it further, the front door opened and the carpenter stuck his head out. He grinned. "Come on in. I fixed enough for us both soon's I seen you sittin' out here. Knowed you'd be hungry 'nuff to eat the south end of a northbound skunk. Come on in. I already got you a cup o' coffee poured."

Cantrell felt like a little boy caught snitching one of his mother's fresh-baked biscuits. He stood and grinned, knowing he must look like a fool, and stepped up on the porch.

He and the man ate breakfast. Quint thought it was as good as any he'd ever eaten, then put that thought down to big-time hunger. About through eating, the carpenter stood, went to the next room, then reappeared carrying the crib.

He put it on the floor at Quint's side and stood there like a child waiting to be praised for a job well done. Then he looked into Cantrell's eyes. "You like it? Is it what you had in mind?"

Quint's gaze took in every inch of it, sanded smooth, all joints fit as though part of the next board—it was the job of an artist. And to top it all off, a mattress of blue denim, stuffed with fresh hay, rested in its bottom.

"Why, man, I didn't expect anything like this. Didn't

figure they wuz anybody this side o' Austin or SanTone who could do this kind o' work. Fact is, I plumb fergot 'bout it needin' a mattress. How much I owe you?"

The man shuffled his feet, frowned, then looked hopefully at Cantrell. "Well, we agreed on five dollars." He took a swallow of coffee, looked at the crib, then at Quint. "If you're thinking I charged too much, even though I done you as good a job as I know how, reckon I could lower the price 'bout a dollar."

Cantrell stared from the crib to the carpenter. "Tell you a little story. I hired a man once, a cowboy. We agreed I'd pay 'im thirty an' found. Inside o' two days I knowed I'd hired me a top hand for regular cowboy's wages. I also knowed it wasn't right to get that kind o' work for what I wuz payin' 'im. I raised his wages right then. That's what I'm gonna do with you. Gonna give you twelve dollars for that there crib, an' figure I got the best o' the bargain." He grinned. " 'Sides that, I figure that breakfast saved my life. I wuz starvin'."

Despite the man's protests that they'd agreed on five dollars, Quint pressed the twelve dollars on him, shouldered Austin's little bed, and headed for Doc's office.

It took only a few moments for Doc to make up the crib and shift Austin to it. The baby lay there, both arms and legs churning the air, and Cantrell would've sworn the chubby little face was covered in a satisfied smile.

They'd hardly gotten Austin settled in his new bed when the door rattled, opened, and Engstrom trudged in—a crib hanging from one shoulder. The first thing his eyes settled on was Austin and the baby bed. "Well, dammit. Figgered I wuz the only one with sense enough to know that baby couldn't spend the rest o' his time in a drawer." He eyed Doc, then Cantrell. "Who done it?"

Quint looked at the crib the sheriff had put on the floor. It obviously had the same careful workmanship as the one he'd had made. "Reckon we seen the same thing, Engstrom. We knowed the baby couldn't sleep in that drawer much longer." He shook his head. "Shoulda said something to you 'bout what I had in mind."

The door creaked on its hinges, swung open, and Waters came in, panting, carrying a crib on his shoulders. Doc, Engstrom, and Cantrell looked at one another, then broke into gales of laughter. Waters stared from them to the two cribs already sitting there. At first, his mouth dropped wide open, his face flushed a bright red, and he sputtered a couple of times; then his anger obviously cooled. His cheeks quivered, and then his laughter drowned out the other three.

Doc was the first to regain his composure. "Men, I got to make an admission. That boy woulda had four beds, but I couldn't talk Olin, the carpenter, into taking chickens and eggs as payment for it. Seems that's what most of my patients pay me lately. Reckon the only reason I take those things in payment is to save them the embarrassment of admitting they can't afford to give me anything else. Fact is, reckon I'd tend their sicknesses whether they paid me anything or not."

Engstrom stared at the two empty cribs. "What the hell we gonna do with the extra beds?"

Doc smiled. "Tell you men something. If y'all don't mind, I'll see to it there are two more babies who'll sleep in their own bed tonight."

Cantrell looked at Engstrom and Waters. "Them beds ain't mine to give, but I figure Doc's got a right smart idea. Fact is, that carpenter feller Olin seemed like a man who could use a few extra cartwheels to jingle in his pocket. If Doc knows of any more babies who need a bed, I'm gonna order a couple more just like he made for us."

Engstrom looked Doc in the eye. "How many more beds you need, Doc?"

Doc Burns held his hand out, fingers widespread, and ticked off on each finger: "Little Jimmy, Sarah, Mary, Frank, and Jedediah." He frowned, held his other hand out to start counting, shook his head, and said, "Reckon that's all. Five beds, three counting these two."

Waters looked at Engstrom. "Cantrell's gonna buy two more, I'll get the other one." He grinned. "The city fathers don't pay you enough to take money outta your pocket at the rate we're spendin' it."

Engstrom smiled, nodded, and said, "Thanks, men. It would just about drag my last dollar outta the bottom of my pocket to buy another."

They all agreed the sheriff had done his share. Then they stood around Austin's new bed and did the things grown men foolishly do when around a chubby baby— ooohd, aaahd, and made silly cooing sounds. They didn't think they were foolish at all, but there were many men west of the Mississippi who, if you told them the sounds and acts were those of Quinton Cantrell and Bart Engstrom, would have split their side laughing—and then called you a liar.

When Engstrom left, Cantrell went with him. "Need to talk to you, Sheriff."

Engstrom nodded. "Go ahead. What's on yore mind?"

Cantrell pushed his hat to the back of his head, thought a minute, then flipped a thumb toward the sheriff's office. "Let's talk in there. I'll make a pot o' coffee. You got enough grounds till I can get to the store an' replace what I done drank up?"

"Don't worry 'bout it. I got enough to last me another week."

They went into the darkened office, and even though it was almost seven o'clock, they lit a lantern. Engstrom's office was on the west side of the building and didn't catch the morning sunlight until about nine. Cantrell went about making a pot of fresh coffee while the sheriff packed his pipe and lit it.

Soon, they sat at the scarred old desk, sipped their coffee, and smoked. After they had finished one cup each, Engstrom stood, poured them another cup, then asked, "What you got to tell me, Cantrell?"

Quint frowned. "Well, gotta say it's maybe got me a little worried. Last night I listened in on a conversation, where I was the one spoken of much of the time. Seems I'm beginnin' to worry this here Soto so much he's askin' Santana to bring his whole bunch to town. Gonna scatter 'em around such that they can get me from in front or behind, whichever works best for them."

"Why's Soto figurin' you're such a thorn?"

Cantrell took a sip of his coffee, blew through pursed lips to cool his mouth, then said, "Gettin' to that. Seems he's been watchin' me. Seen me spendin' a bunch o' time with you, an' he's seen me at Waters's newspaper buildin' a pretty good bit. Sounds like he thinks we're 'bout to uncover who he is, an' don't want that to happen 'cause it'll tear up all he's been tryin' to get for himself around here: Pa Mason's ranch, as well as some business he's staked out for himself."

"You shoulda shot 'im right then."

Cantrell shook his head. "Man, you don't know how close I've come to doin' that several times, but it jest flat wouldn't be the smartest thing I ever did. I figure if we wait for him we can get Santana an' him in the same trap. 'Sides that, when we start gettin' answers to our letters, I figure we gonna know exactly who Soto is—then I'll take 'im. But in the meanwhile, if Santana takes him up on killin' me, I ain't got a way in hell of protectin' myself from every direction."

"What about Cole and Clay?"

Cantrell nodded. "Yeah, they'd side me in a minute, but I already told Cole not to leave the ranch unguarded. Told 'im if he'd taken care of Santana's bunch, then, an' only then, to come to town to help me." He grinned, knowing it showed no humor. "An' gonna tell you somethin' else 'fore you suggest it, I ain't gonna let you side me. Ain't gonna get you killed along with me."

"Not gonna let you do this alone, Quint."

Cantrell shook his head. "That's not the way to play it. I'd helluva lot rather have you sittin' on one of these roofs around here, with a Winchester forty-four overlookin' the street, than to have you at my side. You could help me a lot more that way."

"That's the way we'll play the hand then."

"If Cole can take care of Santana at the ranch, it may not ever come to a showdown." Cantrell's face hardened. "But, despite that, we still don't know who Soto is."

Despite the late hours Howley had kept the night before, he sat at his desk early the next morning. He watched Engstrom and Cantrell come from the doctor's office, cross the street, and go in the sheriff's office. A hot flush invaded his chest; his throat swelled. He pushed his anger aside. A thin smile stretched his lips. He'd have to put up with that meddlesome bastard only a little while longer. Then he'd call the shots for this whole damned town. After

Cantello, he'd make an accident happen to that sheriff—maybe the newspaperman too. Then his thoughts went to the night before.

He'd moved a good bit of the gold coin from his vault, but the way he had it planned, it'd take another day or two to take most of it out—leave only enough to do each day's business.

He allowed himself a self-satisfied smile, and even though it was early in the morning, he poured himself a stiff shot of bourbon, lit a cigar, and estimated the small amount of cash, all paper money, Santana would find in the bank when he blew the vault. No one would ever know but what the big outlaw had taken all the town's deposits. He was certain he could convince the *bandido* leader that the Army, or several ranchers, had pulled out large amounts to meet their payroll. And the beautiful part of it was that Benito Santana could go to no one to prove differently. Then he began to plot how he could expand the B-bar-M to the Mexican side of the border. Get rid of Santana, move onto his land holdings down there, and he'd have the largest ranch he'd heard tell of. He'd be a cattle king.

18

COLE HAD SENT word back for Brad Mason and the women to keep sentries posted day and night for fear Santana might come from another route. But Ma insisted the wives come to the house for breakfast each morning even though they all seemed not to care whether they ate or not.

Despite not feeling well, they all did as Ma wished. Elena drank a little of her coffee, felt nauseous, and left the table to go to her room for a few moments until her stomach settled down. When she came back, Laura had left the table, then Molly followed closely behind. Once they felt better, they picked up their weapons and left to take their turn on watch.

Ma had studied them one by one. The poor dears were just miserable without their husbands.

She stood and poured her husband a hot cup of coffee. "Mr. Mason, I wish you'd convince those girls to stay here at the house. You have enough men to man the wall without them, and don't any of them feel all that well.

Reckon if you were out yonder in the chaparral day in and day out, with the chance of getting shot any minute, I'd feel the same way."

"Ma, I done tried hard as any man could to get them to stay here. They jest flat tell me it's their husbands out yonder fightin' for us, an' the least they can do is help out with the gun loadin' an shootin' here." He shook his head. "Ain't no way I can get 'em to stay here in the house with you."

"Well, Mr. Mason, I'm tellin' you right now, I'm downright worried 'bout the whole kit an' caboodle of 'em. It isn't right for young women to have to do without their men." She smiled at him. "For that matter, it's not right for an old woman like me to have to do without her man."

Brad took her hand in his. "Ma, first place, you ain't old; second place, I reckon you're still the most handsome woman in these parts, an' if they wuz anybody gonna git the achin' in their bodies, or hearts, I reckon it'd be me. Don't think I could get along without you lying in bed beside me. Jest knowin' all I gotta do is reach out to find you, touch you, gives me a right warm feelin'." He sipped his coffee, placed it in front of him, and raised his eyes to stare at her. "Don't reckon I tell you often enough, Ma, but I figure havin' you for my wife makes me the luckiest man alive."

Ma blushed. "Mr. Mason, I reckon sayin' those pretty things isn't necessary 'tween us after all these years. Reckon they're words we both know without sayin' them." She smiled. "But I'm gonna tell you right now, hearin' you say them makes me feel all mushy inside like I did when you stole your first kiss from me."

He turned loose her hand, stood, walked around the

table, pulled her to her feet, put his arms around her, and soundly kissed her until she pushed him from her. "Mr. Mason, what will the girls think if they should come in here right now?"

"Well, heavens to Betsy, Ma, they'd prob'ly turn right around and leave us to have our fun in private."

She walked to the other side of the table from him. "And *in private* is where we're gonna keep it, Mr. Mason." She busied herself picking up the dirty dishes, putting them in the dishpan, and looked at him. "You can pick up that dish towel an' make yourself useful."

Jaime Martinez had brought Vasco Fernandez Cole's message and then left, saying he better get back to the river in case he was needed. Fernandez called his foreman and told him to have the men gather. Then he sent one of his men to each of the three nearest *ranchos* with word that the big showdown with Santana was imminent, informing them where it would take place, and asking them to send any men they could spare.

By then, every man who wasn't out about the *ranchero* on an assigned job had gathered around Fernandez. He looked each of them in the eye, then frowned. "*Hombres*, we have suffered long at the hands of Benito Santana. I have been asked to help fight him, in a fight I believe will rid us of the snake." He pushed a small rock around with the toe of his boot, then again looked at each of them. "I know I'm not paying any of you to fight—but I'm asking that you do it for me this once.

"The *Señor* Cole Mason, most of you know him from the time he and *Señor* Quinton Cantrell spent with us when they were young, wild *vaqueros*. Well, he has come home to try to save his father's *rancho* from Santana, and

I'm honest with you when I say he will save ours for us at the same time. Santana has rustled us blind. The *Señor* Mason has asked for my help, and I'm asking you for yours. How many of you will ride with me this day?"

As one, they stepped forward. His foreman smiled. "*Señor,* it seems that you cannot go without all of us." He turned to the men. "*Vaqueros, vamanos,* saddle your *caballos,* check your rifles, we leave with the *señor* in ten minutes."

Fernandez watched his men, a great swelling in his throat and warmth in his chest. Few of these men were young. Most had ridden for his father before him, and were as faithful to him as they had been to his father.

They all knew he had lost too many cattle to the *bandido* to have money to pay fighting wages. He suspected they knew when he gave them their wages at the end of each month that he'd had to sell off some of his breeding stock in order to do so, and he knew that many of them would refuse to be paid but for the embarrassment it would cause him.

His men were ready to ride, and had used only eight of the ten minutes the foreman allowed. He took his place at their head, raised his hand, and swept it forward. "We ride, *amigos.*"

Late afternoon of the day Fernandez and his men left their *rancho,* Engstrom yelled across the street at Cantrell, "Hey, come on over. I have something to show you."

Quint had his mouth all set for a cold beer, but he changed course, stepped off the boardwalk, and angled across the trail to Engstrom. "Jest gonna have a beer. What's so all-fired important?"

"You'll be happy to wait for your beer when I show

you what I just got in the mail." He took Cantrell's arm and steered him to his office.

Inside, Engstrom went straight for his desk, without first pouring a cup of coffee, which in itself told Quint how excited the sheriff was about what he had in hand. Cantrell was just as happy he'd not been invited for a cup of the mud he smelled simmering on the stove. It was probably the same pot that he'd made the morning before. It smelled like dirty socks.

The sheriff picked up a letter from his desk and handed it to Cantrell. The tall cowboy lifted the flap and removed a single sheet of paper. After reading it, he looked up into Engstrom's eyes. "One letter ain't gonna make the cheese more bindin', Engstrom. We need several more like this. Then I'm gonna take care o' the bastard."

Engstrom nodded. "Yeah, one letter don't do it, but s'pose we get four or five like this one, an' I bet we do?"

Cantrell grinned. "Reckon that bein' the case, I'm gonna open the ball." He smiled. "Sheriff, when we get to the bottom of all this, you're gonna be the biggest hero this town ever had."

"Aw hell, Cantrell, that ain't true. You're the one who dug up all the stuff we needed to try and find out who he is."

Quint shook his head. "No. We gonna leave me outta this 'cause when we get Brad Mason's cows back on his range, I'm leavin' for my home grass. You gonna still be here, gonna maybe run for sheriff again, an' you gonna win, 'cause you gonna be the one who keeps the bank from goin' broke."

Engstrom frowned. "What you mean, 'keep the bank from goin' broke'?"

Cantrell shook his head. "Ain't gonna say any more

right now. Gotta find out for sure, then I'll tell you." He slapped the letter against his palm. "This's reason to celebrate though. I know you don't drink on duty, but I'm buyin', an' I ain't never seen you turn down a free beer. C'mon."

Howley watched from his office window. That damned gunfighter and the sheriff were damned near inseparable. There they went from Engstrom's office across to the saloon. Howley frowned. He'd have to bring the sheriff's habit of drinking on duty to the city council's attention. They wouldn't like that. He nodded to himself. Yes, he'd do that.

At five o'clock he stood by the door as always, and bid the last of his employees good night. As soon as they cleared the door, he closed it and clicked the lock into place.

He went to his desk and removed the bag he'd brought in when he came to work that morning. He pulled the shades and headed toward the vault. Then he changed his mind, and went to the books where transactions were recorded each day. He flipped through the pages, going back two months to ensure he took in payday for the ranches and other businesses. He studied the figures a few minutes, nodded, and went back to the vault. He wanted to make sure he left enough behind to perform business normally.

He filled the bag with as much gold coin as he could heft comfortably, put it on the floor behind his desk, poured himself a drink, lit a cigar, and sat back, his feet on the desk. He'd wait until after the saloons closed before taking the bag to his home.

When he took over the B-bar-M, and reestablished the

bank as a solid, secure institution, then he'd build a larger home, one befitting the town's leading citizen. He'd picked out the spot on which he'd build, a location visible from the main street. People had to be reminded every minute of the day and night who lived there, who held their lives in the palm of his hand—loans and high interest would keep them under his thumb.

He finished his drink and poured another while fighting off the urge to lift the shade and take a look along the street. He could picture in his mind the gunfighter and sheriff going into each saloon, bullying the customers with their presence for a few moments, then moving on to another watering hole. He smiled to himself. That would change. Soon the Mexican gunslinger would be dead, and the sheriff would be run out of town for allowing the bank to be robbed of the citizen's savings.

He knocked back his drink, stood to pour another, looked at the bottle, and shook his head. Wouldn't do to drink too much during such a time. He might get careless. Nope. He'd wait for the drinks until after he'd won the big pot. Why not? He figured he had a royal flush to the town's two pair.

Cantrell helped Engstrom make the rounds of potential trouble spots, broke up two fistfights before they could turn into gunfights, went back to the sheriff's office, had a cup of coffee, told Engstrom good night, and left to take up his station across from the bank.

He couldn't see into Howley's office—the shades were drawn—but the thin seam of light at each edge of the shades told him a lantern burned within. He was satisfied Howley sat inside, maybe having a drink, waiting for the town to quiet down after the saloons closed.

First the tinkling of the tin-panny piano quieted, then windows darkened. The sound of wood hitting against wood said doors were being closed. It wouldn't be long now.

Cantrell fidgeted. He waited another hour; still no Howley. Another half hour, and he'd about decided the banker wasn't coming out. Why the hell was he spending so much time after the town went quiet? Several times he halfway decided to give it up for the night, then figured a few more minutes wouldn't hurt. After all, he'd already wrecked hell out of a good night's sleep.

Inside the bank, Howley sat slumped in his chair, head lolling to the side, his nose twitching with each snore. Then he snorted so loud as to wake himself. He stirred and stared about the room, surprised to find himself still in his office. He pulled his large gold watch from his watch pocket and stared at its face—three o'clock. Damn, those two drinks had relaxed him too much. He stood, picked up the bag, straining with the weight of it, snuffed the lantern, went to the door, pulled it open a crack, and scanned the street. Not a soul moved about. He opened the door, stepped out, and then locked it.

Cantrell, standing in the shadows across the street, had made up his mind to give the banker five more minutes before going to his room and getting some sleep. With that thought, the sliver of light at the bank's window went dark. Tiredness abruptly slipped from the tall cowboy's body. All his senses came alive, alert to everything about him.

Howley stepped cautiously from the boardwalk, looked each direction of the street, and set out toward his house. Cantrell followed, a part of the night's still darkness. Howley kept to the same routine as the night before. He again stood on a chair to push the bag into the high cupboard, stepped down, put the chair back to the table, and turned toward his bedroom, stripping his necktie from his collar as he walked.

Cantrell had seen what he'd thought he'd see. He figured to do this every night until Howley stopped making the midnight raids on his own vault. Quint felt certain that was exactly what he was doing. He ghosted away from Howley's as quietly as he'd come to it.

A huge grin filled his insides. He could picture Santana blowing hell out of the vault and getting only a couple thousand dollars. That Mexican *bandido* would be mad enough to bite railroad spikes.

Cantrell sighed, and stretched and flexed his shoulders. He was tired, and for now, he figured he'd earned a good night's sleep. He headed for his room.

From his perch atop the riverbank, Cole watched a thin spiral of dust approaching from the direction he'd sent Jaime Martinez. He narrowed his eyelids against the bright sun. One rider. That would be Martinez.

In only minutes Jaime forded the river and rode to Cole. "The *Señor* Fernandez is this minute gathering the *vaqueros* from other ranches. He will be here to join us by sundown."

Cole nodded. "Good work, Jaime. We got some hot food cookin' over the brow of the bank a ways. Go get yourself a plate. I'll be there in a minute. Gonna have Clay stand watch up here for a while."

Cole looked in the direction of Clay's bunker and spotted him lying on his stomach in it, looking toward the river. He cupped hands to mouth and yelled, "Hey, little brother, I need you to spell me up here a mite. Gonna feed the inner man."

In only a moment, Clay sauntered up, sweat streaming down his face, one rivulet tracing the scar that ran from the corner of his eye to the side of his mouth. He grinned. "Hi, big brother. Figured you wuz gonna feed yoreself 'fore you let me eat. Go on. I'll keep the bogeyman off'n us while you stuff yore gut."

Cole studied his brother a moment. Except for the scar they'd pass for identical twins. "Clay, I was thinking to let you eat before me, but since you insist on using the worst grammar this side o' hell, I'm gonna eat first. Ma would be downright shamed to hear the way you talk, considering how much time she spent trying to teach you and Quint proper grammar."

"Aw hell, Cole, jest cause that Army school at West Point hammered them fancy words through that thick skull o' yore'n, you done got Ma to diggin' at me agin' 'bout the way me an' Cantrell talk. An' hell, I only been home a short while."

Cole chuckled. "Go on an' eat, little brother. I'll wait."

Clay grinned. "Naw, you go on. I jest wanted to give you a bunch o' guff. Don't figure to miss a chance when I get one. Know damned well you ain't gonna." He walked to Cole's vantage point, leaned his Winchester against his side, and swept the area from which he figured Santana would come. Cole clapped him on the shoulder, then headed for the stew pot.

By the time Cole ate, and came back, Clay could point in the direction from which Jaime Martinez had ridden earlier and say, "Riders comin'. A whole bunch of 'em." He tried to push out a chuckle, but it came out dry and cracked. "Shore as hell hope that's Fernandez an' his *vaqueros,* but just to be on the safe side, I got the men standin' ready to fire."

Cole nodded. "Good work, little brother."

Another few minutes and Clay knew the riders were Fernandez's *vaqueros.* "Stand easy men. That's Fernandez." He looked from the bunkers to Cole. "Gonna go get myself some of that stew, if you left me any."

Cole grinned. "Yeah, I mighta left a little in the pot. Go ahead."

Clay hadn't disappeared over the brow of the bank before Fernandez led his men into the area. Cole hadn't seen him since he and Cantrell had spent a couple of years riding for the Spanish don's father. He ran down the bank, pulled his old friend from the saddle, pummeled him about the shoulders, then stood back and looked at him. "Vasco, *mi amigo.* The years have been good to you, except for that tinge of gray at your temples, I don't think you've aged a bit."

Fernandez smiled. "And you, my friend, can still throw words out like fresh cow paddies. But, for certain, you haven't changed much, except I think I detect a bit more maturity. You're not the hell-raiser you used to be."

"No, my friend." Cole showed him a more sober side. "I don't think any of us would still be alive if we had continued the way we were as boys." He nodded. "Yeah, I've grown up, and so have you." He looked at Fernandez's men and recognized several of them. After getting reacquainted with those he knew, he looked at the don. "You can see how we've prepared to hit Santana when he and his men have their horses crossing the river. I think if you and your men drop back toward the bank here, and dig your bunkers between and behind those we've dug, we'll make a solid line of fire when the *bandidos* are in good rifle range. We should end Santana's rape of our outfits, and by then Cantrell may have Soto identified and taken care of. Then, my friend, we'll hold a big roundup. Each ranch represented can cut out their cattle, and we'll not be much the worse for the time the *bandidos* terrorized our spreads."

"You say we'll hold a roundup. Do you mean our cattle are still where we can get them back?"

Cole nodded. "*Sí*. Cantrell knows where they are being held, but it is rough country, and it'll take every man we have here to gather them."

"Ah, Cantrell again." Fernandez smiled. "He is *muy hombre*. You two have remained *muy bueno amigos* through the years."

Fernandez's words turned Cole's thoughts to Cantrell, and his brother Clay. "*Sí*, we are still very good friends. Cantrell, my brother Clay, and I have our own ranches now. Clay and Cantrell are in Colorado, and I'm in Northern New Mexico Territory. We're all married, no children—yet."

Fernandez's eyes crinkled at the corners, and his mouth quirked as though about to smile. "Time will take care of that, Cole." He shrugged. "Who knows, perhaps the next time we meet, all three of you will have wee *ninos*."

Cole laughed. "You better tell *mi padre* that. He and Ma been pesterin' us somethin' awful 'bout not givin' them any grandbabies yet." He looked from Fernandez to the *vaqueros*. "You better get your men to digging bunkers for themselves. We have plenty of shovels."

Cantrell had watched Howley for five consecutive nights, and each night the banker had lugged the heavy bag from the bank to his home. Quint wondered that there was that much gold in the small town bank. He wondered if it wasn't time he told Engstrom about the late-night excursions Howley made, and what he suspected the bag contained.

Each night now, when Quint went to his room, he cleaned and oiled his guns, honed his Bowie knife, and again checked his throwing knife for balance. He was riding a set of tight-drawn nerves. The gunfight of his life was imminent, perhaps the *last* gunfight of his life. Every time he thought of it, his scalp tingled, his neck itched as though the hairs on it stood straight out, and his back and neck muscles pulled tight enough to hurt.

He thought back on gunfights he'd had, fights in which he'd had to face more than one man, but never more than three. The Durango gunfight had been the worst. Even then he'd not faced the numbers of men Santana would bring with him. But Cole, Clay, and those at the ranch would most likely cut Santana's numbers down, and Engstrom's station on the roof would also help to even the score.

He wondered that he was letting an impending fight get to him like this. He'd not had Elena during those last gunfights. He'd not had to think of anyone but himself. Now he did have her, and he wanted so desperately for their time together to stretch on into old age.

His thoughts shifted to baby Austin. What would happen to him? He couldn't ask Clay and his new bride to take in a baby. He wouldn't ask Cole either. Even though Cole was his best friend, a man didn't just saddle his friend with a life-long burden.

Burden? Hell, little Austin wouldn't be a burden on anyone. Then he started thinking that perhaps he could talk Elena into letting him raise the baby. Hell, he'd make sure the little one didn't cause her any bother. He'd hire one of the wives on the ranch to act as nursemaid during the day and he'd take care of the little chunk at night. He finally defeated every argument he'd posed. There just wasn't any other way he could be certain a good couple, a caring couple, would get the baby.

Howley looked at his watch: four fifty-five. His employees would be leaving the bank in a few minutes. He went and stood at the door, as was his habit. At five o'clock sharp, the last customer left the bank. When the help had also gone, the banker closed and bolted the door. It was time he visited with his *bandido* friend.

He opened the bottom drawer of his desk and removed six sticks of dynamite and caps. He opened the bag, carefully placed the sticks in its bottom, then sat back and sipped his drink. He was in no hurry. He'd wait until midnight to cross the river. He had another drink, wrote a note, and left the bank. He had to see the mute, then everything would be in place.

Santana, sitting at his usual table against the wall in the back of the *cantina*, read the note the mute brought and flipped him an American silver dollar. He'd meet with *Señor* Soto at midnight—but this time without the gunfighter Cantello listening in.

He had three more jobs to do for Soto, three big jobs: wipe out everyone on the B-bar-M, blow the bank safe, and kill Cantello. He'd already decided the B-bar-M would come first.

He hated to kill Cantello. The *hombre* would make a good addition to his gang. He thought a moment, thought of the money Soto would pay for the big gunfighter to be dead. He shrugged and thought, *What the hell, money is money. I'll take it every time.*

He sat there toying with a *cervesa,* only taking a sip every now and then until it was time to leave for his meeting with his still unknown employer.

He drank the last swallow of his *cervesa,* stood, and left the *cantina.* Less than ten minutes later he hunkered down against the adobe wall of the *jacal.*

He'd not settled himself comfortably before Soto rode his horse to the weed-grown clearing in front of him. Soto swung from the saddle, untied a bag of some sort from behind the cantle, and carefully placed it on the ground in front of him.

Without a greeting of any kind, he said, "You find anybody who knows how to handle dynamite?"

"*Sí, señor,* I have such a man."

"All right. There's dynamite and caps in that bag yonder. Handle it like you would a baby. My friend at the bank tells me there is an Army payroll placed there for safekeeping until the Army payday. And to make it sweeter, he said the ranchers have their money there for safekeeping after a trail drive in which they all took part." He chuckled. "Sounds like everything is working our way."

"*Sí, Señor* Soto, but what will you get from the bank holdup?"

Soto's voice hardened. "That's not a helluva lot of your business. But like I told you before, I want control of the bank, and if it is out of money—I can take it over. Now, when do you plan to do everything I have asked?"

Santana's face turned hot, and bitter bile boiled into his throat. He'd killed men for talking to him in the manner

Soto had. He swallowed his anger. "The B-bar-M first.
Then I ride to Presidio with my men, all of my men, and
we take care of the *Señor* Cantello. While the people are
hiding behind their doors to keep from getting in the way
of the flying bullets, I'll have me and three of my men in
the bank. Then, *vamanos,* we all go across the river at the
same time. Cantello is dead, I have the *dinero,* and you
will have the Mason's *rancho,* and the bank."

Soto nodded. "Sounds slick as a newborn calf. It better
work the way you have it laid out, or you won't see
another payday from me."

Again, Santana fought down his anger. "You do your
part, *Señor* Soto—I'll do mine."

Soto toed the stirrup, looked down at the big outlaw,
and kneed his horse into a gallop.

Santana stayed hunkered against the wall until the
sound of Soto's horse disappeared in the distance. He
didn't feel right about this. He didn't trust Soto, but how
could the man double-cross him? He thought on that a
moment, then decided he'd play the cards the way they
fell.

19

COLE WATCHED THE sky lighten in the east. Soon the sun would be up, and another sweltering day would be upon them. He sipped his cup of coffee. His nerves pulled tight. He nodded, and looked at Fernandez. "Soon's it's good light, let's get our men in their bunkers. Know it's gonna be hot enough to paper hell a mile, an' they gonna sweat bullets 'fore this day is done, but I got a feelin' this is the day Santana's gonna make his last desperate move. He's gotta. His numbers are down to what he's gonna have to have to even think he can take the ranch. When we surprise him here, that should be the end of it." He swallowed the last of his coffee. "Even if he's lucky enough to get away, I don't figure he'll be able to collect another gang of cutthroats. His reputation as a leader will be ruined."

Standing at his side, Fernandez stared toward where he believed the outlaw gang would approach. He nodded. "Think you're right." He chuckled. "I'd like to be close enough to see his face when we open up on him from here." The don nodded. "I believe as you do. He'll think we have to defend the ranch from behind those thick walls. He'll never dream we'd leave it unprotected to fight here beside the river."

Cole grunted. "You're probably gonna get your wish. We wait till they get into the river, you're gonna be able to see more'n their faces, you'll see their eyes."

Fernandez feigned a shudder. "Makes you wonder if we're lettin' them get too close."

Cole, taking him seriously, shook his head. "No. We need their horses in the water. That way they'll not be able to run away fast enough to get out of rifle range before we empty every saddle."

"Okay. What's the signal for us to begin firing?"

Cole had already told his men to wait until he fired, then to open up with everything they had. He wanted no prisoners. He told Fernandez what his orders were. "Hate to do it that way, *amigo;* some of those men have families." He shook his head. "But I can't think of any other way we'll be rid of their kind for good."

"I know your feelings, my good friend. Those of us on my side of the river have long suffered at their hands. It is time we take action."

Cole tossed any remaining grounds from his cup. "Okay, let's get the men settled down. No movement of any kind. If anyone has to relieve himself, he'll do so right in his bunker. It might be the difference between living and dying."

The sun moved higher into the heavens, and with each minute the slight breeze seared the men as though blown from a blast furnace. To move to a more comfortable spot meant having the sunbaked earth burn through their clothes. They held their positions, covering rifle barrels with parts of their clothing to keep the sun-heated steel barrels cool enough to hold steadily.

Cole pulled his watch out and glanced at it for at least the hundredth time: quarter of ten. Then a glance across the river. A swirl of dust boiled up in the direction from which he expected Santana to ride. He judged the riders to be about a half mile away. His voice was quiet in the hushed expectancy, but loud enough to carry to the farthest man. "Steady, men, steady. This'll all be over soon. Take a deep breath before shooting, then when I fire, let 'em have it."

Cole's muscles relaxed. His senses sharpened. It was always like this before a battle—or a gunfight. The jitters, the nervous talk, the loud laughter would wait until it was all over.

The horses drew nearer, then the lead rider broke clear of the chaparral on each side of the well-worn trail. Santana rode at the head. When only a few feet short of the water, he held up his hand and signaled his men around him. Damn! Cole wondered if something had spooked the big outlaw.

Santana was obviously talking to those around him, then he held up his hand for all to see and swept it forward. They gathered around and rode in a bunch into the muddy stream. Cole, his eyelids slitted against the bright sunlight, felt like celebrating. Santana's men riding clustered in the middle of the river was more than he could have hoped for.

Before the lead riders made the north bank, every one of the outlaw's band had entered the stream. Cole leveled his Winchester, aimed, and fired. A rider went down. Before he could jack another shell into the chamber, the bunkers erupted with a steady crack of rifle fire.

The muddy waters of the Rio Grande melded the red gore spilling into it to a dirty orange. Men screamed. Some pitched from their saddles to sink below waters churned to a froth by the frantic horses; others fell into the water and tried to swim, only to catch a bullet from the second volley fired by their still unseen enemy. Those remaining on their horses tried to bring their rifles to bear on an enemy they could not see—and while trying, they died. The stench of gunsmoke caused those in the bunkers to cough. The smell burned the backs of their throats.

Cole drew his sights on the man he wanted most— Santana. The man was magnificent. He tried to shield those that he could with his body while urging them to retreat, to get back on the Mexican side. But there were only four left for him to direct, and one of them died before reaching the bank. Cole fired, and missed. The moment Cole squeezed the trigger, Santana leaned from his saddle and grabbed a man by the shirt collar to drag him from the water. His act of mercy saved the man. He now had only three men of the thirty he'd entered the river with. Riding behind them, he cursed, yelled, and waved his arms for the three to get into the chaparral. They disappeared from Cole's view. As he'd told the men—the killing, suffering, yelling had lasted only a few minutes.

The Mason and Fenandez crews began to spill from their bunkers, yelling, clapping one another on the shoulder, and laughing through gunsmoke-caused tears. Cole yelled, "Get the hell back in those holes. Stay there until I make certain they're not hangin' back, hiding in the brush waiting to get a good shot at you."

He wondered how to be sure they'd gone, then did the

only thing he could think of. He stood, and walked along the top of the bank, betting on the chance none of the remaining outlaws could shoot straight enough to hit him. No shots. They were gone. "All right, men, come on out. We've got a nasty job to do. Dig those holes deeper. We gotta bury those we killed."

Cole searched the riverbank for Fernandez, spotted him, and headed that way. He passed Clay on the way, clapped him on the shoulder, looked into his eyes, smiled, and nodded. He didn't have to say anything. His little brother would know how he felt about seeing him. He told Martinez to take a count, see if any of their men were hurt.

He walked up to his longtime friend Fernandez, hand extended. "It's over, *mi amigo*. Did you lose anyone?"

"No. One got hit in the shoulder, another creased along the ribs." He sighed. "We were lucky."

"Not luck, Vasco. Surprise was on our side, and by the time they figured we were firing from bunkers, it was too late. We had 'em whipped."

He looked the length of where the battle had taken place. Shovels flashed in the sunlight, deepening the holes that had saved the lives of good, honest cowpunchers. Those holes now became graves. He looked at Fernandez. "Can you have your men ready for roundup in two days?"

Fernandez nodded. "We are ready now, *señor,* if you are."

"No. I want to get back to the ranch, let them know we are all right. Let them know it is over and we can get on with our lives. I've got to see what's happening in Presidio. Cantrell's there, and if he's found who Manuel Soto is, he may need help."

Fernandez chuckled. "Unless Cantrell's changed, *muy mucho,* it'll be Soto who needs help."

Cole smiled. "Reckon I just want to be there to see what he does."

Fernandez nodded. "Good. I'll go with you, but first I'll send my people back to my *ranchero.* They can tell *mi esposa* that I am all right, then they can ready the chuck wagon for the roundup, and get their own gear in shape." While talking, he loaded fresh shells into his rifle. "As I said, we'll use my chuck wagon. It is only a small thing I can do for you. You've given us back our lives."

Cole shrugged off the thanks. "*De nada,* you'd do the same for me. Come, we'll go to Pa's ranch. You can meet the wives. Then we'll head for Presidio."

Cantrell leaned against the wall of the stage station. He'd taken to meeting every stage that came in, watching the mail sacks tossed to the ground, and following the postmaster into the office while he sorted it.

The postmaster, Buck Lydle, glanced up while he stuck another letter into a cubbyhole. "Cantello, you an' Engstrom must have a secret lover staked out somewhere the way y'all sweat out the mail when it comes in."

"You find us a bunch o' letters or we'll stake *you* out." Even while he spoke, Lydle tossed two letters to the counter, then another, and another, until Quint held seven envelopes in his big hand. He flipped through them, grinned, and said, "Reckon you missed gittin' staked out this time. These are some o' them me an' Engstrom been expectin' " He stepped toward the door, and twisted to look over his shoulder. "Thanks, Lydle. Know you worked extra to git me these 'fore anybody else come for theirs."

Only a minute or two later he sat in the sheriff's office, tossed three of the envelopes to Engstrom, and slit the flap on one of those he held. He scanned the page, then slowly read each word, allowing a smile to break his lips. Finished, he looked at the sheriff. "If most o' these letters follow the way this one done, I'll tell you right now I know for sure who Manuel Soto is. An' I don't figure we need to wait fer answers to the rest o' them letters 'fore I move on him."

" 'Fore *you* move on 'im? How 'bout me?"

Cantrell frowned. "Tell you for a fact, Bart. All I got is a hunch, but it's a strong one. I figure Cole's done had his fight with Santana—an' whipped 'im."

He stopped to pack and light his pipe, then stabbed Engstrom with a penetrating stare. "If Santana got away, he's gonna come here lookin' for me. If you can keep that big outlaw off'n my back while I take care of Soto, you gonna have your hands full without tryin' to give me any help."

"You think many of his gang will escape Cole's men?"

Quint shook his head. "Don't know. Fact is, if we can surprise Santana—take him without us havin' to pull iron, that's what I wanna do. I want to talk to him. Won't take but a few minutes. I think I can tell 'im somethin' that'll make him want Soto as much as you an' me do. Then he's gonna be so mad our job's gonna be to keep 'im from killin' the slimy bastard."

"You figure Soto's gonna let us take 'im alive?"

Cantrell shook his head. "Don't know." His face sober, he said, "This one letter I read says he's faster'n a rat-tlesnake. I might have to kill 'im." He shrugged. "At first I figured I wanted 'im alive so's I could sweat out where he's got the loot he stole. I believe now I know where it all is. If I do, it ain't gonna make no difference if I kill 'im deader'n a outhouse rat."

"Where you figure he's got it stashed?"

"Okay, Bart, here it is." He started at the beginning even though some of it Engstrom already knew. Then he told him about watching Howley take heavy bags of something from the bank over a period of several nights. He told him about Soto setting Santana up to rob the bank, and furnishing him with the dynamite to do it.

A glimmer of understanding showed in Engstrom's eyes. "Yeah, Quint, go on, but I think you've already given me the answers."

Cantrell leaned across the desk. "Sheriff, Nat Howley—Charley Butts, or whatever he'll be callin' himself tomorrow—is Soto. I don't need them other letters to convince me o' that, but the one letter I've read describes him right down to his liking for expensive cigars. It also says he's fast, maybe the fastest man west of the Mississippi."

Engstrom smiled. "Yeah, an' from where I'm sittin', I could spit on the only other man I've heard described that same way. You gonna fight 'im, Quint?"

Cantrell shook his head. "Don't want to, but I got a hunch he's gonna force me to. He ain't gonna take kindly to losin' all that gold because of my snoopin'."

He took another swallow of coffee. "I expected you to ask me why he'd want Santana to rob his bank." He leaned back and grinned. "But I reckon an old law dog like you has done figured it out."

Engstrom nodded. "Yep. You've told me Howley's done stripped his vault of all but probably just enough to do his daily business with. Santana'll rob the bank, get a couple of thousand dollars. Howley'll squall that he wuz robbed of many thousands. The gold you saw him takin' to his house at night was probably the life's savings of the people around here, plus what he stole in them robberies on the way down from Dodge.

"It costs him a couple thousand to make maybe half a million, an' if Santana wants to come huntin' him—well, like we've heard, he's fast with his gun. He figures he can kill Santana, start the bank up again, take over the B-bar-M, an' be sittin' pretty with nobody suspectin' him of anything."

Cantrell grinned. "Don't know why I wuz worried 'bout tellin' you what I figured wuz goin' on. Reckon I wuz mighty slow in comin' up with the answer, myself."

"Hell no, Quint, you solved this an' laid it in my lap."

Cantrell shook his head. "Ain't laid nothin' there yet. We gotta catch Howley doin' what we figure he's gonna do." He packed his pipe, struck a match, and let it burn down to his fingertips while he thought about their problem. He slung the match to the floor, sucked on his two burned fingers, then asked, "If I can get Santana to tell us what he wuz promised, would you be willin' to let him ride back across the Rio Grande, free of any charges?"

Engstrom leaned back, stared at the ceiling a moment, then nodded. "He gives us Howley, he can ride any damned where he wants."

"Good, but 'fore you let him ride off, I want him held for about a week."

"Why?"

Cantrell grinned. "Figure it'll take 'bout that long to round up them cattle he's been stealin', and to drive 'em back to home range. But even though he hired out to kill me, I figure he and I got to where if things wuz different we coulda been *amigos bueno*. You see, if I get a chance to talk to him before we go to the bank, I figure to tell 'im just what we gonna do. Too, he paid me half of ten thousand dollars to find out who Soto is. He wuz gonna give me the other half when I told him the answer, an' proved it. I'm gonna give 'im his five thousand back, and tell 'im to forget the rest." He glanced at the old Regulator Clock behind the sheriff's desk—almost two o'clock.

"I figure Cole's had 'bout enough time to get to the ranch, tell our womenfolk about the fight, and head for here." He stood. "Reckon he'll be ridin' in with the crew anytime now. You still need to take your place on the roof. I'm gonna try to get behind that big *bandido* bastard 'fore he can decide to carry out the robbery. If he knows we got 'im in a cross fire, I figure he'll talk before fightin'."

Engstrom walked to the door with him. "You be careful, boy. I'll be where we agreed on. If you see Cole, have him place his men in stores on each side o' the street."

Cantrell headed for the livery, figuring Santana would ride there and leave one of his men to hold the horses, while he and one or two others took care of blowing the vault. Cantrell slipped into the back stall and waited.

The smells of the livery were of hay and horse droppings, odors to which Cantrell was accustomed. He had waited in the dark, hot confines of the stall about fifteen minutes when the sound of several horses came to the back of the stable. The door opened and riders led their ponies into the darkened runway.

Cantrell eased his Colt from its holster, held his breath, and waited to hear the *bandido* give his men some orders. Instead, he heard Cole. "You men, scatter up and down the street, step into whatever businesses there are, and watch for Santana."

Cantrell had heard enough. "Cole, it's me, Cantrell.

Keep your men here a minute. I got somethin' to say to 'em." He stood and walked from the stall. "I'm gonna ask you how the fight at the river came out after a while, but first we got business to take care of here."

"Yeah, but I'm gonna tell you anyway. We killed all but four of Santana's men—"

Cantrell cut him off. "Figured you'd get most of 'em. Now what's left'll be comin' here to get me. I don't want none o' you buttin' in to my fight. I'm gonna try to get behind that big *bandido,* get a gun on 'im, an' do a little talkin'. If you figure you can get the three men with him under yore guns, do it. It'll give me a better chance to talk without havin' no gunfire."

Cole stared at him like he'd lost his mind. "You crazy? That's one of the most dangerous men in Mexico. You can't talk to him."

"Five'll get you ten, I can, an' will, talk to him. I know a few things don't neither one o' you know, an' when I tell 'im, I figure he'll play my game down to the last chip—then I'm lettin' 'im ride back across the border. I don't figure there'll be a shot fired 'less o' course Howley starts the ball. He does, I'm gonna have the last dance."

Cole smiled. "So the banker's Soto." He nodded. "Makes sense." He turned to his men. "All right, don't do any shootin' till Cantrell opens the game. I'll stay inside the forward stall till you get your gun on Santana, Quint."

This time of day, Presidio sweltered under the late afternoon sun, and most people either stayed inside or took a *siesta.* The town lay quiet. The sound of a lone horse stepping through the street's heavy dust broke the stillness. Cantrell waved the men to the side of the runway, out of sight.

The horse passed, the rider looking to neither side.

Howley. Cantrell grinned. "Our friendly banker's gonna make sure he ain't around when Santana hits the bank. He musta seen 'im ridin' in. All right, stand by."

The men melted into the dark stalls on both sides of the runway. In only moments, four riders came through the stable's big double doors, Santana slightly in the lead. They climbed from saddles at the same time. The big *bandido* took the reins of the four horses and handed them to one of his men. "Stay here about ten minutes, then bring the horses to the front of the bank." He raised his arms to untie a package from behind the cantle of his saddle.

"Just keep yore hands busy where they are, Santana. I got my colt pointed straight at yore backbone."

Santana froze. Then, as though asking a friend to have a *cervesa,* he said, "That you, Cantello? Didn't figure it your style to take a man from behind."

"Benito, you know damned well it ain't my style, but I gotta talk, an' I couldn't figure no other way to keep you from shootin' 'fore you talked. Tell your men to rest easy. They got 'bout fourteen six-shooters pointed at them."

Santana's men held their hands away from their sides while Cole's men came from their hiding places and disarmed them. "Okay, now we talk." Cantrell stepped to Santana's side, removed his sidegun, patted him down for other weapons, looked at the bag he knew must hold the dynamite, then nodded toward it. "If that's the explosive Howley got for you, tie it back to your saddle. You won't be needin' it."

Quint glanced at the men Cole brought with him. "Keep these three men here. Don't hurt 'em. I figure to let 'em ride back to Ojinaga when I get through with Santana." He again stepped behind the big outlaw. "You an' me, *amigo,* are gonna go visit the sheriff. He ain't got nothin' on you. He ain't gonna arrest you. The reason I'm takin' you to him is 'cause he's part o' the talkin' we gotta do." Quint holstered his Colt. Then the two walked across the street to Engstrom's office, Cantrell a couple of strides behind Santana.

In the sheriff's office, Cantrell poured each of them a cup of coffee, told Santana to sit, and he started talking. He explained that Howley was taking the outlaw for a sucker. "Gonna take you over to the bank when we get through talkin' an' show you what I mean. Howley has all but emptied the vault you're s'posed to blow apart. You see, *amigo,* I done the job you paid me for. Howley is Manuel Soto. I ain't gonna keep yore money—gonna give you yore five thousand back. You get to keep it."

He sipped the hot liquid in his cup, then put the cup on the desk. "After I prove to you the vault is almost empty, we gotta git Howley back to the bank. I figure if we blow a couple sticks of that dynamite you brung to town, he'll figure you done robbed the bank, an' he can come in yellin' that he's lost whatever he had in the vault. Figure he's gonna say somewhere 'tween a quarter and a half million dollars." He stood. "And, Santana, you always played square with me so I'm gonna tell you right now, my name ain't Juan Cantello, it's Quinton Cantrell. Brad Mason's been a father to me since I wuz knee-high to a jackrabbit."

Santana showed no surprise. "He simply looked Quint in the eye. "Makes sense," he said in English. "I never heard tell of a gunfighter named Cantello—but I tell you now, *señor,* I 'ave hear *mucho,* of one whose *nombre es* Cantrell."

Cantrell pulled a deerskin bag from inside his belt and

handed it to the *bandido*. "Here's yore *dinero*. It's all still there." He stepped toward the door. "Let's go see if what I got figured is right."

On the way to the bank, Quint told Santana he'd have a crew in Mexico rounding up the rustled cattle that belonged to the B-bar-M. "Fernandez'll have his crew there too."

Santana only shook his head. "Damn, *amigo,* you ain't gonna leave me much." He shrugged and grinned. "Well, as you Texians say, 'win some, lose some.' "

A few moments later, in the bank, Cantrell told one of the employees to open the vault. The man shook his head. "Mr Howley doesn't allow anyone in the vault but him, Mr Cantello."

Engstrom stepped to the front. "I'm tellin' you to open the vault. The law is tellin' you—now open it."

The teller went to the vault, fiddled with the dials a moment, pulled at the door, and it swung open. Engstrom led Cantrell and Santana inside it. Cantrell was the first to speak. "Reckon I wuz right. She's bare as old Mother Hubbard's cupboard."

Santana tapped his thumb against his chest. "I, Benito Santana, 'ave more in my pockets than Soto leave me to take from here. I theenk I keel heem when I see heem."

Cantrell shook his head. "No. Let's play this out the way I said. Have your man take a couple sticks of that dynamite out back and explode it. Then we wait for Mr. Howley to show up." While he talked, he dropped his hand to his holster and thumbed the thong from the hammer of his Colt. What he'd not told Engstrom, or Santana, was that if Howley, Charley Butts, or whatever his name was, could handle a six-shooter like the letters said, he'd not go with them peacefully. Cantrell figured he'd have to kill him.

Santana sent a boy to go tell one of his men to bring the explosives to him in the bank. Five minutes later his rider came through the door carrying the sticks in his hand. After the outlaw leader told him what to do with them, he left.

While they waited to hear the explosion, Engstrom herded all the employees into a back room of the bank. "Don't want none o' you gettin' hurt. Soon's this is over, you can come out." He'd not finished when two loud, earthshaking bangs rent the air.

Cantrell, a cold smile splitting his mouth, said, "Won't be long now." Then, true to his estimate, hoofbeats pounded to the front of the bank. Then Howley ran inside panting.

"What happened? What was the explosion? We been robbed?" His eyes fell on Santana, then Engstrom, then Cantrell; then he noticed they were the only ones in the dusty-smelling room. "What the hell's goin' on here?"

Cantrell grinned. "Figured to let you know your scheme didn't work. It didn't work as far as breakin' Brad Mason—an' it didn't work as far as stealin' all the money in the bank. I know where you got it stashed, but you ain't gonna have no use for it anyway. The gov'ment's gonna salt you away for a long time for that payroll holdup you pulled up north o' here."

Then he pinned Howley with a look that could penetrate steel. "Somethin' else you need to know. I ain't a gent by the name o' Cantello. My name's Quinton Cantrell, an' I hear you fancy yoreself as bein' fast with that hogleg you got under yore coat. If you think you're that good, have at it." Without shifting his gaze from the banker, he said, "Santana, Engstrom, don't neither o' you take a hand in this. I owe this bastard for all the misery he's done caused Ma Mason an' Brad. Move to the side. Don't want none o' you catchin' any lead this slime might throw."

The thin veneer of gentility slid from Howley. His face hardened, his eyelids drooped to only slits, and he fingered a button on his shirt. He looked Quint in the eye. "Heard 'bout you a long time, Cantrell, but it's all been talk. Ain't seen none o' your graveyards, ain't seen anyone who ever actually seen you in a gunfight. Fact is, I figure you for a lot o' smoke."

Cantrell stood there, relaxed, allowing a slight smile to crease his lips. Inside, his stomach churned, his neck tingled. Then Howley's hand moved in a blur to the inside of his coat. Cantrell's right hand flashed to his holster. Howley's handgun came out spitting fire and smoke— but the end of Cantrell's Colt blossomed a split second before Howley's.

A slug tore at Cantrell's belt, another streaked fire along his thigh, but the button Howley fingered only a moment before had disappeared, and the one above it had also turned to a small black hole oozing red.

Both bullets knocked Howley back a step. He regained his balance, stepped forward, tried to trigger another shot, but his hand fell to his side. "Yeah. All the talk 'bout you—wasn't just talk. I'll tell folks I seen you pull a gun—pull a gu-gun." He fell on his face.

Santana was the first to speak. "Even eef he lived, *señor,* eef he say he seen you make the draw, he'd be lying. Ain't nobody can ever say they see you pull that forty-four. Whew. I'm *mucho* glad I wasn't dumb enough to push our little differences."

Engstrom went to the back room, told the employees to come out, and told them the bank was closed until the town council could bring in a banker and that no one in town would lose a penny.

Back at Engstrom's office, Santana looked Cantrell in the eye. "*Señor,* eef I geev you my word I'll not hinder the roundup of the cattle, will you let me cross the border tonight?

Cantrell studied the big *bandido* a moment, then in the pure Castilian Spanish he'd learned from Fernandez years ago, he said, "Somewhere in your past I figure you had another name, an honored name in your country." He nodded, then looked at Engstrom. "*Sí,* I will take your word for it, *amigo.* How about you, Bart?"

In pure Texian, Bart said, "Hell, I got no wanted posters on 'im. Yeah, let 'im go."

They shook hands, and the big *bandido,* whom Cantrell thought of as a friend, walked from the sheriff's office to—perhaps one day go back to being a gentleman.

Quint and Engstrom went to Doc's office. Waters's turn at taking care of Austin had ended. If Cantrell had his way, none of them would have to worry about the baby hereafter.

He told Doc what he planned. Doc agreed, as did Waters and Engstrom.

Cole took his crew to Mexico for a roundup, while Cantrell, Doc, Engstrom, and Waters packed the crib onto a packhorse. Cantrell held the baby to his chest and toed the stirrup, reaching down to shake hands with his friends. Then he rode for the ranch.

• • •

Ten days later, Brad and Ma Mason, Quint and Elena, Cole and Laura, Clay and Molly all sat around the table. Finished with breakfast, they drank their last cup of coffee before leaving for their separate homes.

Brad looked them all in the eye, one at a time. "Gonna tell y'all somethin'. Ain't a one o' you gonna say different. That there little Austin's gonna be my an' Ma's grandbaby just like he was yore own." He looked at Quint and Elena. "Know y'all gonna take good care o' him. Only thing I want is a promise you'll bring 'im to see us at least once a year." He wiped at his eyes. "Danged dust in this here country is hell on a man's eyes." They all laughed. Elena wiped her eyes then and said, mocking Cantrell in her finest Texas drawl, "Reckon that there damned dust done got in all our eyes at the same time."

Ma stood and looked at each of the wives. "I reckon none of these girls are going to admit to it, but I'm here to tell you right now, Mr. Mason, whoever visits us after about nine more months is gonna be bringin' us a grandbaby. Every danged one of them's been havin' mornin' sickness for the last two weeks. They figured they'd caught some sort o' chilblains. I did too at first, but then all o' them come down with the same symptoms—sick in the mornin' and spry as a young filly come sundown." She pinned each of them with a don't-fib-to-me look. "Any of you told your husbands yet?"

Each of them turned a rosy pink, and each admitted that she'd told her husband she *thought* she might be pregnant.

Cantrell felt his face turn hot. "Well, dammit, it must be somethin' in this here Big Bend soil what's good fer a man an' a woman. Course, with little Austin, me an'

Elena's one up on y'all already." He turned even more red. "What say we all come back for Christmas, once these first are born?"

Brad laughed. "Hot damn. Bet we gonna have 'em sneakin' off to their bedrooms like a couple o' young'uns jest findin' out boys an' girls are different."

"Mr. Mason, we'll have no more of your crudeness. I declare."

No one knows the American West better.

JACK BALLAS

☐ *THE HARD LAND*   0-425-15519-6/$4.99

☐ *BANDIDO CABALLERO*

                        0-425-15956-6/$5.99

☐ *GRANGER'S CLAIM*

                        0-425-16453-5/$5.99

The Old West in all its raw glory.